THE DAY DREDES

Shayna Grissom

Shayna Grissom

CONTENTS

CHAPTER ONE

THE NIGHT DREDES

The corridor blurred as she struggled to catch her breath. Her heart pounded so loud, she swore it was on the verge of stopping altogether. Gasping for air, she collapsed against the dark, wainscoted wall. He was waiting for her somewhere in this labyrinth of hallways. He was always waiting for her.

This was her house, and this was her island. She wasn't about to let a scary old story about Sallows Hall get the best of her.

This scene had played out so many times in her dreams, but never had she dared open the door. That single horrid door waited at the end of a hallway that stretched on forever. The peephole shone like a beacon to what was her doom. Clamping a hand over her mouth, she choked on her cries. All this time, the night dredes that plagued her were not dreams at all. These were memories played out over and over—each time more distorted than the last.

Don't do it. Don't look in the peephole. You know he's waiting for you.

But she did it anyway. Daniel had gotten into the room by accident. Her sweet, gentle fiancé. His voice cried out for her from behind the door. How long would she leave him in that room?

"Destiny, please!" he pleaded.

She hated herself for all the times she never opened the door. As punishment, she made herself glance into the peephole—to behold the horror. Shutting one eye, she pressed her face against the door and into the glass lens.

Huge, rusted chains hung from the ceiling and corners of the room. Embedded in the walls were rusted skewers, threatening anyone who sought respite in that room. Parts of the wall swelled on their own as if the walls were breathing. Maggots fell from the cracks and splits in the shiplap. The ground was a bloody mess with bits and pieces of what—she didn't know.

Despite herself, she jumped when a vivid, green eye stared back at her, eclipsing the room. She let out a shriek and stepped away as she always did. The man in the room sounded like her fiancé. He had green eyes like her fiancé, but he was the monster.

"Open the door, Destiny!" How his voice trembled.

She hesitated, and he pounded so hard on the door, she expected it to break. According to the diary, the Green-Eyed Monster lived behind this door, but that couldn't be her Daniel. That was hundreds of years ago.

"Open the Gods' damned door!"

Once again, torn between running and opening the door. He frightened her, and the diary said he belonged in there as punishment for his crimes, but perhaps Nathaniel was mistaken. Daniel couldn't have been one of the fabled monsters of the island. That was over four hundred years ago! The stories couldn't be true. It just wasn't possible.

Gritting her chattering teeth, she stole a second glance through the peephole. The man in the room was leaner, with longer hair, but there was no mistaking it. This was her fiancé. He smiled at her gruesomely with a mouthful of blood. It dribbled down his face. He was trying to show off. Her hand tremored on the handle; she didn't think she could go through with it.

"You must open the door," a child's voice rang. "It's the only way to break the curse."

What curse was she talking about?

Daniel had both hands on a spike. "I can't stay another moment in here," he said. "I'm going to end it."

"Oh no you don't!"

Destiny was not about to let Daniel go. Not this time. Monster or not, he was her Daniel. He was willing to accept her faults; she would accept his as well. She opened the door and stepped inside.

CHAPTER TWO

GHOST HUNTERS

The boat's engine cut without warning. The passengers bolted upright from their seats and surveyed the dark, choppy waters. The fog was so thick that they had no idea the island was upon them until the boatman's heavy boots thumped toward them, a thick reflective rope in his hand.

"Are we here?" a passenger asked.

The boatman was an Icelandic fisherman they had heavily bribed to come here. No one in Scotland would take them. They might have found someone in Norway, but the trip would be twice as long. The wind-worn boatman had on a thick wool cap and a large neon yellow parka.

"Well, yeah," the boatman scoffed. "If I were going to kill you, I'd have used cheaper rope."

The boatman trudged to the side of the boat before docking. The old fisherman anchored the boat to a half-rotted dock. "It's not illegal to be here, just frowned upon. I've already taken a few Americans. Why not a few more?"

"You said there is a homestead nearby?" Jeremy asked.

The boatman nodded as his gaze attempted to pierce the impenetrable fog blanketing the coast. "Eton and his sister, Kerry. They arrived not long after the island did."

The group went silent. The boatman described the island as if it had just risen from the ocean's depths. It was by all accounts what had happened. In the triangle of countries in the Norwegian Sea, an island appeared as if it had always been there. It baffled scientists. The fishermen panicked. For Jeremy, it was an opportunity.

"You certain you want me to come back tomorrow?" the boatman asked.

"We'll be fine," Jeremy said, offloading his camera and lighting gear. Ryan helped Tiff get off the boat before stepping on the dock himself. "You said there are people on the island. If we run into any trouble, we will find them."

The three passengers waved as the boatman drifted back out to sea. His boat was a shadow in the fog when the engine sputtered to life and puttered its way back to Icelandic shores. Off the dock, the trio set out to investigate the mysterious new island. Jeremy had been promoting this segment of his online show for weeks now.

The sand gave way to a beaten trail that forked in two different directions. A handwritten sign saying "Grocery" pointed to the right. The left trail skirted underneath the blanket of fog.

"Satellite photos indicated a mansion on a hill," Jeremy said. "I'm guessing this trail will lead us to it."

The island was like any remote part of Iceland. The grass was short and a vivid green that would make any homeowner in LA jealous. The island's steep incline promised a harrowing hike before them, but the group had anticipated that—Jeremy and Ryan went hiking all the time, but both men were panting hard with the gear.

"This place is incredible," Tiff said. She took photos with the professional camera her parents had bought her for this trip.

"I can feel some mad vibes here, man," Ryan said. He pulled at a loose dreadlock that had fallen from his hair tie. "This place has a story to tell."

Jeremy was fumbling with a device he'd made himself. It could read Electronic Voice Phenomena and Electromagnetic Fields at the same time. He found it too hard to set up both everywhere he went, so the combination only made sense. It was also smaller, more portable, with patent filed with his name on it. If the Ghost Hunting community wanted to use his design, they would have to use his patent.

"Well," Jeremy said as he wiped the sweat from his forehead. "I'm not picking up any of those mad vibes yet."

Ryan wrapped his arms around Tiff and pulled her in for a kiss. For them, it was the spooky romantic getaway of a lifetime. Her woolen cap scratched his bare chin. The lavender essential oil she dabbed on her chakra points lingered in the cool air.

"You really think something is here?" Tiff asked.

They came across stone fences sectioning off different parts of the land. It was common in villages to delineate land with stone fences. Back in the day, a father usually divided his land for his sons that way. There were only a few of these fences, which meant the population was small. Jeremy took out his camera and rotated it so that it faced him as he made a slow circle.

"This is it!" he said. "This is the mysterious island. We just arrived forty-five minutes ago. For those who are new to my channel, I am Jeremy Sands, and this is my buddy Ryan and his girlfriend."

Tiff's nose scrunched at being relegated to "the girlfriend."

Ryan caught her expression and added, "Tiffany Meyers is an award-winning photographer."

Jeremy rotated the camera away from them and towards the trail. "So far, we've seen little. There is some stone fencing. We have yet to see the mansion, but I think we're going to be encountering that soon."

Jeremy held out his camera as the group marched up the trail. "The forest from this angle appears small, but it actually inhabits nearly a third of the island. The mansion itself is a few miles from the cliff face."

"The mansion," Ryan agreed. "That place will have a story to tell for sure."

"Dude," Jeremy shot him a look before turning off the camera. "Do a dab, please?"

Ryan laughed, but Tiff flashed Jeremy a sneer.

"I didn't bring all that here. I got a vape, though."

Pulling out a palm-sized device, Ryan and Jeremy took turns smoking. Jeremy offered the vape to Tiff, but she shook her head and turned to take more photos. The guys continued to pass the vape while Tiff came upon a beaten path.

"Hey guys," she said after a short time.

There it was, bearing down on them. Much like the island, they didn't come upon it so much as the mansion found them. There was still a distance to walk before reaching the house, but the three of them stood in the shadow of a stately mansion. The dark stain of wood contrasted with mortared stone around the entrance and the base of the house. The roof was a patchy, swollen mess that had seen better days, and the glass windows were clouded. Wild heather and vines entangled with shutters and the several chimneys the house boasted.

Jeremy pulled out his camera once again and spoke to it. "Here it is! The secret mansion. Untouched by man for, well, we're not sure how long. They estimated the mansion was built in the fifteen hundreds.

It's a Tudor style, which is consistent with the time. What secrets does it hold? We're about to find out."

"Jesus, man," Ryan gasped. "Look at the size of that place. How did we not see it from the shore?"

"Probably the incline," Jeremy said.

"Incredible," Tiff said. She snapped photos in rapid-fire succession.

"Glad you came, babe?"

The ghost hunters stood at the steps of the mansion. The sun was setting, but it was too overcast to see the Northern Lights. The island developed a warm glow from all around, except for the bleak black hole that was the mansion.

"Let's go in," Jeremy said. His followers were eager for this segment. It would take his career from self-produced online content to streaming channels or even cable TV.

"It's going to be dark in, like, less than twenty minutes," Tiff warned.

Ryan didn't respond. He was too busy touching the stones of the house. He inhaled deeply into the wood siding before pressing his ear against the exterior as if he expected it to speak to him. Ryan patted it lovingly before giving the stones a full lick with his tongue. Jeremy shook his head at the sight.

"Whenever you're done making out with the house." Jeremy motioned to the front door.

"I'm getting a feel for it, man," Ryan said.

"Well, your girlfriend wants to go when we just got here."

"You're the one who said you didn't want to be here when it got dark," Tiff fired back.

"I was just trying to keep the boatman chill. He really didn't want to bring us out here," Jeremy countered. "Besides, what kind of ghost hunters run away from a haunted house at night?"

"You're so fucking rude," Tiff spat.

Jeremy gave her a sardonic shrug and turned back to Ryan—who was still *feeling* the house. "Well, you guys can do what you want. I need to get some readings and get to work."

"We stay," Ryan said as his fingers traced the stone. Tiff's hands rested on her hips, annoyed that he gave her no choice in the matter.

Jeremy opened the door and said, "It's not locked."

A groan echoed into the empty foyer as the daylight illuminated the room for the first time in what was likely centuries. "We are the first people to enter this house since it was originally inhabited." Jeremy narrated into the camera.

His backpack was on the floor, and he was now wearing his head-lamp. Ryan pulled a matching helmet out of his backpack while Tiff turned the phone's flashlight setting on. She rolled her eyes and opened the shutters, allowing the remaining daylight to shine through the milky windows before turning off her flashlight.

"Well, that just killed the atmosphere," Jeremy said.

Tiff slid her phone into the pocket of her leggings. "Better than killing my phone battery."

"Come on, guys," Ryan said. "Let's keep going."

They entered a room through two swinging doors and found a kitchen. It had two counters that stretched the entirety of the room, a cast-iron stove, pots, and pans. There was nothing spooky about it. It was old but functional. "Hey, we can cook breakfast tomorrow!" Ryan said as he opened the stove. "This thing is pretty neat."

Another door led to the backyard, where an overgrown hedge maze grew. Tiff's camera came out once more as she took pictures of the maze, the porch, and the second-story balcony that was nearly swallowed by a climbing rosebush.

"How did these grow so big?" Tiff said, her camera lowered.

Ryan's brow creased as he stared at the cherry-red blooms. "Your mom is into gardening."

Tiff stared at the rose vines that wrapped around the chimney. "I remember how proud she was when her roses grew to twelve feet—that's like the max. These are insane."

"A mystery for sure," Jeremy said. If he cared about the anomaly, it was fleeting. "Look at this!"

Ryan and Tiff followed Jeremy into a large room with cords strung along the ceiling and large wooden troughs. Heavy rollers with handles and baskets full of pins made the room's intended use obvious.

"This is pretty state-of-the-art for the fifteenth century," Jeremy spoke into the camera. "I'm not a historian by any means, but I did my homework on homes around this time. We will need to have a few follow-up episodes to unpack this place."

Jeremy ducked and weaved around the mechanics of the room to make certain it was all on camera before pulling out his EVP device. The instrument whined and buzzed. Its indicators wavered as Jeremy watched it record through the camera. "Some strange readings here."

He followed the readings around the room and stopped where Ryan had stopped. The furthest trough on the right. All the machine's dials went into the red before inexplicably stopping. Jeremy tinkered with the knobs and said, "What the hell?"

"It's getting dark," Tiff warned.

Ryan stared hard at the last trough on the right. It was empty, but Ryan's pupils dilated as he stared at it. "We should find an excellent base of operations. Not here."

The trio made their way out of the laundry room and came upon a massive staircase. "That is one majestic mother-fucking staircase," Jeremy said. "A whole circus could run up and down those steps, man."

They had to watch their step as some stairs had rotted, and the splintered railing was not all that reliable. The only thing that had lived here lately was rats. Nests were in every corner, and rat shit was everywhere.

Ryan remained quiet after leaving the laundry room. He trailed behind his friend and girlfriend, heavily smoking his vape. Tiff was already making her way up the first flight. She checked the first door on the left with her flashlight.

"There's a fireplace in here," she said.

A dark, hand-carved coffee table and several end tables accompanied a red velvet sofa and loveseat set. The room had a rocking chair with a wicker seat and high-backed leather chairs. There was a table pushed up against one wall with several added dining room chairs where a crystal punch bowl sat. There was pink stuff caked inside, but they didn't dare touch it.

Leather-bound books were on the bookshelves. The mantle of the fireplace had a carving of some sort of wolf on a hilltop. The eyes of the beast stared at the intruders, watching their every move.

Ryan picked up one of the many crystal cups scattered around the room and admired the exquisite cut of the glass. It was a shame that rats pooped everywhere and chewed on what was once an expensive rug. The wallpaper was peeling from walls swollen with water damage.

The fireplace had a healthy stack of wood beside it. It was dusty, and the smell of rat piss overpowered the stink of mold, but it was safer than spending the night outside. Ryan pulled a presto log and a lighter out of his backpack and placed it in the hearth. A warm glow filled the room as the fire grew.

Tiff wasted no time in lighting all the candles she saw around the room. The once-polished furniture was now dull, but there were indentations in the seats and worn spots on the armrests.

"This place was someone's home once," Jeremy said. "Look at all these books."

Along the wall was a floor-to-ceiling bookcase stuffed with leather-bound books. They were printed books. "These would have been expensive," Tiff said as her fingers tickled the spines. "Print books were rare during the fifteen-hundreds. Incredible."

"Everything here would have been expensive," Jeremy added. "Makes you wonder why they would just up and leave after going to such lengths to care for it."

"They didn't leave," Ryan muttered into the fire.

While Jeremy played the scientist, Ryan was the spiritualist who created a unique dynamic for the show. The problem was that Ryan genuinely believed his unsettling musings, and it often put him in a weird mood. Tiff and Jeremy exchanged a glance before Jeremy said, "You still got that vape on you?"

"I'm out," Ryan said, reaching for his bag. "But, I got this."

He shook a bottle of whiskey, and Jeremy smiled. Tiff let out a sigh and dusted off a sofa before sitting down. The velvet didn't have the shine that new fabrics did, but it was soft and still plush despite its wear.

What they meant to be a serious ghost hunting expedition turned into trespassing and getting drunk. Tiff sat with her legs crossed as she read a book from the shelf. Her leg twitched every time either man laughed. When the drunken conversation proved too much, she stood up and said, "I'm going to check this place out."

"You sure, babe?" Ryan said.

"Yeah," Jeremy slurred. "You're not a ghost hunter. You don't even believe in this stuff."

"Bullshit, she believes my abilities," Ryan said, taking another swig from the bottle.

"Yeah, she believes in your feelings but not my scientific findings. How does that work?" Jeremy asked.

Tiff didn't respond. She put on Ryan's headlamp and armed herself with her phone flashlight before leaving the room.

"I think she just wants to get away from us," Ryan said.

"Well, no one likes to be sober around drunk people."

"It's her lifestyle. I respect it."

"You going all vegan now too?" Jeremy teased.

"It's better for your body and the environment, dude."

Jeremy laughed and threw another log on the fire they were hovering beside. It was getting colder in the house. Condensation was forming on the windows, and if they moved too far from the fire, their breath would create clouds in the room.

"You've changed since you started dating her," Jeremy said as he dug around in his backpack before he produced a bag of beef jerky.

"Who doesn't change when they're in a relationship?" Ryan asked, digging through Tiff's backpack to pull out mason jars with pre-cut vegetables. "You see things from their perspective. You make compromises."

Jeremy's face went sullen. "Maybe that's why I don't do relationships. I'm not willing to compromise. Everyone I know is having kids or engaged. This lifestyle makes relationships hard. It makes everything hard."

"But you believe in it, and you do incredible work," Ryan said. "You've got a booming website with almost three million subscribers. You've got donations coming in from all over the world. Did you ever hear from that TV executive yet?"

"My lawyer's going over the contracts now," Jeremy said with a smile. "We want you in on it, of course."

"Man," Ryan smiled with delight. His long arms wrapped around his knees as he looked around the house. "I'm so down, bro."

"I had to get you in on it," Jeremy chided. "You're the one who's always willing to come. I would've starved if you didn't buy food. Now, look at you, munching on carrots like a fucking rabbit."

Ryan snorted a laugh. "I love doing this, man. I know I get weird sometimes, but it's cool, you know?"

"Yeah," Jeremy nodded. "Enough of this lovey shit. Let's listen to some music!"

Ryan looked up at his friend, who was now plugging his phone into a speaker. He raised his eyebrows. "You sure about that? This place is hot. What if we miss something?"

"It's fine. We'll just rock out for a minute until we sober up. Then we'll go searching. We're plugging in old school," Jeremy said. "I don't want to drain the battery with Bluetooth."

"Is the camera still rolling?" Ryan asked, motioning to the camera and the EVP machine beside it.

"Oh yeah, both are always on. I edit the shit out of everything later. Those readings were promising. This house will make us famous!"

***

Tiff jumped at the sudden noise and let out a defeated growl. "Great, now they're drunk and blasting music," she muttered. "I guess I'll be the ghost hunter today."

Rounding the stair railing, she looked at the other areas on the second story. Opening a double-door, Tiff found a huge dining room with a long table. She walked along the table and counted all the chairs.

There were sixteen seats plus one on each end. What were these people like, and how did they live on this island?

The stained-glass doors were a stark contrast to everything else in the home. They were a beacon of light and beauty, untouched by time. Her fingers traced the outline of the orange glass fox before opening the door to the balcony. She had to push a little hard than she liked. The doors hadn't moved in a long time. It was only after she had the door open that she learned why it was hard to push the door. Rose vines wrapped around every nook and cranny. Those incredible roses wrapped around the banister and pressed against the doors as though they were desperate to get in.

"Well," she said. "Found the balcony."

The music blared from the family room as Tiff went up the stairs to the third story. She found many sections were closed off with locked pocket doors. With two different wings locked, Tiff found a hallway unlike the others. Its red carpet runner was missing. She told herself that the singularity was the only thing that brought her to this hallway, yet it did not explain the urge to open the first door on the left.

The bedroom was once occupied. They'd made the bed up with a yellow quilt, and there were matching pillows. The open dresser exposed a young woman's clothing. The vanity had belongings scattered across it. A rose stem—the petals must have long rotted away. There was a pin with a red rose made from fabric, a homemade doll, and a rattle. The drawers to the vanity held the things a young woman would use: hairpins, homemade jewelry, and little treasures most collected throughout her life.

"Oh god, Ryan was right."

The quilt was crumpled, and the pillows scattered as if someone was lying on it after they made it. Tiff snapped pictures—relying on her flash to light the room. They would not be cover photos, but they could be of some use to Jeremy and Ryan's ghost hunting expedition. Maybe she could sell them.

The flash of the camera illuminated something on the floor. She bent down and picked up a tennis shoe. Tiff couldn't wrap her head around it. It was rudimentary and homemade with wool and leather. It even had a Nike logo sewn onto the side. How would sixteenth-century islanders know about Nike? This didn't add up. "Whoever lived here had style well before their time," she muttered as she took more photos of the shoe.

Tiff had checked many of the rooms on the third floor, and only the one showed signs of life. They'd stripped everything else down to just basics, like unmade hotel rooms. All the rooms were uniform in style and fashion. They may never have been used. Why would someone create such a massive home for no one to live in? It showed status, not use.

Whoever lived here before was wealthy and educated, but why live here at all? Scientists theorized that there was some sort of atmospheric bubble around the island that made it nearly invisible. The people who lived here must have gotten stuck in that phenomenon.

There was a room on the fourth floor that was made up. The room still held lingering traces of perfume. It smelled musty, something a mature woman would wear. Tiff flinched at the sight of a skinned wolf pelt on the end of the bed. The inhabitants of this island had to rely on all resources.

The face of the animal was still attached but pressed and sewn down. Great gleaming teeth the size of her fingers and shiny glass eyes made her shutter. Tiff marveled at the size of the wolf as she photographed it. The headboard of the bed was a hand-carved rendering of a fox on a hillside. The same image on the stained-glass in the dining room doors. Was it the family's crest, perhaps? She took photos of that as well.

Goosebumps rose all along Tiff's arms as she beheld a wing of the fourth floor. The doors were half open and half in their pockets—roughly splintered along the door frame—as if someone had ripped the doors open in a hurry. Her bottom lip trembled, but Tiff walked into the hallway. It appeared no different from the others with its red runners and occasional side table.

The hallways wound around and around; Tiff lost track of how many rooms there were. They were small for bedrooms, but that was common for old mansions. The air in this hallway was different somehow. Dense, like breathing in a sauna, but frigid.

Tiff gasped as she came across a section of the hallway wall that had been partially demolished. It was as though someone smashed a hole right through it. The fragments of wood and debris still lay on the floor. Lifting her camera up, Tiff took a series of photos until something caught her eye. She paused and lowered her camera. Behind the wreckage was a hidden hallway, sealed up from the rest of the house.

"Hey guys!" she shouted, but they couldn't hear her. Tiff ran down the stairs and burst into the family room. Both men were so startled that they flailed around screaming. It would have been comical if they were not in an abandoned mansion on a magically appearing island.

"What the fuck?" Jeremy asked.

Tiff was trying to catch her breath from running down the stairs. Ryan was on his feet and wrapping his arms around his girlfriend. "Are you okay?"

She laughed between gasps, "I'm out of fucking shape."

"Well, you're like what?" Jeremy asked. "A buck fifteen and twenty-two? You haven't seen a gym since you sat on the bleachers and intentionally failed gym in high school."

Tiff tilted her head and asked, "How did you know that?"

Jeremy shrugged. "Every high school has one." He got to his feet and picked up his camera. "I'm guessing you found something."

"Yeah," she nodded. "It's incredible."

***

The three of them stared at the massive hole in the wall. Jeremy was investigating it with his instruments and his camera while Ryan touched and investigated. Tiff stood back with her arms crossed as the men theorized about what had happened.

"I'm not getting much in terms of readings. The EMT is higher than usual, but that could just be the plumbing." Jeremy tapped the copper tubes that ran up the side of the wall like a maze. "It's important to note that this home should not even have plumbing. They barely had toilets at this time."

"They never tried to clean it up," Tiff said.

"This could have happened after the inhabitants left the island, or maybe it was part of the reason," Jeremy explained. "By the way, I tested the plumbing... for science. None of it works, probably never did."

"It blew outward," Ryan said. "See how the wallpaper rips away from the wall? Something inside this hallway wanted out."

Jeremy stepped inside. "Looks like a bathroom right here. The plumbing is destroyed. Maybe the pipes burst, and it caused the hole."

"No," Ryan said. "You said yourself the plumbing never worked. Besides, there's no water damage."

Tiff stepped in behind Ryan and gazed down the hallway. "It's no different from the others," she said. "Why wall this one up?"

"Someone didn't want anyone to find it," Ryan said gravely.

Jeremy was still checking out the elaborate plumbing that ran along the walls in a maze of copper tubes. Tiff found it equally compelling and snapped photos while Jeremy recorded it. "There's some sort of residue on the pipes too." He pulled out a small plastic tube with a cotton swab inside. Jeremy popped the lid and took a sample with the Q-tip. "Look at that," he said, holding the sample up to the camera. "Can't wait to see what that is."

Music still blared from downstairs. "You didn't turn it off?" Tiff said.

"Well, you kind of scared the shit out of us," Jeremy explained.

The more they traveled the hallway, the more Ryan veered off and touched a wall or stared at a window. Tiff and Jeremy wanted to check every room and compare the slight differences this hallway had from the others, but Ryan scratched at his dreads and chewed his nails in the hallway.

"Dude, don't you even want to look?" Jeremy asked.

Ryan folded his arms and bit his bottom lip, shaking his head.

"Babe, what is it?" Tiff asked.

"We shouldn't be here," Ryan said.

"Come on, man," Jeremy whined. "There are no signs of EMP or EVP."

Ryan shook his head and pointed at a door at the end of the hallway. "Why would anyone need a peephole on an interior door?"

Jeremy lifted his eyebrows. "Oh man, you think it might be a dis-appointment room?"

Tiff winced. "A room to hide a family's ill or disfigured child."

Jeremy marched towards the door with his camera strapped firmly to his hand. Tiff chased after with her camera, ready to capture whatever lay in that room. Ryan paced and put his hands behind his head. "Guys..."

Ryan's warning didn't reach them.

"Guys!"

Before Tiff and Jeremy could reach the door, it swung open on its own. Neither waited to see who or what opened the door. All three ghost hunters turned to flee without looking back. Their screams could be heard over the music and throughout the vacant hallways.

They ran out the front door, leaving all their belongings behind. The music continued to roar. It was a dubstep remix of a jazz song that no longer resembled what any generation before it would recognize as music.

A worn leather boot kicked the speaker across the room, where it smashed into the wall and ricocheted into the corner. The music yanked to a halt.

CHAPTER THREE

THE ROOM OF PAIN

Destiny sat up and gazed at the room. She had avoided this place her whole life. She'd cowered in fear of it since she was a child, yet there she was, sleeping in it. Many things, such as the chains and spikes, remained, but the chaotic energy inside had evaporated, revealing a hollow room.

Someone was beside her. She hoped, whoever he was, that he was still breathing. Placing two fingers near his nose, she could confirm that he was. That brought a little relief until it occurred to her he might have been the reason she was here.

"Hello?" she asked while gently patting his shoulder.

The man let out a groan and rolled over, exposing his face. It was her fiancé, Daniel—only he was drastically thinner. His brown hair had grown to his shoulders. A lean, striking face cut away from the baby fat. Gods, he was handsome, but she didn't love him for his looks. It was his unyielding kindness that she loved most.

He would have been just as handsome if he remained unchanged. That, of course, brought about the question of why such a transformation had taken place. She touched her face, and from what she could tell, she was the same.

She shook his prone body. "Daniel, wake up! I'm frightened."

Daniel groaned and patted her gently. "It's all right. It was just a dream. Go back to sleep."

She smiled. Even in this state, he was trying to comfort her. Perhaps it would have worked were they not in such a terrifying place. "Daniel, wake up!"

He rolled over and opened his eyes. Daniel had the most amazing green eyes, like her father. Like the monster detailed in her ancestor's journals that once violated her dreams every night. Only now, his eyes did not set her nerves off at all. It was just as she always hoped. She could gaze into his eyes without consequence. She gasped with relief.

Daniel was just as alarmed by the room as she was. His eyes watered, and he tensed all over as if expecting a threat to emerge from the windowless space. "Where are we?" he asked.

"In the room for the Green-Eyed Monster. If there truly ever was one."

Daniel wasted no time in getting up. His black trousers threatened to slip down his narrow hips, but he adjusted his leather belt to the closest setting. She averted her eyes to avoid embarrassment. Daniel may have lost weight, but his pants did not scale down with him! He'd discarded the black formal jacket and simply wore the loose black linen shirt underneath.

He extended a hand to help her up, and she took it. "Well," he said. "Let's get out of this place." He scowled at the room in disgust, and she was relieved he was of the same opinion. Destiny took his hand,

and together, they left the room of pain. He gave her hand a squeeze, and she stopped, nibbling on the edge of her fingernail.

"What happened here?" Daniel asked. "It's all so different from what I remember."

She nodded with a furrowed brow. "Yes, it feels like recalling a dream or a childhood memory. I know it to be true once it's said, but it's all rather hazy."

His shaggy hair added an element of rebellion to his image she hadn't imagined before. She rather liked it. "It is an odd feeling."

The hallways were as she recalled, but they weren't. A great deal of time had passed since the last time they walked these halls, but how could that be? The runners were dirty, and mice had chewed at the edges. The windows were so cloudy that they only omitted a veiled light. Wallpaper peeled and fell from the corners, and piles of leaves had collected in the corners.

They made their way through the winding halls until they encountered a massive hole in a wall. Daniel investigated the wall and could only shake his head. "I don't remember anyone blasting a hole through your house."

"Look at the state this place is in," she said. "It's as though it were untouched for hundreds of years." There was more resentment in her tone than she meant to reveal. While her memory wasn't perfect, she remembered this house was a source of deep-seated pride. For it to go to the wayside like this made her feel sick.

Lifting her black lace skirts, she stepped over what was left of the wall and craned her neck. "What is that noise?"

Daniel stepped a few paces ahead, motioning for her to stay back while he attempted to understand it. "I don't know, but it sounds violent."

Despite his warning, she followed the sound. It was strange, but there was intention behind it. It provoked confusing emotions within her. "I think it's a type of music."

"That is not music," Daniel said. "Just stay here. I'll have a look."

He left her at the top of the stairs, biting her fingernails. He wanted her to stay put, but she couldn't help herself. Treading down the steps, she found Daniel in the drawing room. The sound was blaring from a round gray device with a series of tiny holes in it. Daniel gave the thing a swift kick, and the music stopped.

"Why did you kick it?" she asked, rushing to the creature's aid. What if he had hurt it?

It didn't appear too damaged, but the noise no longer came from it. It was a strange tube. Perhaps she could get the music to play again. She found three buttons, but they did nothing. There was a hole in the side, and Destiny scanned the floor before finding a cord connected to another unusual device. It was small, like a pocketbook, and glowed a vivid blue.

"Don't touch it," Daniel said. "We don't know what it is."

Daniel paced around the room with his fists balled. He was so distraught. She hated the state he was in; it wasn't like him.

"Are you all right?" she asked.

"I don't know. I remember this place, but things are different," he said, storming around the room. "Everything is old and in disrepair, but I don't remember it being that way before. It just doesn't make sense."

As a man of science, Daniel did not like the unexplainable. She was inclined to agree with him that something was dreadfully wrong. She could only make one conclusion, as stupid as it was. "Maybe we were sleeping for a long time," she said, still cradling the gray tube.

He stared at her with those green eyes and stopped pacing. Her skin flushed. They were recently engaged before this happened. Gods, he was so striking! To think he was her fiancé, though she supposed they would put off their marriage given the circumstances.

"I don't know what is happening. I just know that I missed you," he said.

Her eyes watered, and she moved towards him and embraced him. "I missed you too."

They held each other in the decaying mansion, and the need for answers lessened. He kissed her then, and she felt herself melt into him. Their kiss grew more passionate, and their hands searched one another until Daniel broke free. She wanted to slap him for doing so.

"We should check the other rooms," he said. "See if anyone else is still here."

It wasn't exactly what she had in mind, but Daniel was probably right. They searched the house—the parts her mother hadn't closed. They found no one else, but they came to the same conclusion.

"Destiny," he said, holding her hand as they walked through the decrepit mansion. "The last thing I can recall is the night of our engagement party."

"Same," she admitted. "With the punch bowl and the cups where they are, the dinner plates laid out, and the pan in the oven, I think it may very well have been the last night for everyone on this island."

There was no sign of their family. Only reminders of an evening long ago. Her heart hurt with the prospect, but if something horrid had occurred while they were in that room. They needed to know what. Daniel pushed open the door of her bedroom with one hand while she hid behind him, fearing what they would find.

"It's empty, too."

Everything was exactly the way she remembered, except her shoe was on the bed instead of on the floor. She would never have put her shoes on the bed. It must have been the visitors from the other night. Her wardrobe was open, but her clothes were unmoved. Dust covered her vanity table, but everything was where she left it.

It was only yesterday that Daniel's sister was drawing the laces of her corset. Abigail begged her to push through her phobia of green eyes. She practically carried her to the drawing room for the proposal.

"Daniel," she asked. "Do you notice something different about me?"

He smiled. "It's rather hard not to. You're no longer afraid of my eyes. The last thing I remember was you and I searching for the Green-eyed Monster's room."

On the night of their engagement party, she and Daniel went on a hunt of sorts. She feared the family lore so greatly then. Perhaps finding the room resolved her phobia after all. She recalled Daniel did not want to go, but it wasn't polite to gloat over being right.

"Do you still have the diary?" she asked.

Daniel patted his pants pockets and produced a small, leather-bound journal. He extended it to her, and she hesitated before taking it from him. To think the stories in this journal once had so much power over her.

Night dredes, her mother used to call them. Nightmares that would be so intense they rendered her hysterical and drenched in sweat. What had befallen this house the night of their engagement party?

"Are you all right?" Daniel braced her shoulders. He swallowed hard and gently stroked her face with a thin hand.

"I'm fine," she said, with both hands on the diary, reminded of another significant event that night. The Sallows ring. It was an emerald-cut ruby with a trio of diamonds on each side where the gold was attached to the ruby. The ring passed through the direct descendants of Nathaniel Sallows, the first settler of Sallows Island.

"We should check the cellar," she said, facing the window.

"Why?"

"According to the diary, the room in the basement housed all the monsters... most of them, at least."

Daniel didn't ask further questions as they made their way to the mansion's cellar. Her mind was buzzing with questions that all came to a halt at the bottom of the basement steps. She gasped, using both hands to cover her mouth.

Daniel tilted his head and asked, "There was once a door there, right?"

Indeed, there was. A great solid wooden one that was walled off along the edges to prevent anything from opening the door again. The door was nowhere to be found, and a large black void had taken its place.

"The Sallows were charged with safeguarding the world from the monsters in that room," she said, feeling the smooth stone of her ring. "They all escaped on my watch."

Daniel shook his head. "That's not fair. We don't know what happened. We don't even know if the monsters were real. It was probably just a story to cover up a king's illegitimate son."

He didn't put it together, her sweet fiancé. He was trying to make her feel better, but she knew it to be true. Daniel pulled her in close and kissed her temple, and despite herself, she relaxed against him.

"I'll cover it up," he said.

She pushed past his embrace and returned to the drawing room and to the devices that remained. Picking up the smaller of the two items, it responded to her touch by glowing bright enough to light her entire face. The glass screen wiggled and asked for a combination of four numbers. It was what was called a PIN. She pushed the numbers and watched the device deny her access, whatever it was.

It made her smile, but when she tried to show Daniel, he shied away. He even took a step back from her. It was the device he disliked, but it felt like rejection all the same.

"I'm going to have a look around," he said, leaving her alone.

Destiny didn't want him to be afraid. She wanted him to be curious with her. Guilt struck her then. When she feared the most ridiculous of things, Daniel never pushed them on her.

She didn't mean to upset him. Her mind had Daniel painted as a curious, bookish person, but the man she was with now was fearful of the future. Sitting on the sofa, she continued to meddle with the device. Sometimes, it would buzz in her hand when she got it wrong; other times, it didn't.

It had its flaws. It didn't always register her fingertip, and sometimes, it would go black and do nothing before she pushed a flat button along the side. Daniel might have been struggling with this harder than she was, but that didn't mean he wouldn't come around. He needed her support and her patience, and she was more than willing to provide it.

After much fiddling with the device, she tapped one, two, three, and four on the screen, and the device was finally unlocked. She was giddy with her discovery. A whole new world was waiting behind the buttons.

There were people in clothes unlike any she had seen before. Women wore clothes so revealing that it made her blush. How would Daniel react to women wearing transparent gowns? Not all people did this, only certain people wore such things on *red carpets*, but the average woman wore trousers these days. She could get behind that.

While she didn't have a reference for how much time had passed, it must have been centuries. She didn't know what year it was when they were last awake, and she didn't remember it being something that concerned anyone. Days, weeks, and years meant nothing to people who lived and died on the same little island. They lived by the seasons and the harvest.

She struggled to read many of the words, and even then, the context was confusing. One picture was of an island, and the words *Mystery Island Appears* lettered the top of it. Her mind swam at the possibility of that being their island.

It was several hours later that Daniel sulked back into the drawing room with a defeated expression on his face. She set aside the device and patted the place beside her on the sofa. He obliged, but his shoulders stooped, and his head hung low.

"I don't understand what's happening," he said, shaking his head.

She sensed that something had broken that night, but how to explain it? She stroked his back. "Something happened the night of the engagement party. Something we can't explain with logic."

Daniel put his head in his hands. "You think the monsters were real after all?"

"We may never know," she said.

"What do we do?"

This was something he could understand, for it was ingrained in all Sallows. "We do what we've always done," she said. "We survive."

Chapter Four

SHOP TALK

Jolted awake by pounding and screaming at the cottage door, Eton stumbled out of his cot. He grabbed the baseball bat he kept by his bed as a precaution for weirdos. Kerry stood outside her bedroom with a blanket wrapped around her shoulders, wide-eyed and alert.

"What the fuck is that?" she asked.

He answered by lifting his baseball bat to let her know he would handle things if they got out of hand. Eton opened the door a crack and stopped it from being pushed open further with his foot. Two guys and a girl nearly fell in. They were franticly trying to get inside.

Eton stepped outside, ready to face whatever chased the group into the cottage. The fog was constant on the island. He listened for anything, but all was silent. Kerry watched from her bedroom door, waiting to hear an explanation.

"Dude," the guy with dreadlocks breathed. His hands were on his knees as if to steady himself, but what were they running from?

The girl had been crying. Her makeup streaked down her face in black smears. The older, balder guy was facing the wall. He said nothing. Eton had gone from dead sleep to high alert, and now he was just annoyed.

"Who are you guys?" he asked.

"I'm Jeremy," the balding one answered. "That's Ryan and Tiff."

"Hey, aren't you the ghost hunters on YouTube?" Kerry asked.

"That's us," Jeremy said.

Cool. Well, now that they made their introductions...

"I get why you would come here," Eton said. "But can we get an explanation?"

"Something's there," Ryan said as he talked with his hands. "Something that is way out of our paygrade."

"Do you guys want a drink?" he asked. "I got these cans of Rose wine..."

"No!" all three said at once.

"Kombucha it is," he said, opening a small freezer to produce bottled drinks. "We only arrived two weeks ago, so we're not set up all the way."

"There's this hole and a door," Ryan babbled. "It has a peephole on the inside..."

Eton hadn't watched the show, but he assumed ghost hunters believed in ghosts and probably saw them everywhere. Especially on a spooky island that appeared out of nowhere. That was why he and his sister were there, after all. To cater to tourists.

"Okay, okay," Eton said. "What happened? A little more slowly this time."

He listened to the story and didn't get what was so paranormal about it. They were trespassing, getting drunk, and playing loud music when a door opened. "I didn't realize anyone was living there," he said. "Bart is the only one brave enough to come out here, and he didn't mention bringing anyone else."

"Maybe they came on a private boat?" Kerry offered.

"From where? There's only one place anyone can dock," Eton said.

"So much of my equipment," Jeremy muttered. "Even my phone. At least I still have the camera and the EVP reader."

The guy was distraught. He could sympathize. His last phone cost over two months' rent. "I'll tell you what, the three of you can take my room for the night. I'll sleep in Kerry's room."

"I appreciate it," Jeremy said.

It took some time to get back to sleep. It wasn't just Kerry's snoring because of her retainer or the three guests staying in his room. It wasn't even the fact that he was lying on freezing cold ground. What kept Eton up that night was the fact that the internet bill was staggering. He had already paid thousands to lay the groundwork for internet on the island, but the cable company tacked on so many fees that the internet bill was over seven hundred dollars.

Kerry didn't know, but they were about to lose her only access to the outside world. Eton had to hurry and get the store running. At this rate, they couldn't afford to stay the rest of the month. Just outside the window, a drip fell with enough consistency that Eton could focus on the sound. It pushed him into a restless sleep. His last thoughts were on the squatters and trying to live with his sister without internet.

The next morning, Eton woke with chilled hands. Even the tip of his nose was cold. He pulled a beanie over his head and came out to find Kerry standing by the coffee pot, wrapped in a blanket. "Morning."

"Morning," he replied. "Have our guests woken yet?"

Kerry shook her head. "Their door is still closed."

He would enjoy however many mornings and coffee and videos he had left until they flipped the switch. How the hell was he going to tell her? "You know, Kerry," he started. "I think we're too invested in our modern conveniences."

"Uh, huh."

"Our society is a frazzled, anxiety-ridden stress ball because we have access to so much information but are powerless to use it in a meaningful way."

"I use it in a meaningful way," Kerry argued.

"Well, yeah, you use it to learn how to make stuff for the store—which is pretty cool, but people figured that stuff out without the internet. I bet if you put your mind to it, you could learn it on your own."

"Yeah, I'd rather just use shared information, thanks."

He rubbed his brow bone. This wasn't going anywhere. After his second cup of coffee, he traveled to the outhouse behind the cottage. "Hey guys," he said to the sheep and chickens in the covered pens.

After feeding the animals, he returned to the cottage and canceled the second refrigerator. He couldn't afford it with that internet bill stepping on his neck. Besides, there wasn't a lot of room in this cottage. He had hoped to prove himself an entrepreneur, but the half-assembled racks and boxes on the dirt floor, accompanied by a worn, old fridge, weren't what he had in mind.

With a resigned sigh, he began assembling the racks and shelving. His bedroom door remained closed and grew more suspicious with each minute. He didn't notice the paper on the cash register until after he checked his bedroom. All three of their guests had left before he or Kerry woke up.

"Well, it seems they left before we noticed," he announced.

Kerry stood by the antique register, staring at the note. Her face was pale. His stomach dropped, fearing the worst. He stood beside Kerry and stared at the note. It read: "*IOU 500 dollars—thx.*"

"They took all the bills from the till." He couldn't believe it. "Our first customers, and they rob us."

"I'm so sorry, Andrew—I mean Eton," Kerry said as he sulked out of the cottage. To her credit, his sister accepted his name change. He told her it was because he wanted to keep a lid on his identity after going viral in the worst way possible, but honestly, he just thought Eton was a way cooler name.

"We need some wood."

He chopped at a log with his full strength, but it only made a tiny cut. He threw all his weight into hit after hit, unable to strike in the same place twice on the wood round. He didn't understand why the delivery tow boat owners laughed when they pulled away from the shore until now. He assumed they underestimated him like everyone else did. While flailing at the wood round, he thought that if they knew just how much of an idiot he was, they would have never left him on that island. A fucking failure was all he was.

He hacked at the wood until he was in pain and couldn't lift the axe over his head anymore. Fuck it, he had a generator anyway. He fed the chickens and the sheep. Initially, he wanted to buy a cow, but now he was glad he didn't get one. There was no time to care for that many animals. Kerry tried talking him into getting a horse. The thought made him laugh hard enough that the pair of sheep ran to the other side of their pen.

"What are you laughing at?" Kerry asked.

How long she was standing behind him?

"Just about how Mom and Dad were right and how fucked I am."

"Well, most people pay with a debit card anyway," she said, shifting from one knee-high boot to the other. Her five-hundred-dollar boots she bought in New York last fall.

Eton spread his arms out wide and gestured, "What people? There's no one here. There were supposed to be a shit ton of tourists in need of basic supplies on the island that *magically appeared* out of nowhere.

No one is here to use their debit cards, and even if they did, we're about to lose our internet because I can't afford it."

"What?" Kerry's eyes went wide, no longer the optimist.

"I spent thousands getting internet here. The cable company tacked on so many shit fees that unless I come up with seven hundred dollars from all these customers"—he yelled into the vacant hillside—"we will have no internet. No talking to your girlfriend, no surfing the internet, no way to take debit cards."

Kerry unclenched her jaw and searched the ground as if it would have her precious internet. Her eyes were watering, and Eton struggled to find an ounce of sympathy. He was too angry and too busy feeling sorry for himself.

"You don't even pay rent. How did you go broke so fast?" she accused.

"Oh, I know, it's going to be so hard spending the next few months without internet," he said. "If you're lucky, we'll be forced to go home sooner than that. Our parents can spend the rest of their lives reminding me about the time I tried to open a business using my college savings."

"I need to call Holly," Kerry said. She turned around and ran back into the cottage.

With the animals fed and the wood not chopped, he forced himself to go back into the cottage to finish building the store. He couldn't even sell cans of wine to hipsters, but they would at least set the store up with the little keychains and shit Kerry made.

He lost a great deal of motivation setting up the shelves and items because there were no customers, but also because he found himself overwhelmed with taking care of the animals and making the cottage livable. He wasn't much of a handyman, but he'd taken a few semesters of wood shop in high school.

In her bedroom, Kerry was talking to her girlfriend. He stopped feeling sorry for himself when he heard how hard his sister was crying. He bowed his head. "I'm such a dick."

Kerry didn't want to come here. She wanted to stay in Maine with her friends and her girlfriend or maybe go on one of those senior trips. Instead, his sister was forced to come with him to this island because his parents wanted this "phase" that was her and Holly to run its course.

"Hullo?" A scratchy old man's voice sounded.

He turned and forced a smile when he wanted to cry. "Hey, Bart."

The man was in his sixties and lived a few hours away. His shaggy white hair and weathered face were always a joyful sight. He was wearing his lucky suspenders today.

"Hey, I can walk around in here!"

Eton was too upset to talk about it. "Did you pick up a trio of younger people this morning?"

"No, must have been the Norwegians."

"Explains why they needed all the money from my till."

"Oh no," Bart took off his hat.

He glared at the can of twelve-dollar wine in his hand and set it on the shelf.

"Yeah."

"You know, Iceland officials are saying to steer clear of this place until they investigate it, but they won't do that until it's named our territory. UK thinks it's theirs, but Norway wants to use some metric way of determining whose jurisdiction it falls under."

"So, what you're saying is that people won't come here from Iceland, and Norway is still not talking about it, so I might get some bored Scottish tourists, but that's it."

Bart shrugged with his hands in his acid-washed jeans. In that moment of awkward silence, they could hear Kerry burst into sobs from her bedroom. He sighed in defeat. "I can't pay my internet bill."

"I never understood the thing," Bart said under his mustache. "But it's how the girl talks to her friend, yes?"

Eton nodded. "She hates it here."

"Maybe invite the friend for a visit. Could be useful to have another set of hands out here."

It was a good idea.

"I'll probably have no choice; Kerry will be even more useless if I don't."

"Excuse me?" Kerry's strained voice came from behind him.

Bart's sagging brow raised, and he said, "I'll be back in a few days. Hopefully, your luck will have turned for the better."

"I'm useless?" she said, crossing her arms.

Eton really didn't want to fight with her. They were both beyond upset as it was. "Do you want to bring Holly out here or not?"

Kerry's face strained between emotions. She wanted to be angry, but she was too excited by the prospect of having Holly stay with her on the island. He didn't mind; he thought Holly was the coolest shit to ever happen to his sister. If anyone could get this place moving, it would be her.

"I have to call her," Kerry said as she dashed back into her bedroom.

He laughed, and the tightness in his chest eased. He would give this place a few more weeks tops before liquidating all the inventory. Bart would sell the animals quicker than the cans of Rose wine, but he would have Kerry home in time for spring semester. He would work with his dad for a few years just to keep the complaining to a minimum while he tried to figure out what to do with his life.

The generator's constant roaring faltered, and the lights he had rigged around the store dimmed and refused to return to their full capacity. "Shit," he groaned.

This was the last thing he needed. He went back outside to see what was wrong with the generator. Trying to keep the stone cottage warm meant he needed space heaters or to get better at chopping wood. The belt on the generator was okay. He checked the oil and gas and noticed the oil was way lower than it should have been, and there was a small dark line that led from the oil compartment to the grass below.

There was an oil leak in his generator somewhere. He was having a hard time staying on the bright side, but he was at least competent enough to have bought more oil and fuel than he needed. The generator was second-hand. He bought it off someone Bart knew. He anticipated it not lasting long, but he had hoped it would last longer than a few weeks.

Kerry had left her cave and came out to see what was going on. She was wearing makeup, which meant she was talking to Holly. "What was with the lights? I lost connection."

"Just my life falling apart," he said. "Nothing to worry about. I'll make sure you can still use your extra bright lighting mirror to put makeup on—in the literal middle of nowhere."

"Jesus, Eton," she said. "You're such a dick."

"Today I was bankrupt by your internet bill and robbed by hipsters!" he said. "How the hell does someone get robbed by people who can't even figure out which way is up on their several-thousand-dollar cameras?"

Kerry snorted and couldn't stop laughing. Eton was trying to stay mad, but it was no use. He felt as though he were cracking at the seams. "And now, my generator has an oil leak, which means one of us needs to get better at chopping wood because once I'm out of oil, it's going to get mighty cold. Internet will be the least of your worries."

Kerry's face dropped as Eton's emotions went from anger to humor to near tears. She wasn't laughing anymore. "Maybe I can ask—"

"Nom" he said, pointing the generator dipstick at her. "No. I can't ask them. They made it clear that this was a fail or fly thing."

"I was going to ask Holly," Kerry said.

Eton's eyes went wide. "Your girlfriend? We can't ask your girlfriend. She lives in New York; you know how expensive it is to live in New York? People look at obituaries for places to live."

"Holly has money," Kerry said.

"I'm not asking your girlfriend for money," Eton said. "We just need to make adjustments."

"Adjustments." Kerry crossed her arms and gave a look that promised she would pay him back for the suffering he had put her through this summer.

"We need to take it easy on the generator," Eton said. "The leak is small, and I can top off the oil for a while, but it will get worse. We will use daylight and candlelight and only charge our phones once a day."

Kerry groaned.

"No more laptop. No more videos online."

"I hate this place," Kerry stomped around. "I swear to fucking god it's cursed. Nothing has gone right since we've been here, nothing!"

He had to agree with his younger sister. It was like the island wanted them gone. The generator was the most current in a long line of unforeseen issues that even his most careful planning couldn't avoid. All he could do was nod at Kerry's assessment.

"First were the coyotes that killed Peabody," she said. "We had everything reinforced with chickenwire, and the pen was fully secure, but the next day, Peabody's remains were smeared across the front yard."

He'd been waiting for her to bring that up. Kerry had fallen in love with the chicken and named it Peabody. His goal was to become as self-sustainable as possible, and he'd explained that they were going to eventually eat Peabody, but Kerry wasn't having it.

The night they put up the chicken coop, something got in there and mutilated the chicken, leaving its body like a warning. It didn't eat it. It pulled the poor thing apart and decorated the countryside. "I still find feathers," he agreed.

Kerry was on a rampage. She was now pacing back and forth as she continued her rant. "Then, after Peabody, was the pallet that was filled with maggots. Almost as disgusting as Peabody."

"Okay," Eton interjected, "But that may not be the island's fault. That was an issue with the warehouse that delivered it. Who knows how long it was—"

"No, Eton. It wasn't like that until it came here." Kerry said. "You checked each pallet and signed off on them. Maggots can't even survive in Kombucha! Nothing can survive on Kombucha!"

Hipsters could.

All he could do was shrug. He didn't know why or how. He opened his mouth to speak but realized he would not get a word in while his sister was venting.

"Don't even get me started on the Norwegians!"

"I think they are the reason our friends took our money," he said.

Kerry stopped pacing for a moment. The Norwegians were a trio of fishing brothers who had tried to charge double what Bart would to transport them to shore. They were part of a bigger group spread along several boats that lined the dock and mocked them when they first set up shop.

"The ghost hunters probably saw a boat and flagged it down at the dock and got the Norwegians instead of Bart."

"Cash up front, more cash at the dock," he agreed.

Kerry cursed under her breath and threw the tantrum he was too reserved to throw himself.

"Thank you," he said.

"For what?"

He capped the generator and stood up, wiping his hands on his pants. "Thanks for not blaming me for ruining your life."

"Nah," she said. "I blame our parents."

"You've got about four more years until you can't blame them anymore. After that, it's all on you," he warned.

"Who do you think is the bigger disappointment?" she asked. "The college dropout or the lesbian?"

He shrugged. "I don't think they will feature either of us in the yearly Christmas letter."

They laughed and went inside, saying farewell to their internet and cellphones. To their lighting mirrors and coffee machines. The last thing they watched on video was how to chop wood before packing it away.

That day, the store came together and actually looked like a real convenience store. Shelves were up, and items were stocked. Sometimes, Eton impressed himself. Kerry was too busy figuring out how to knit a shawl of her own design.

Chapter Five

LOOK! CATS!

They could view so much of the world from the device. Everything was scarcely recognizable; even people no longer looked like people. Their flawless, painted faces were plastered everywhere. She touched her own face and wondered if the people of this world would think her ugly or strange. Would they know she was not of this time?

"Destiny."

His voice cut through the noise in her mind, and she jumped. "You startled me."

Tension mounted between her brows, and she set the device down. It was all too easy to get lost in such a world that she wondered if it was real. Much like the stories within books. They painted a different picture than reality.

Daniel was smiling for the first time since they woke up. "Come have a look at this."

Taking her hand, he led her down the stairs and out the front door. The daylight was intense after dwelling in such darkness. She squinted and allowed her eyes to adjust. A curious call came from above.

It was a bird of some sort. It had a white and gray body with an orange beak. "A seagull?" she asked.

She had only seen them in pictures. They were common on the mainland, but for whatever reason, they did not come to the island. Destiny was told that the island was too far from larger lands, and that was why the gulls did not occupy it, but they were here now.

"There's more," Daniel said. He practically dragged her down the hill with his excitement. Near the edge of the island, she could hear barking. Hands around her waist in case she lost balance, her fiancé instructed her to peer over the edge.

On a small sandbank at the bottom of the cliff was a group of fat, round things with whiskers. They were seals! Destiny giggled with the discovery, well aware of Daniel's intent stare. "It seems we have guests."

"If they are here now, why weren't they before?" he asked.

"I don't think they could find the island before," she said. "I was reading things on the device."

Daniel did not want to hear about it. He pulled away, but she dug her nails into his arm. "There were articles about an island appearing out of nowhere. A scientific marvel."

His ears perked at the mention of science. "What do they think it is?"

"Daniel, these people study science. The device had articles and articles about so many discoveries. It can explain so much."

He was so reluctant to meet her eyes then. It was like Daniel wanted to be as excited as she was, but something held him back. "But do they know why the island is only visible now?"

"You, of all people, should know science is merely a theory waiting to be disproved. They think it has something to do with the atmosphere. 'Climate Change.'"

Daniel chewed on his lip and nodded. "All I know is that if seals and seagulls came through, it's only a matter of time before people do."

She hoped for it. People meant they could leave the island for the first time. The first Sallows to leave since their family was first sent here. "Would that be such a bad thing?"

"We need answers first."

Still clutching his arm, Destiny relented and rejoined him. He was right. They needed answers before they could leave. Her mother said her family was banished to the island as a punishment for witchcraft. Nathaniel's diary claimed the Sallows defended the world from monsters. Another theory was that Nathaniel was, in fact, the bastard son of the king.

If there were indeed monsters left on the island, she and Daniel would need to deal with them before going anywhere. "We owe that much to our family's legacy," she said.

***

Returning to the mansion was a reminder of another hurdle. What would they do with Sallows Hall? There was no way the two of them could repair it. She looked at Daniel, who was scanning the entryway as though thinking the same.

"One thing at a time," he said. "We start by cleaning the spaces we use the most and working our way out."

She took the drawing room while Daniel went upstairs, probably to clean her bedroom. Giddy with the prospect of having her fiancé in her room, she set about removing the rug and taking all the dishes to the kitchen. What if he stumbled across her underclothes?

Night had fallen by the time she finished sweeping and repositioning the furniture. Through the foggy glass, Destiny beheld another marvel of the new world. She thought it was a figment of her imagination at first. A trick of the glass or a strange reflection, but there were green lights in the sky!

"Daniel?" she called outside the dining hall.

"Up here," he shouted.

Hurrying up the stairs, she found him in her room, stripping the linens off the bed. "I figured we would want these washed, eventually."

"Look outside."

He did, and the sheets dropped from his hands. "What is that?"

"Another marvel we could not see until today."

It was like the world was beckoning to her, pleading with Destiny to leave the island and seek all the things it offered. She craved the freedom, the newness, but there were so many questions that needed answers.

"Are you hungry at all?" she asked.

He furrowed his brow and shook his head. "You'd think I would be by now. Are you?"

She shook her head. "I'm not tired at all."

"Nor am I."

What did it mean? Not so much as a wisp of hunger. She had been working in the drawing room for hours. No sweat and no fatigue. Daniel was experiencing the same. There were no fires lit in the house, and she was not cold.

"Would you just look at this?" she said, leaning toward Daniel with the phone. He no longer shied away, but an air of reluctance remained. His lips went thin as he stared at her. He took the device and flipped through the news articles.

"These are recent science articles," she said. "It's like books. Unlimited books."

The screen grew dim, so she tapped again. The sound of his breath catching as she pressed her chest into his side was enough to make her squirm. He didn't resist, even with the device in her hand.

"You have to let it know you're still reading; it's just a machine."

He scrolled through the pictures of smiling people. He shook his head as if the words and pictures meant nothing. "It's fascinating, really." His sarcasm was muted for her benefit.

"Just try," she said. "You might find something to connect to in this new world. Something good."

Daniel read a news title 'Climate Change: What you need to know to survive the oncoming glacial melt.'

Of course, he'd find that story of all things. She scrolled down to another title, but this article had a video. The moving pictures startled Daniel at first, but the content quickly negated his fear.

"Look! Cats!"

The couple watched images of cats knocking things off counters and laughed as their owners pleaded for them not to. They watched cats chase things, snuggle, frighten dogs. Soon, it was her fiancé who was scrolling and selecting videos. She was happy that Daniel was warming up to the device.

"I know things have changed a lot," she said. "But deep down, the things that matter still matter."

More videos came on the screen. This time, it was cats with babies. They laughed and laughed until the sun came up. "I want a cat one day," she told Daniel.

"What about a baby?" he asked.

The question flustered her. They hadn't even said their marriage vows yet, though she supposed it didn't matter anymore. He wanted to have a baby with her!

"I guess one of those as well," she grinned.

"How about five?"

She cringed at the number. Five babies were less romantic than one. "Let's just start out with one and go from there."

"Do you think we'll be able to have children?"

"We won't know until we try," she said. She hadn't thought about it, but now that he mentioned it, maybe it wasn't a possibility for them because of what had happened to them—whatever that was.

Daniel watched the screen grow dim once again, only this time, a spinning circle popped up, and the device went black. She tried to push the button, but nothing would happen.

"I think it ran out of fuel," he said.

That made sense. She nodded before resting her head on his shoulder. "I know you don't want to, but I think it's time we see if there are others on the island."

"Do we have to?" he sounded like a boy who didn't want to do his chores.

"There is a whole world out there. Do you want to stay in this house forever?"

He wrapped his arms around her and squeezed, playfully rocking her back and forth. "I just want you all to myself!"

"Then come with me."

She dressed in her most modern attire. A plaid dress that was lying on the bedroom floor. It didn't fit her well. It was too tight around the chest, but from what she'd seen on the device, clothing didn't need to fit appropriately anymore.

"We should bring the device with us," he said. "Maybe we can return it to whoever left it."

Instinct told her to snatch the phone out of Daniel's hand and never let go. She realized this was a sort of effect of using it to begin with. She noticed he hadn't let it go since she had given it to him. What a strange power it held.

Swallowing this need, she nodded. "Yes, we shouldn't keep what isn't ours."

To her disappointment, the island appeared no different than she remembered. The early morning mist still clung to the rocks and moss. The forest was closer to the house than she remembered.

"Watch your step," Daniel warned. "There are deer pellets everywhere."

"I imagine the population has overgrown since..."

Destiny felt dread brew in her stomach. Something awful must have happened to the rest of the family, and something in her heart told her it was no mystery what.

"Daniel, whatever happened, I think it had something to do with the basement. In fact, I'm certain of it."

He gazed at the morning horizon. He frowned and nodded, "I'll get it sealed up."

The shore was lined with seals and seagulls. "It's as if they've always lived here."

"Look at all the trash," Daniel said.

Her smile faded as she saw what he was referring to. There were several bins filled with what was once bagged rubbish. The birds were picking away at the shiny black bags, and now garbage was strewn everywhere.

"Someone else lives here," she said. "We should let them know."

It didn't take long at all to locate the new residents. There was a sign at the dock that said, "Grocery," and an arrow to show which way to go. She braced Daniel's arm. Partially because she was thrilled to meet new people but also because it was once Daniel's home. She couldn't fathom what was going through his mind then. Seeing the only home he had ever known inhabited by strangers.

It was a small cottage shared with his two siblings and both parents, far too small for the five of them. Made from stones and wood with a thatched roof. The new residents had replaced the thatching with tiles, and the windows had taping along the edges, but otherwise, it was the same as she remembered.

Daniel's face was unreadable. She looked up at him with pleading eyes, hoping that he would find something positive to say, but he said nothing either way.

"Are you okay?"

Daniel had his hands in his pockets as he regarded the cottage. She regretted that she ever asked him to come. "You can go back," she said. "I can just—"

"I'm not leaving you on your own with these strangers."

"I'm just sorry," she said. "This was your childhood home."

"My mother hated this house," he said at last. "It was always too cold, and with the time my father spent fixing this place, he could have just built another."

"Why didn't he?"

"Don't remember," Daniel said, giving her a sad smile. "I guess he just wanted things to stay the same."

The door swung open, and they came face to face with a man. He was around their age, with blue eyes and dark, thick brows. His hair was tucked into a tight-knitted hat around his head, but Destiny could see his fringe poking out here and there. He was tall, nearly as tall as Daniel, but with broader shoulders.

He was wearing a red and black plaid shirt that was similar in design to the print on her dress. "Hey!" he said, noticing the similarity. "Twinsies!"

She did not know what he was saying. Bursting into giggles, she found herself unable to stop laughing. Daniel squeezed her hand, and she covered her mouth to stifle it. The man didn't dwell in the doorway. He opened the door wide and said, "Come on in! We're open!"

"Thank you," Daniel said through a locked jaw as they stepped through the door.

"My name is Eton. I'm the only store to be found on the island. If you need something you don't see here, just let me know."

She gave a nod to the man, and he stepped behind his counter. Overwhelmed by all the things. So many things! What did they all do? She resisted the urge to reach out and touch everything like a small child. Instead, she walked along the rows of shelves and tried to read their labels.

Daniel stood in the room, but it was as though he were somewhere else. Sometimes, he would pick something up and examine it before glaring at it and before putting it back down.

"Is there a brand you prefer?" Eton asked.

Daniel turned to the shop owner and slipped his hands in his pockets. "No, I just recognize this from all the garbage left outside."

Eton's eyes went wide, and he said, "Excuse me," before stepping into one of the cottage bedrooms. "Cursed, I tell you!" A young woman shouted from the other room.

The shop owner reemerged from the back room. "We will have that cleaned up in no time. Would you guys like some coffee? Tea?"

"No thanks," Daniel replied.

Since they woke, Destiny hadn't felt thirst either. It seemed like a distant problem. One she couldn't imagine having to begin with.

She found an arrangement of soaps and bath salts. She smelled each one of them. Delighted by the citrus and lavender fragrances. They reminded her of something warm and safe. She grabbed one bar of each scent and brought them to the counter before going back for more things.

She felt Daniel's eyes on her, but he said nothing as she found more items to purchase. While money may not have been used on the island, Destiny did know the fundamentals of how it worked. Books could be more valuable than gold. Soon, the counter was full of items, including hats, gloves, bottles that promised to give energy, funny little clippers, pictures on small cards of hard paper, and small crinkly bags.

Eton looked down at the pile, then looked her in the eyes with a smile that made her want to giggle. "Did you find everything you need?"

"Daniel needs to buy new clothes," she said.

"Okay, what size are you, Daniel?"

"I don't know," he admitted.

Eton came from around the counter and approached him. He studied Daniel up and down. "You look about my size," he said. "You want to step in here for a minute?"

"Sure," Daniel followed the store clerk into a room. There was an exchange, and Eton stepped out of the room, shutting the door behind him. She smiled at him.

"Have you been here long?" she asked.

"Almost a month."

Daniel stepped out wearing pants that presumably belonged to Eton. The pants only elongated his legs and gave him a sharper appearance. One that made her knees tremble.

"They are a little long, still too big around the waist, but you have a belt. I don't know how long you're going to be here, but I can order some stuff online, and Bart can bring them here," the store owner said.

"Online?" She tore her gaze from Daniel's legs. "Like on this?" She held out the device.

Eton tried his best to hide his alarm, but his pause was long and telling. She was out of fashion but not stupid. He knew who this phone belonged to.

"Um, yeah. Exactly," he said. "You guys doing some cosplay?"

"Precisely," Daniel said.

"Right on," the store clerk said. "I appreciate the dedication."

"Yeah. Sometimes, things don't go as planned, though," Daniel said, gesturing to his pants.

Eton gave a full laugh. "I've been there. I've lost my pants in weirder places."

Daniel walked with Eton towards the counter, where Destiny waited. "Just get me a few pairs of trousers, pants, and shirts. Any will do."

"Okay, it will take several weeks to ship. Bart comes every few days. You can come back and check in on the status whenever you'd like."

"Very good," Daniel said.

"How would you like to pay for all of this?"

Destiny placed a chunk of gold the size of a large pocket watch on the counter. It made a clunking noise as it hit the table. Eton nodded while staring at the gold. The shop owner tried his best to keep his expression under control, but his skin was turning bright red.

"I take it that's real," Eton said without breaking his gaze from the nugget.

"Of course." Daniel straightened.

Eton's eyes narrowed. "You're not just cosplayers, are you?"

Daniel and Eton were having a stare off, and Destiny was feeling warm all over. She didn't know how to answer his question. Daniel tried to play along with whatever Eton initially thought they were, but it seemed the jig was up.

It had been her idea to bring the gold nugget. She was hoping to use it to barter their way to shore, but there were no boats, and this was the only sign of life. They had lots of gems and gold. Things brought over by Nathaniel Sallows but totally useless on the island until now.

"Do you want the gold or not?" Daniel asked.

"This is worth more than all the things you bought..."

"Keep it," Daniel said, sliding the nugget closer to the shopkeep. "Our little secret."

Eton's eyes went back to the gold, and he shook his head, "This isn't something I can say no to."

"We have a deal?" Daniel extended a hand.

Eton nodded. "Certainly. Anything you need, just let me know."

The clerk put the gold in his pocket and was bagging the items when a younger girl walked in from what was once Daniel's bedroom. She had long, brown, wavy hair. She was wearing a sweater three times too big and thin pants underneath. She also wore a pair of boots, like men wore when they went hunting.

"The birds tore into the bags. We need to either double bag them or get some heavy lids."

"This is my sister, Kerry," Eton introduced. "She will work here for the winter. Kerry, this is..."

"Destiny," she replied. "And this is Daniel."

"Our first customers!" Kerry smiled. "Cool."

Destiny loved Kerry's eyes. Her makeup was so sophisticated. The most she had ever worn was some rouge on her cheeks and lips. Kerry's skin was dewy and with a flawless finish. Bronzed lines sculpted her cheeks, and there was purple pigment around her eyes.

"Do you guys want me to help you carry this?"

"No," Daniel said. "I can manage."

Eton led them to the door and opened it for them. "Thank you, guys," he said. His eyes met Destiny's, and he said, "We were robbed the other day, and you just saved our asses."

"Robbed?" Daniel's voice rang with concern. It forced Eton to tear his gaze away from her, and she shook off whatever feelings lingered.

"Yeah, these people came pounding on our door the other night with some shit about the mansion being haunted. They were so spooked, we let them stay, but the next morning, my till was empty. I was about to pack my bags before you came along."

He was staring at her again. Destiny swallowed hard and ignored it. "This is not ours," she said, holding out the device. "We thought perhaps it was yours, but that is not the case."

"This probably belonged to one of them," Eton said.

"See if you can't use that to get your money back," Daniel said with a nod.

"Dude," Eton's eyes welled as though he were about to cry. "I don't even know what to say."

"You live on the island now," Destiny told Eton as she smiled at Daniel. "We help one another get by."

"Just so that you don't go talking about us," Daniel reminded them.

"Of course," Eton said. "It's no one's business."

"Good," Daniel said.

They walked along the path with three large, full paper bags. Destiny didn't speak for a long while. She wanted to let Daniel work out their encounter without her attempts to sway his reasoning. Once the mansion was in sight, she couldn't help but prod him.

"That went well," she said.

"Yeah," Daniel agreed. "We've got a point of access to the new world, and they seem happy enough to leave us be."

She should have been happier with his positive outlook. Daniel agreed with her that not everything the new world offered was bad. Some of it was rather nice and even convenient. The store clerk and his sister were happy to provide them with the things they needed and keep their presence on the island a secret.

But part of her was also unhappy with the answer. She wanted to see what life was like outside the island. It wasn't fair to want so much from Daniel straight away. To leave everything she ever knew to dive headfirst into a new world was a foolish idea.

"Yes," she agreed. "Let's go home and do some housecleaning."

Daniel smiled at the notion before looking down at her, carrying a bag with one arm. "Is that heavy?"

"Not at all." It was light as a tuft of cotton.

"I can go back and ask the clerk to carry it for you," Daniel said. "I'm sure he would."

The way Eton watched her wasn't lost on Daniel after all. Destiny had hoped it went unnoticed. "He was just trying to be helpful."

"I'm sure," Daniel said.

"I didn't realize you were the jealous type."

Daniel had to think on that. She enjoyed watching the range of emotions that flickered on his face while he debated it in his head. "I didn't think I was, but then again, it's not something I've ever encountered before."

She gave a thoughtful nod to his answer. Many things were different about them since they woke up. They were in love in their youth, and it felt as though they were relearning one another as adults. The love was still there and stronger than ever, but the person was different.

It was a long walk. By now, carrying anything should have been a little cumbersome at the very least. Daniel marched on, full of energy, and she kept up without issue. Not a gleam of sweat on his brow. Was it connected to their lack of human needs?

"Daniel," she asked. "Have you..."

He turned to her, waiting for her to finish. She couldn't believe she was blushing over something so stupid. They were adults. "Needed to use the outhouse?"

"I've wanted to ask you the same question, but it's not right to ask a woman such questions."

"I haven't," she admitted.

"Nether have I."

Clearly, their bodies were stronger than ever, but they were no longer performing basic human functions. "Are we still human?"

"I'm not sure," Daniel said. "But I think we will find the answers in the house."

She agreed. "We have our work cut out for us."

"Good thing we don't need sleep anymore."

It was a joke, but the ramifications were too intense for her to bear. If they were not human, it meant that there were even more answers to find before they could consider leaving—if they ever could leave.

CHAPTER SIX

TIDES OF FORTUNE

Eton turned to look at his sister and dragged his hands across his face. One minute, they were on the verge of returning home, and the next? They could keep the internet on. Not only that, but they would have a way of getting back at the people who stole from them.

"Wow," Kerry said. "I can't even..."

He plugged the phone into the nearest phone charger. "That asshole will need to pay up now."

"That couple, though," Kerry said. "They were weird."

"I think they're the ones the ghost hunters saw at the mansion and thought it was haunted."

Kerry laughed and crossed her arms. "They're not ghosts."

"No," he agreed. "I think they're squatters, and they've been here for a long time."

"Pretty sure the guy didn't like you."

"Yeah," he said. "The woman was cute, though."

Kerry raised her brows. He shouldn't have said anything about the woman. They were most likely a couple, and he had a bad habit of getting in between couples. His sister would not call him out on it today, at least.

"Just how long do you think they've been squatting?"

"Their clothes were homemade. And the dude's pants were way too big. I think they were probably here since they were kids, maybe even born here."

"Like Amish people?"

"Maybe." He took off his beanie and scratched at his head through the thick brown hair before putting it back on.

"Do you think they are a couple or related...or both?"

He gave an awkward laugh. The thought had occurred to him. "I don't know. I just know I need to get Bart over here ASAP because I got this to exchange," he said, pulling the lump of gold out of his pocket.

"Holy shit!"

"Yeah," he said. "This might be enough to keep us going. And if the ghost hunters give us the five hundred back, we're set for the month."

Kerry's face lit up. "Does that mean we can use the internet again?" she asked.

"Not yet," he said with gritted teeth. "When we have customers who use the internet, we can keep it on during store hours, but they charge me by usage out here, so we can't use it unless we absolutely need to."

It was a partial truth. The internet was an added expense that they didn't need. He still had to pay off the last bill, but after that, he intended to keep it off. It wasn't just about the money. Since they put the phones and laptops down, productivity had increased.

The two of them had stalled for weeks on setting up the store. After they got off the computers, they had the shop up and running in a day. Kerry had taken on the role of caring for the animals and the shop while he had figured out how to chop wood and was improving the cottage's insulation so they wouldn't freeze at night.

His whole body was sore, but it was a good ache. The kind after a solid workout, only this was just everyday life. He wanted to come out here to get away from technology and live off the land, but with everything going on, he craved the normalcy that the internet provided. On the mainland, it was essential for jobs and living, but out here, it was a hindrance.

Kerry was trying her best not to pout. He felt bad about it, but she was so lazy when she could just hide in her room and talk to her girlfriend whenever she was available. He knew she didn't want to be here, but maybe their parents had more than one reason to make her come.

"Okay," she said with a sigh. "But I want to FaceTime Holly at least once a night."

"Sure," he said, "An hour tops. Did you talk to her about visiting?"

Kerry shrugged. "She has a lot going on right now, but she said maybe next month."

"Cool."

"I'm going to check on the chickens," she said as she trudged out of the room.

Eton hated disappointing people. He didn't like saying no. It wasn't any easier saying it to his sister. He felt responsible for wrecking her "free year" even when she clearly didn't blame him. Still, if he hadn't declared the world too dependent on technology and gone on a soul-searching business escapade instead of just admitting college was too hard—their parents would have sent Kerry off to Europe for a year instead.

He checked the phone the couple gave him, and it still wasn't ready to be turned on yet. Instead, he called Bart. He was willing to gamble that the ghost hunters would show up the moment he made it known that he had their phone. He didn't want to be a dick about it, but he had no qualms about playing dirty.

***

Eton met Bart at the dock and hopped onto his boat. The fisherman was making this trip just for him. "Hurry up, Eton," he said. "The missus is angry that I'm taking time away from fishing. Says we're losing money."

"Bart, my man," Eton said, strolling to the dock. "I'll pay you double whatever you make in a day with fish."

Bart's coarse brows wiggled. "Oh ho! You got a big fish yourself!"

Eton laughed at the metaphor and imagined the scowl on Daniel's face if he had known he was being referred to as a big fish. Kerry didn't like the idea of being left alone in the store, but she put on a brave face.

"If something comes up, just go to the mansion," he told her. "Daniel and Destiny are weird, but they won't hurt you."

It was an odd assurance but one that they both appreciated. Daniel may not have liked him all that much, but he was confident that the man wouldn't hurt Kerry or let anyone else hurt her. Neither would Destiny. When they said they took care of their own on the island, he got the feeling they meant it.

"Well, boy," Bart called. "I hope it's a same-day payment." Eton pulled out the gold and showed the fisherman. Bart's eyes lit up. "How the hell did you get that?"

He told Bart about the couple and his suspicions while they sailed to Höfn. The fisherman could only shake his head. "In all my years," he said, "I've never had an island just appear like that."

Eton had read about the island on the news and talked to the locals about it. There wasn't any one person who discovered the island. It was more like everyone was out fishing, and there it was. Bart was no exception.

"I saw it on the horizon and thought my navigation went kaput. I've sailed this area going on forty years, never saw the damn thing before. I got on the radio, and there were half a dozen ships out there, just like mine. Asking the same thing; where did that island come from?"

It only increased the mystery that was the couple on the island. If the fishermen didn't see it, how did the couple's families see it? How did that mansion get built when no one knew the island was there to begin with?

"These days, you can't even take a shit without the government knowing," Bart railed as he steered the boat. "That island appeared out of nowhere, I tell you."

Eton was feeling a little unsettled. Bart wouldn't lie about it, and neither would the other fifty fishers in town. He believed them, drunk as they were. Three different countries all confirmed his story, but it was a hard pill to swallow.

He had read theories about weather anomalies that could camouflage small bits of land. The compasses he bought to sell at the store never worked. He assumed they were defective, but maybe the island had some weird magnetic thing that threw off technology. He just knew that islands didn't appear with fully built several-hundred-year-old mansions on them with people already living there.

"I just wish that local authorities hadn't told everyone to stay clear," he said. "I mean, I get they wanted to make sure it was safe, but they could have made that decision before I moved to the island."

Höfn was traditionally a harbor town, but these days, it was more of a tourist hot spot. He didn't have time to check out the rest of Iceland, but from what he understood, this area was uncharacteristically flat for the country. The air was crisp and clean, like most port cities, but it had an earthy quality about it that most didn't.

Anything a tourist could want on a vacation was here. Horseback riding, geothermal baths, bunch of theme parks for kids. The lobster festival was a tremendous hit every summer. The place was full of young, adventuring backpackers and hikers.

His dad worked at the Coast Guard, so they'd heard the news before everyone else. It was his chance to be the first shop on what would become a tourist hotbed. His plan was to charge in and ask for forgiveness later if there were any issues, but people avoiding the island altogether wasn't the problem he expected to encounter.

Bart took Eton to a little storefront painted a bright white with a pine shiplap interior. There were a lot of random items for sale, from jewelry to instruments. He got the feeling that it was a pawnshop or something like that. He didn't speak Icelandic and certainly didn't read it, so he would rely on Bart for a good deal.

Another old, rugged, white man wearing a wool cap greeted Bart familiarly. Bart spoke to the man in Icelandic before turning to him, "Okay, show him what you got."

Eton pulled out the gold lump and set it on the counter. The man's face went blank, and he looked at Bart and asked something.

"He wants to know what karat it is."

"No idea."

The man was talking excitedly and waving his hands as he spoke while Bart translated, "He wants to test it for purity. He thinks this is pure gold that was melted into a nugget. This was something people would do hundreds of years ago. They would keep this kind of, eh, lumpy gold and gems to give as dowry."

He shrugged. "How much can I get for it?"

After the shop owner tested to confirm that it was a solid chunk of twenty-four karat gold weighing five point six ounces, he walked out of the store with nine hundred Króna. A little over seven thousand dollars.

After giving Bart a generous tip, he promised to meet the fisherman back at the dock within a few hours. Bart liked to be home before dark. "I need to go buy something nice for my wife," he said as he danced down the street.

Bart had been with the same woman his entire life, and anytime he had a little extra money, he would bring her home something. It was super romantic, and Eton wished he had something like that. It was probably why he was so attracted to women in relationships.

Eton supposed he interpreted women in relationships as attractive because they looked like they had their shit together. Only after he wrecked everything did he realize it wasn't *her* he wanted, but the *relationship*. It was part of the reason he left Maine and college. He'd burned some bridges that shouldn't have been burned.

Using his phone, Eton found his search for the ghost hunters was not all that hard. The main guy, Jeremy, was actually famous for his findings. The guy, Ryan, was in the contacts, and with one phone call, Jeremy Sands agreed to meet him not too far from Hotel Höfn.

The scraping of sneakers against the sidewalk announced a fast-walking, upright sort of dweeb. Eton was taking advantage of the

Wi-Fi while he waited but wasn't the least bit surprised to look up and see Jeremy Sands glaring at him.

"You got my phone," he said.

"Nice to see you again," Eton said, trying his best to contain his smugness. He rarely got all high and mighty, but how often did someone get to catch the person who nearly ruined him? A rich thief didn't make things any easier. It was hard to not gloat over retribution when a rich guy stole from a poor one.

"Yeah, look," Jeremy said. "I'm sorry we took your money. I was going to send you a check. Those guys at the shore wouldn't take us off the island without some upfront cash."

"The Norwegians."

Jeremy frowned. "Sounds like you know them."

"We've had dealings."

"They refused to take us anywhere but Norway, and those people were not happy to hear where we came from. We had to call my lawyer; it was ugly."

"You were that desperate," Eton laughed. "Couldn't you just wait for me to call someone?"

Jeremy's face went dark. "You don't know what we saw in that house."

Eton was pretty sure he knew but didn't want to spoil the fun just yet. "Well, do you have my money?"

Jeremy handed him one-hundred and twenty-five thousand Króna, "Paying you back, with interest. I really am sorry, man. That place just had me so spooked, you know?"

Eton shrugged and couldn't help but feel sorry for the guy. He wanted to believe that Jeremy intended to pay him back. There was no point in not believing him. It would just be him hanging on to negative energy that served no purpose.

"Here's your phone, by the way."

Jeremy's eyes bugged out of their sockets. "You went in the house?"

Eton shook his head. Keeping a straight face was killing him. "No, the people who live there gave it to me after you left. I don't think they meant to startle you. I think you guys scared them as much as they scared you."

The ghost hunter still wasn't willing to back down on his story. "No," he shook his head. "No, there was no one in the house. Not living, at least. If you saw it, you would understand. I went over the tapes and the EVP. There were so many voices in that house."

"Voices?"

"Yes, voices on my EVP like I've never heard before. My team's still cataloging how many distinct voices are present in the footage. Some of it we're not even sure is human."

Eton wasn't too familiar with what EVP was, but from what he understood, it was a device that recorded ghost voices. "Is that even a real thing, man?"

"Dude, I get it. I'm usually the one who needs convincing, but when I ran around that house with my camera rolling, I did not hear voices other than mine, Ryan's, and Tiff's. We can line up the footage with the EVP and confirm voices other than our own are going on at the same time. Multiple conversations going on at the same time!"

"It's like there are layers over layers of conversations happening all at the same time, all similar but slightly different. It's like the spirits are acting out a story on re-run. I don't know how to explain it. It's real, man. It's the realest thing I've ever done."

He didn't think Jeremy was lying. Crazy people thought they were telling the truth. Then again, Jeremy didn't seem unbalanced. Arrogant, maybe, but not crazy. Eton was overall conflicted about what he was hearing and wondered if he should warn Destiny about what Jeremy was saying.

"Okay," he said. "I should get back; Kerry is there."

"The girl?" Jeremy said. "She's alone there?"

He didn't need douchebag almighty worrying about his sister. "She's fine," he defended. "And she's not alone."

"All right, man, just take care out there, okay?"

This guy had the balls to tell him how to take care of his shit? Eton could only shake his head and leave before he said something he'd regret later. "Yeah, you too."

Eton walked away from the encounter with a sense of bewilderment. What the actual hell just transpired? He didn't expect Jeremy, the guy who stole from them, to express so much concern. He supposed the man's priorities were honest, but his methods were not. His eyes ached from staring at a small screen again for the first time in several days, and he rubbed them as he stepped onto the dock.

He found Bart in his captain's quarters, humming happily.

"So, what did you get her?" Eton asked.

Bart smiled with large yellowed teeth. "I got her a pair of earrings. I'm going to give them to her tonight when I come home for supper."

Eton patted the fisher on the back. "Well, let's get you home in time."

"Aye aye!" the fisherman cried as the motor roared to life.

CHAPTER SEVEN

IN DEATH DO US PART

The drawing room was littered with all the things she had bought from the store. Destiny played with the items sprawled around her like a child during the Sabbath. Letting out a squeal of delight while Daniel scowled at the peeling wallpaper.

"We've got more water damage," he said. "Just tack it on to the list, I suppose."

He did a double-take before grinning at her. "Those little trinkets make you so happy."

She put on the knitted gloves and inhaled the scent of the wool. Her eyes met his, and she nodded. His expression softened, and he went to her before kneeling at the edge of her horde. "You make me very happy," his deep voice purred.

The night dredes had dominated her life until she woke up in the room of pain. Once terrified by the very idea of green eyes, now she couldn't get enough of them. Did that make him a day drede? "Daniel..."

He took her hand and kissed the top of it. "I know I asked you once already, but considering the circumstances, I felt I should ask again. Destiny Sallows, will you be my wife?"

She laughed at how absurd the question was. Of course, she still wanted to marry him. Only when she laughed, his face shadowed with doubt. "Yes, Daniel," she said. "Always yes."

Sitting on her knees, she pressed against him, and her lips connected with his. They had kissed several times before, but this time it was different. There was a stillness about it. A quiet understanding that lingered along their mouths. There would be no ceremony—as the leader of the island, she was the only person able to officiate a wedding anyhow.

As if he could read her mind, Daniel stood, pulling her up by the waist before lifting her up. He carried her to the door only to whack her legs against the half-open pocket door. The dry wood shattered and sent splinters and chunks into the hallway and over the railing. Daniel cringed as fragments landed on the first story; their clatter echoed throughout the mansion.

"Are you all right?" he asked.

She wasn't hurt. At least, she didn't think she was. Rotating her feet, she said, "No harm done."

But Daniel remained unconvinced. He set her down to assess the damage. Squatting down, he looked through the newly made hole in the door. "The entire door has to go," he said.

Destiny didn't feel a thing. Were they so strong that such things could happen? Maybe she was a monster too. It was just a musing, but it cast a dark shadow in her heart. Was it just coincidence that she found her green-eyed fiancé in the room? What if they were the monsters somehow?

"Daniel," she whispered. "What are we?"

"I don't know," he said, staring at the broken door. "I don't know."

***

"We don't have any soap," Daniel grumbled while looking around the room.

"Oh, don't we?" she said, running out of the room to return with a bar of soap she had gotten from the store.

Holding it up to Daniel's nose, he lurched his head away, rejecting the soap initially. Perhaps he was just concerned that she would miss and shove it up his nostrils. Daniel leaned in and sniffed. "Lavender. That's lovely, really."

She knew he would like it. The soaps were handmade and reminded her of the soaps their family used to make. No doubt he felt the same. Daniel took the bar and read the description on the paper wrapper.

"Handmade in France. No dyes, no additives, and no parabens, gluten-free...what are parabens? And Gluten?" he asked. "Should we be worried about these things?"

Couldn't he just be happy? "It's French."

Daniel shrugged. "I suppose it's good since it doesn't have all those things."

They rolled up their sleeves and washed everything in the trough before putting the clothes through the ringer. Daniel pinned them to the cords he'd restrung along the walls so they could dry. "They would smell better if they dried outside, but I don't want to alert anyone to our presence," he said.

Why would that be so bad? "They should know," she said. "We've always lived here, and this is our island."

"We need to know more about what we are before we try to interact with others."

It was something that had been sitting in his mind too. She went to put another dress through the ringer, but when she turned the handle, it got stuck. She tried going backwards and forward again, but it was being stubborn. She gave it a hard push, and the solid wood handle tore clean from the ringer.

She stood there, holding the handle in disbelief. Daniel rushed over to see what had happened. "Are you all right?" he asked, taking her by the shoulders.

"Look what I did!" It wasn't so much frightening as it was exciting.

Daniel cocked his head and said, "Well, I guess we won't be using that anymore."

The thick metal screw that held the handle in had shredded through the solid wood dowels that pressed the clothing. She had ripped it clean off like a dying branch off a tree. There was no mistaking it. This was not something she could have done before.

He hugged her close, took the handle, and tossed it into the corner. "The wood was probably weak from time and use," he explained. "I wouldn't be surprised if termites had been here at some point."

"Where are they now, then?"

"The termites?"

The question was absurd. He wouldn't know the location of the termites any more than she would. Still clutching the handle, Destiny let loose a cackle. The whole thing was so ridiculous. Daniel's chest let loose a laugh as well. "I'm glad you're laughing because I didn't think I could hold back much longer."

For the rest of the day, they swept and cleaned all the debris from the bedroom before retiring to the drawing room so that she could play with all the things she had bought from the store while Daniel read a book on Plato's theories.

"Do you want me to start a fire?" she asked, sitting on the ground surrounded by her modern marvels.

"Are you cold?" he asked.

She shook her head. "I remembered always needing a fire before," she said. "I thought it would be more comforting."

"The additional light would be nice, but the smoke from the chimney will get people's attention."

She disliked feeling like an intruder in her own home. If anyone was an intruder, it was the people who'd made the island their home without her permission. Not that she minded the new arrivals, but she didn't enjoy hiding. "If you won't do it, then I will," she warned.

"Okay," he said, snapping the book shut and standing. "But we need to decide what to do when people return because they will."

What exactly did he think was going to happen? Worst-case scenario, they would force them to leave. That wasn't such a bad thing. Then again, broaching the subject with Daniel was a sticky one. They always postponed the discussion of leaving, but they were always too busy to search.

"These things are so neat," she said, changing the subject.

"I'm not sure what most of that even does."

"Neither do I, but I'm sure we will learn."

"Hm."

That didn't seem to be the topic Daniel wanted to discuss either. She was determined to make the best of it. With a slight grin on her face, Destiny moved to all fours and crawled towards her husband. "I'm sure we have lots to learn," she said playfully.

Daniel's eyes moved towards her. Tossing his book aside, he pulled her onto the sofa. "Just be mindful of the doors," she teased.

His face scrunched with laughter as his nose met hers. "Perhaps we should just walk to your bedroom. Then I will carry you over the threshold."

Taking Daniel by the hand, she led him up the stairs and to her bedroom. It was about time they consummate their marriage. If he had put it off any longer, she would have carried *him* over the threshold!

He hesitated when they got to her door. She assumed it was because he wanted to carry her over, only he was paler than usual. "Don't tell me you're nervous," she teased.

Daniel's eyes fell to the floor. "I know men are not supposed to be nervous about this sort of thing, but it just feels like I've waited an eternity to be with you. Now that we're together, I keep waiting for something to separate us."

"I won't let that happen," she said, kissing his hand. "I promise."

He said nothing else as he swept her off her feet and carried her into the bedroom.

***

Freshly laundered bedsheets were the best thing ever. She pressed the quilt to her face and inhaled the clean scent before airing the blanket across the bed. While she was making the bed, Daniel was beating the drawing room rugs over the banister as if he was taking out his endless angst on them. She snickered but paused when he overheard her.

She took her time hanging up her clothes, not wanting to disturb Daniel. Her bedroom would have been immaculate except for the peeling wallpaper in a few of the corners. She went to open the window to help dry out the room, and she noticed a soft spot in the window frame. Gently poking it, Destiny realized the wood here was rotting and would need to be replaced.

"Daniel," she said over the railing. "We have some rot around this window, too."

Plumes of dust wafted to greet her. Destiny waved it off. Daniel was shaking the carpet runners over the stairway. They reeked of mold and ammonia.

"More on the list of things to do."

She helped Daniel beat the dust off the furniture and sweep the staircase before opening every window possible. This old house needed as much fresh air as it could get. With everything swept and dusted, the house was better but not quite up to standard.

"We'll need to take down all this wallpaper," she said.

"I can't help but wonder if it's just too much for the two of us," Daniel said. "I know we don't sleep, but even if we work non-stop, it will take decades."

She crossed her arms over her chest and looked out the window. It was beginning to rain. "Maybe we should consider leaving."

"Where would we go?" he asked. "This is our home. And the monsters... There is still so much we don't understand about this place."

"We've seen no sign of them. It's just us. It will always be just us."

Daniel nearly dropped the broom in his hand as he stared at her, speechless. She smiled on the inside and pretended not to notice his reaction. She loved rendering her husband speechless. She glanced out the window just as three dark figures came up the hill.

"People are coming to the house," she said. A swell of panic rose in her chest. Daniel was at the window in an instant, looking as well.

"It's not the store clerk."

"No," she agreed. "Do you think it's the intruders?"

"I don't know," Daniel said. "I'm going to lock all the doors. Stay here."

Daniel's footsteps pounded on the old floorboards as he raced around the first story. There were four entrances but countless windows. She chewed on the edge of her nail as she wondered if those windows opened or not. She couldn't remember.

She stood outside the drawing room and waited for Daniel to come up the stairs. The people were knocking on the door when he skirted around the banister and up the steps. This was ridiculous.

"Daniel, this is my house," she said. "I'm just going to tell them to leave."

"We don't know who they are or what they want," he said, taking her hand and leading her upstairs.

They were rattling the door, and she heard the voices get louder as one declared the window could open. She saw them for an instant before Daniel pulled her away. The intruders wore matching uniforms and had shiny strips on their coats.

"People have been here, all right," a man with a thick accent said. "I can see footprints in the dirt over there."

As they ran up the stairs, she dug her feet into the stair landing and gripped the bannister. Daniel shot her a warning glance, but she wouldn't relent. She wanted to hear what they had to say.

"Looks like they're doing some housekeeping."

"Window is open, room is all clean. It's freezing in here, though."

"A fire was built sometime last night," a man with a cleaner drawl said.

The couple hurried up to the fourth level of stairs while the people conducted their investigation.

"Yeah, the tip reported by that *ghost hunter* has some truth. There are people living here. Looks to be squatters."

"They are taking care of the place," the man said. "No signs of drugs or alcohol. There are signs of permanent residency, but there's no way people could live here without a heat source; they'd freeze to death."

"So, squatters who show up, clean the house a bit, then leave?" The thickly accented man laughed.

"I'm guessing it's the Americans trying to spruce up the place for future customers."

"You think he was lying when he said he'd never been here?"

"Absolutely. I think he probably has friends, and that was who the ghost hunters saw."

Daniel tugged on her hand, and she moved away from the staircase. The voices carried well enough that she could hear, even from outside her mother's bedroom. They didn't seem to be traveling closer, and Daniel was starting to relax his grip on her hand.

"You want to check out the rest of the place?"

"No. It's colder in here than it is outside. We'll be back with some researchers next week anyhow."

"I don't see the trouble as long as they're not doing any harm. I want to get home before the game starts."

"We still don't know if this island will be under Scottish law yet or not."

The couple waited for several agonizing minutes before a window squeaked shut and the door closed. She and Daniel exchanged the same worried expression. Change would come, ready or not.

Daniel turned around and stood before her mother's bedroom and said, "Do you want this room to be cleaned as well?"

"Are we not going to talk about that?" she asked, motioning to the downstairs.

"I'll nail the windows shut and board the door," he said. Daniel was staring at the bottles on her mother's vanity and entirely missing the point.

"It doesn't matter if you do that. They will come back and with more people."

"What do you suggest?" Daniel's tone was sharper than she liked.

Destiny didn't answer. She only scowled at him with her arms crossed. He bowed his head apologetically. "I'm sorry," he said. "I didn't mean to take it out on you."

"I hated that as much as you did. We can't go back to the way things were before. If we want to live in the new world, we need to follow their rules."

Daniel leaned against the door frame and looked at a wet spot forming on the ceiling. "At least we know the store clerk didn't rat us out."

"No, it was the people who woke us."

"Do you think we can trust him and his sister to help us?"

"I don't think we have a better option."

Daniel frowned. "I don't want you alone with him."

She disliked the implications of what her husband had just said. "I wouldn't question you being alone with his young, beautiful sister with her flawless skin and curling hair."

"I don't want to fight about it," Daniel skirted. "Just decide how you want to go about this. I'll follow your lead."

She struggled to contain her emotions as he walked down the stairs and out of sight. He wanted to nail them into the home like an undertaker wanted to nail the lid shut on a coffin. He was in denial. She was experiencing it as well in some ways. Daniel would not leave the island unless he had to.

The men in the uniforms called them "squatters." She would need to know what that meant and if there were any rights for these people. It seemed this island did not belong to any other country for now. That was something she'd need to learn about as well.

She didn't want to go downstairs and face Daniel just yet. Instead, she sat at her mother's vanity and played with all the things Helicant left behind. She wished her mother were here. Mother would know what to do. What happened to her, to all of them?

Mother was so old to begin with. She couldn't bear the thought of something terrible happening to her. Mother was the most terrible thing to happen to anyone on the island. She smiled at the thought. There was no way anything in that basement could harm Helicant Sallows.

After much thought and debate, she went downstairs to the drawing room, where she found Daniel on the loveseat. He was sitting upright, with his hands on his knees, just staring at the rug.

"We need to do two things," she told him. "First, we need to learn all we can about how the new world sees this island. Second, we need to uncover the truth about what happened. No more putting it off."

Daniel glanced downward at his voluminous pants and white formal shirt before looking her up and down. Destiny would have loved this, but his catty response ruined it.

"I've already got clothes on the way," he said. "It seems like it's you who needs to get with the times."

Destiny didn't know whether it was the sarcasm or the overall attitude, but she didn't like it. She didn't like how hard she had to work at being cheerful about their situation and how he struggled to accept anything. She didn't always feel optimistic. Sometimes, she wanted to bury her head in the sand too, but she couldn't, or he would bury them both.

Grabbing the nearest thing—which happened to be small nail clippers—she threw them at her husband with all her strength. Daniel dodged the projection, and it went into the old, worn wood. There was a new hole in the drawing room floor. She let out a frustrated cry as she marched out of the room.

"Destiny," he called softly.

Nothing he could say would make it better. Running to her bedroom, she slammed the door shut. She would have locked it if she had a lock. Destiny paced around her room at a furious pace for a few minutes. When her need to break things lessened, a profound sadness took its place.

Curling up on her bed, she had a good cry. After a while, she heard a knock at the door. Destiny wiped her eyes dry but said nothing. Daniel came in quietly and sat beside her. "I'm sorry," he said. "I should know better than to comment on a woman's clothing."

Was he really that dense? "That's not why I'm upset."

"I know," he said. "I was just trying to make a joke. It wasn't a very good one, was it?"

He curled up behind her and held her close. "It hasn't been a great day for us, has it?"

She could only sniff and wipe her face.

"I think it's because you're right," he said. "We're cooped up in this house all day and night. It's not healthy."

"I need you to be more positive about this. I can't carry the both of us all the time," she told him.

"I know," Daniel said. "I've been nothing but a grump since we woke up. I'll work on it."

She needed him to improve his mood about the new world. He needed to adjust to their circumstances because she needed him. They would ultimately have to exist in the new world. This was the only home they ever knew, and she understood that need to protect it, but they couldn't protect the island by hiding in it.

CHAPTER EIGHT

TWO BIRDS, ONE STONE

Eton was chopping wood when the couple came walking down the path. A chore that was once futile was now just a daily exercise. Going to the gym several times a week couldn't compete with these results. Daniel was still wearing the same clothes as last time, but Destiny was wearing a white cotton dress. It was old-fashioned but fit her every curve.

"Morning, guys," Eton said.

"Morning," Daniel replied.

"I don't have the clothes you ordered just yet, but I can check the tracking on them."

"That would be nice," Destiny said, pausing awkwardly as she played with her fingers. "We actually have a few other questions we were hoping you could answer as well."

Eton had a lot of questions for them, too, but he couldn't just throw them out there. He would have to finesse the situation. It's not like the couple could make an island appear, but maybe they had some answers. He was pretty sure they were here before the island appeared, so maybe they knew more.

He brought them into the store and opened his laptop to check the status of the order. "Well, it looks like it's going to be delivered by the end of today. Bart will pick up the package and bring it the next time he comes to visit. So, probably another two or three days."

"I will need some new clothes as well," Destiny said. She was leaning over the counter just slightly, and Eton couldn't help but gaze into her soft brown eyes.

"I suppose you don't know your size either," Eton said.

Destiny shook her head, biting her lip ever so slightly. Eton didn't think she was intentionally flirting, but it sure felt that way. "Hey, Kerry?"

Kerry took Destiny into her room with a measuring tape and did whatever girls did when they shopped for clothes. Eton found himself alone in a room with Daniel, who was comfortable with awkward silence. If his grin meant anything, it was that Daniel enjoyed the discomfort.

"So, have the two of you been married long?"

"We're newlyweds," Daniel said.

"Congratulations, man," Eton said.

"Thank you," he said stiffly. "I think Destiny mentioned earlier that we have some questions."

"Yeah."

"What country owns this island currently?" Daniel asked.

"Well, that is a good question…" Eton looked up the most recent news about the island with his laptop. "According to this article from yesterday, the provenance is still being deliberated over. It seems like it's a tie between the UK and Iceland, but Norway might contest it if there are resources they want."

"What about the original owners?" Daniel asked as he leaned over the counter to read the article.

"There aren't any as far as anyone knows."

"What if there were?"

Was that what they were? Somehow, their family survived on this island in some sort of bubble until one day, that bubble popped? "If you had proof that it was your island, I imagine it would remain that way."

Daniel froze at the sound of Destiny giggling in the other bedroom, then his entire face softened. The man didn't like Eton all that much, and that was fair, but he loved his wife. Eton couldn't blame him. Destiny was total Wifey material. She was going to be such a good mom too.

"We had some visitors this morning," Daniel admitted, his eyes still on the bedroom door. "It gave Destiny a fright."

She was so fragile; it made sense why Daniel was so protective of her. She was like a butterfly. He couldn't help but share the same resentment as Daniel. Destiny did not deserve to feel unsafe. "The ghost hunters?"

"No, some people in blue uniforms. They had thick accents but spoke English. Our ghost hunter friends sent them."

"Fucking Jeremy."

Daniel's brow crumpled, and Eton told him the story about returning the phone and confronting the ghost hunter who had robbed him. "Dude was convinced the house was haunted even after I said that actual living people were in the house. He must have gotten butthurt and tried to call the police."

"What is a ghost hunter, anyway?" Daniel asked. "Is that even a real job?"

"He looks for paranormal stuff. You know, ghosts, monsters, and whatnot. I'm sure your family had spooky stories."

Daniel laughed. "Oh yeah, we have some chilling tales here on the island, but what would Jeremy do if he actually found a monster?"

"Probably run away screaming like he did from your mansion."

Both men had a good laugh at that. Was it his imagination, or did Daniel's laugh have a sinister undertone? His eye teeth were pointy and were on display. It gave Eton the willies.

"A monster has nothing to fear from Jeremy," Eton said. "It's the government they'd need to worry about. Anything out of the ordinary, and they'd have it dissected like a lab rat in minutes."

Daniel's expression went stoney, and his back straightened. Eton couldn't blame him. The way people disregarded anything that wasn't like them was one of the shittiest attributes of their species. Eton suspected he and Daniel had a lot more in common than the guy wanted to believe.

Daniel leaned toward the counter. "I feel as though we can trust you," Daniel whispered. He swallowed hard at the proximity between them. "You must know by now that we live in the mansion. We have for a long time."

"Hey man, it's cool," Eton said, taking a step back. "I support your claim to this place. You somehow found it way before anyone else did. If given a chance, the Icelandic government probably wouldn't have allowed me to set up shop here, but they will have a hard time getting rid of me now that I'm here. They will have a harder time getting rid of you. The fucking government, man, they're almost as bad as the major corporations that own this world."

Daniel leaned on one elbow and nodded. "So, you came here without the king's permission?"

"If I didn't, some corporation would have bought their plot on this island with their countless millions. I couldn't afford to ask for permission, and neither can you," he said with a point of his finger. "Fuck the king."

"Fuck the king," Daniel gave a defiant nod.

"Iceland doesn't have a king, though." He figured it was important to update Daniel. "Most countries don't these days."

"So, they are republics?" Daniel asked. "Like the Romans?"

Eton was a college dropout, and this guy was clearly more schooled than he was despite living on a secret island. "More or less. Anyhow, I guess the mystery everyone is trying to figure out is how the island suddenly appeared."

Daniel shook his head like he had no idea.

"Yeah, dude, this island just emerged out of nowhere a few months ago. With today's satellite technology and high fishing population, there's no way they could have overlooked it all this time. It was like the island just appeared."

"That's not possible," Daniel said.

"Right? And you guys have been here the entire time?"

"Much longer than a few months," Daniel said. "I can guarantee that. Our ancestors built this house, that mansion, and the cottage on the cliff. There's also a freshwater well beside the mansion."

Eton was happy to hear that. They had been using jugs of water Bart had brought from his boat. "Really? Do you mind if we use it?"

"Not at all."

"I got to ask, though," Eton said. "How do you keep up the mansion?"

Daniel gave a sort of gloomy expression. "To be honest, we can't. We just focus on the rooms we use and just ignore the rest."

"Right," Eton agreed.

Destiny emerged from the room with Kerry. She was all smiles as she was telling Daniel all about the outfits she had picked online. Kerry beamed with pride. She was nodding along with the things Destiny was saying, as if she had helped her rehearse it.

If they had lived here their entire lives, like Daniel said, then the island belonged to them. It wasn't their fault the island was some strange anomaly. He couldn't just stand by while the government came and claimed what wasn't theirs.

"I'll do my best to keep people away from the mansion," Eton promised as the couple left. "They're just curious. I'll look up squatter laws for you."

"Much appreciated."

"Thanks!" Destiny waved as the door closed.

Eton and Kerry waited for several long minutes before saying anything about the couple.

"They've been here since before the island appeared," Eton told his sister.

Kerry nodded while staring at the door. "It's like they were Uber-homeschooled."

"I told Daniel about nobody being able to see the island. He had no idea, but they are freaked out. The prick that stole from our cash register called Scotland Yard."

"No shit?"

Eton gave her a knowing nod. "I think they are all that's left of some Amish type of village."

Kerry's face scrunched up. "Do you think they're inbred?"

He didn't want to think of Destiny as being inbred. She was too cute to be inbred. "Maybe like distant cousins or something."

"So weird."

"How did things go in there?" he asked, gesturing to the bedroom.

"She's super sweet. Pretty awkward, but I think that's to be expected considering the limited contact."

"He doesn't like me very much."

Kerry gave him a knowing look. "I wonder why..."

Eton could only shake his head. It's not like *everyone* knew. "Yeah, 'cause the Amish know what happened back in Maine."

"It doesn't take a social media account to figure out that you like her."

Eton winced at the comment. Part of the scandal back in Maine was because of social media. What happened didn't quite go viral, but it was enough of a situation that everyone he knew also knew about what happened between him and Brie.

"That's not why I'm anti-technology," Eton said. "It just convolutes everything and..."

Kerry wasn't listening. She was texting someone before leaving Eton to his own devices. "Oh," she returned. "I almost forgot this." Kerry dropped a gold nugget twice the size of the last one. It clunked on the laminate tabletop. Eton raised his hands in shock and glared at her.

"You know they overpaid last time," he said. "You can't just take thousands of dollars worth of gold from Amish people. It's not right!"

She had already left the room.

Eton groaned. He didn't want to hang on to their money when he could barely handle his own finances. Eton took out a notepad and began running a total for the couple. Every time they came in, he would put it on their pre-paid tab. In the meantime, he'd stick the latest gold nugget in his suitcase until he had an excuse to go to the mansion and return it. Eton had to get back to work. He had a never-ending woodpile to chop.

***

"What did you learn?" Destiny asked the moment they were away from the door.

"Do you remember there being any proof that the Sallows owned the island?" Daniel asked.

"It depends on who you talk to," she said. "The popular story was that the King of England himself issued the decree that brought the Sallows here. That he gifted the island for the supplies and killing the monsters. Or at least containing them. Mother had a different theory."

"What did your mother think?" Daniel asked. "I think you told me once, but I can't remember."

"She said that Nathanial Sallows was an illegitimate heir to the throne. The king was obsessed with monsters and thought himself an expert on witches. He declared Nathanial's daughter a witch and sent them all here to avoid a curse she supposedly placed on the world."

"Two birds, one stone," Daniel shrugged. "Did your mother have any kind of proof that the Sallows owned this island?"

Destiny shook her head. "I don't think so. Anything relevant to the mansion and its history could probably be found in the mansion on the cliff. Aunt Sophie had the first settler's diary and a map of the mansion."

Daniel nodded slowly. "I seem to recall something about that as well. Wasn't she the one who told us ghost stories as children?"

"Perhaps for everyone else," Destiny chuckled. "Mother threatened to push her off the cliff if she read those stories to me."

They laughed, but she was quite certain her mother was serious about that threat. Mother was the one who had to deal with her night dredes. Father died a little less than a year after they started. Mother blamed Nathanial's diary, but the night dredes started before she read it.

Daniel told her that Eton thought tangible proof would settle the dispute over who owned the land. It wasn't for certain, but it was a safe assumption. Apart from that, there were also rights for people who dwelled in an area for as long a time as they had.

"This could actually work," Daniel said with an optimistic tone. "If we can find the document from the king, we may be safe. Otherwise, we just state we've been here our entire lives. The buildings are enough to prove how long our family has lived here."

Maybe having more control over the island would soothe Daniel and make him more open to the new world. If it helped him adjust, she would support it. They would find proof of their ownership and fight to keep the island—for now, at least.

She smiled at him, "I can't wait for you to see the undergarments I ordered."

His grin was uncontainable. "I'd sooner have you wear none at all."

"Oh, then you'll like these," she laughed.

Daniel did a double-take and laughed, but the laughter and the walk came to a sudden halt. They came face to face with what they could only describe as carnage on their doorstep.

A doe, Destiny suspected, was ripped to shreds just outside their home. All at once, she gasped as she clung to Daniel. Bracing herself as nausea wracked her body. The poor animal was broken beyond reason. Like some macabre gift basket.

Who could have done such a thing? Certainly not Eton or Kerry. There was no one else here. Daniel approached and kneeled by the head and stroked it gently. "What happened to you?"

Something horrid. "Daniel..."

"She was dead before this happened to her," he said, examining the body. "The body was stiff when it was broken, and there are bite marks around the flanks. I think a wolf attacked her, and then something brought it to us."

She winced and turned away. "I don't want to know. Just get it out of here."

"I will give her a proper burial," he promised. "While I'm at it, I'll make sure she didn't leave a faun behind. I think she was too young, and it's not breeding season, but just in case."

Avoiding the mangled corpse, Destiny went inside. She could hear Daniel picking the doe up, but she didn't dare look. He would care for the poor thing. The front door was partially open. She didn't remember shutting it or not, but the hairs on the back of her neck pricked.

Swallowing the lump in her throat. Destiny noted the dampness on the marble as her shoes slipped ever so slightly. The daylight through the windows illuminated the wet smear on the ground. No footprints. A trail.

Destiny followed the trail as it made its way through the entryway and to the kitchen. There was a stillness in her mind, unlike how she felt when she saw the doe. Whatever this was, it had every right to be here, just as she did.

Down the broken old steps and into the cellar, the water churned with the dirt and made a muddy path right into the pitch-black hole.

She stood and stared at the space where a door once was and nodded with understanding. It was comforting, in a way. She and Daniel were not alone on the island. The others had been here all along and would reveal themselves in time.

CHAPTER NINE

SECRETS KEPT

Destiny remained wrapped up in the sheets as Daniel lit some candles. They had spent the last few days in bed. While their lovemaking was romantic, it highlighted the less normal things about them. They did not need to rest or eat. They really could spend the rest of their lives tumbling in bed if they wanted.

She never told him about what she'd seen in the basement. It wasn't right to keep secrets from a spouse, but Destiny simply did not know how to explain it. She didn't see anyone, just a wet trail. That, and Daniel was so cross after burying the doe, she feared he would retaliate on whatever did it.

"What do you think of the sister, Kerry?" he asked while he fumbled with the lighter she'd bought from the store. He held it in front of his face and pushed the button several times before sparks produced a small flame. "This is rather nice, by the way."

She thought about the girl, then gave a slight frown. "She is nice but self-absorbed. It's probably her age more than anything, but she is more interested in her image on the internet than anything else."

"That's the place on the devices with cats and babies, right?"

"And where they order clothing sometimes. She checked her profiles on social media several times and showed me how it worked a little."

Daniel gave a considerate pause before asking, "What is the point?"

"They talk to other people. Like long-distance correspondence but with pictures and videos."

Daniel rejoined her in bed. "Like distant relatives and old friends?"

"Anyone," she said. "They can also meet new friends. That's how Kerry met her friend Holly."

"Well, that sounds rather nice," he said. "Not insincere at all."

"That's what I thought, too," Destiny said. "It surprised me she had so many friends when she doesn't have all that much to say."

"That might just be her age," Daniel agreed. "I remember my brother behaving similarly, but he wasn't the brightest, come to think of it."

She couldn't remember much about his brother. Destiny's memory was slowly fleshing out around her as she found and touched things. A silver spoon in the kitchen reminded her of a time when she was sick with a fever, and her mother fed her soup. The hedge maze outside brought back all the times she had spent learning its secrets as a child.

Her whole life was here, but it was a distant shadow of who she once was. Destiny remembered being afraid of things that she'd never worry about now. She recalled her fears plaguing her mind, awake and asleep. Green eyes consumed Destiny's dreams of a locked door. Looking at Daniel now, she couldn't imagine how she could be afraid of such beauty.

"Promise me something," he said.

"What?"

"It's not that I distrust you. I distrust Eton. The way he looks at you. I don't like it. Promise me that if he tries anything, you'll let me know."

"And just what would you do if something happened?" she said playfully.

Daniel's glowing green eyes went dark, and he said, "Whatever it takes."

***

The LA-based number popped up on Jeremy's phone, and he couldn't bring himself to answer. As soon as they got back, he'd uploaded and edited a video to send the producers for the TV show. It was rough but full of the most compelling evidence of paranormal activity.

He hadn't even gotten through all the EVP yet. The audio was so dense he had to split it into seventeen different filters. It was a miracle that his software could even handle it. When the voicemail icon popped up, he didn't wait to hear the producer's opinion.

"Hi Jeremy, we got your video—neat stuff. Listen, we need to work through some ins and outs—"

Jeremy deleted the voicemail. The producer had told him enough. They were not willing to sign him yet. Which was a shame for them because his viewers had jumped up another six hundred thousand since he announced the investigation of the island.

"If that's how you want to play it," he muttered before dropping the video into his YouTube uploads. The bar lagged forward at a snail's pace—it was over four hours, even after he had edited as much as he could. The affiliate links and podcast tours were lined up. He just needed to pull the trigger.

Another segment of the EVP had finished filtering. Jeremy pulled up the audio files and continued to unravel the mystery. He could determine that everything he caught was about one night.

It was an engagement party for a girl named Destiny. She was afraid of the groom—green eyes? The family was strange and cultish. They spoke a dialect far too common for the sixteenth century. Typically, that would scream 'hoax' in his mind, but there wasn't a way to trick EVP as far as he could tell. He slouched, clicking on the triangle icon, awaiting what would come next.

"What happened?" the old man asked.

"Tell your truth, Destiny," the fiancé said. "Your safety is the only concern here."

Jeremy chewed at the cap of his pen. This was where things got weird. In most of the audio, Destiny Sallows says no to Daniel. Sometimes Destiny goes missing later that night. This clip has her saying yes to the proposal, which was the first out of seventeen versions.

"He threatened to rape me!" Destiny said.

"Are you certain he wasn't joking?" Coral asked. "He's crude, but—"

Jeremy was certain they were talking about her cousin Drew. He spun around in his chair and checked the map of the mansion. He had been documenting where each person went at what time. Destiny claimed that Drew tried to rape her...but he had audio of Drew getting it on with Abigail on the fourth floor. Man, that audio was some first-rate porn too.

There was no way Drew could have been chasing Destiny around the maze while he was shagging Abigail. He gave Destiny a drink and talked some shit, but he left when she told him to leave her alone. Jeremy mapped out the voices and checked again.

The only person who was outside with Destiny during that part of the night was Daniel. Not just in this audio track—but all seventeen tracks. Daniel was the one who chased his fiancé around in the dark and framed his cousin. This was some first-rate soap opera shit.

"Hah!" Jeremy said with a laugh. He was willing to bet Daniel was the reason Destiny went missing in some of those audio tracks. "Just what did you do, Daniel?"

***

Destiny spent the better part of the night sweeping. She swept the stairs. She swept the entryway. She swept the kitchen. After sweeping the dining room, she did it all over again.

She longed for the days when she slept half the time. Occasionally, she would try to sleep. She would lay there with her eyes closed in remote stillness for hours. Not for a single moment did she flitter out of consciousness. She came close once, but her husband came stomping in, so she gave up and went back to sweeping.

Meanwhile, Daniel was on a rampage in the cottage by the cliff. He was determined to find things related to how they got like this and anything that could prove their ownership of the island. She tried to go with him, but Daniel was rather insistent that she stay behind.

"No, I do better work on my own," he said. "You should stay here and get some more work done on the house."

Well, she had done all the work, and now she was tired of it. Bored with sweeping and wiping and sorting. She took a walk along the trail to the cottage her Aunt Beth and Uncle Edward inhabited. Drew, her cousin, also lived there— once. She shook that horrid memory from her mind.

The house itself remained mostly intact, but the greenhouse where her aunt grew medicinal herbs had collapsed in on itself. Rough winds had torn windowpanes from the frame, and freezing winters had shattered what remained. The greenhouse only stood because of constant care, but it still made her sad. Witnessing the demise of something so prominent in one's youth. Time had corroded everything, but why not them?

The house had fared better. The once sturdy roof kept out most of the storms but did nothing to stay the mice or deer that found Beth's dried plants. In the corner of her late aunt's chemistry room, she found several bottles, and a few of them were in a basket labeled *Helicant*.

Her mother had a vanity full of bottles and tonics to keep her young. Only none of the bottles in the basket resembled the things on her mother's vanity.

Something clicked in her mind then.

A snap of a memory from long ago. She and Daniel... They had drunk something from her mother's vanity. It was Mother's supposed 'immortality potion.' She thought it was just a story her mother told her at night to keep her mind off the night dredes.

Rushing back home, she ran up the stairs and into her mother's room to find the bottle. It was unlike all the others. Amber crystal with a strange, wood-like stopper with countless holes in it. It was a material they didn't have on the island. She opened the bottle and inhaled. The water they refilled the bottle with had long evaporated. Nothing else remained.

"I have a potion that extends life," Mother said one night before tucking her into bed.

"Why didn't you drink it?" she asked. Mother slipped her sleeping dress over her head and buttoned the back before brushing her blonde hair.

"I drank half," Mother said.

"Why?" she asked.

"No one wants to live forever," Mother said.

She didn't understand as a child. Who wouldn't want to live forever? Though now it made sense. Forever was a long time. She supposed it would be okay if she could spend it with Daniel. They only drank a quarter of the potion each. If that was indeed what extended their lives. Then again, her mother was gone, as far as she could tell. Mother wouldn't have left her unless she had no choice.

She went downstairs to see if Daniel had come home, and he hadn't. Slapping her hands to her sides, Destiny went down the stairs and into the drawing room.

Lighting some candles, she read *Bovo-Bukh* until the sun began creeping over the horizon. She loved *Bovo-Bukh*. Princes in disguise were her favorite, but she hadn't intended to spend so much time reading. She let out a gasp when the horizon's colors danced in the sky.

Then again, there was nothing else to do. Daniel wanted to research on his own. She missed him terribly and grew anxious because he wasn't equally distraught by their separation. He wasn't a neglectful man, so this behavior was odd for him. She disliked being ignored so.

No, she wouldn't go running to him like a frightened child. He would come to her. She was Helicant's daughter and heiress of the Sallows Island. She did not need any man. At least that is what she told herself while she read well into the night. When day broke through the windows, Destiny threw the book so hard it broke through the half-rotted wall.

It had been several days since she had last visited with the store clerk and his sister. If Daniel was in such dire need of space, she would visit with the only other people on the island.

When she stepped out, she had to shadow her eyes with her hand and squint at the morning light. It was so bright. She stepped back, grabbed the freshly cleaned parasol from the coat rack, and took it with her. It was heavily starched black lace with little clay-painted beads. She wasn't certain, but she thought one of her aunts had made it.

From where she stood, tiny boats dotted the horizon. They moved so fast. One of them might have brought her clothing. She reminded herself that it would take time for such things, but it was exciting to wait for a package. It felt like Sabbath.

"Hello?" she asked before stepping into the cottage.

"Oh hey," Kerry said from where the kitchen once was. Now it was a slightly concealed corner of the cottage where Eton and Kerry made hot drinks and washed dishes. She rounded the corner to find Kerry flipping a tray over.

She watched as Eton's little sister peeled away parchment paper to reveal a large block of swirling colors. With a great big knife, she then cut them into smaller blocks. She inhaled and recognized the scent.

"Soap?"

"Yeah, I learned how to make my own," Kerry said with a smile before realizing who she was speaking to. "Of course, you probably do this all the time."

"No," Destiny said. "It wasn't my job, but I am familiar with how it's done. I think yours are much prettier."

"Your husband then?"

Destiny shook her head. "There were once a lot more people here. We don't know where they went."

"Like, they died?" The idea struck Kerry's poor little face. She regretted even mentioning it.

Were they dead? Destiny didn't think so, but how to explain such things. "I'm afraid so. It was all very sudden."

"I'm so sorry."

"Thank you." Destiny found Kerry to be much more sincere than she initially suspected. "This smells minty."

"It's peppermint and tobacco."

The door opened with a groan, and Eton stepped in. He had his hat off and was wearing a thin white shirt with no sleeves. His trousers were much tighter than anything she had ever seen a man wear. She turned bright red at the sight. She was staring at his wide shoulders and lowered her gaze, only to lose her breath at the sight of a distinctive outline near his left thigh.

"Hey," he greeted. "Nice to see you."

Her ears were red hot, and she wasn't certain where to turn. She didn't want to look at Kerry and risk giving away her embarrassment, and she couldn't stare at Eton any longer. "I just love these soaps," she said. "Have you smelled them yet, Eton?"

She could feel him stand beside her. He smelled strongly of sage and something she didn't recognize. He took a bar and held it to his nose. "That's awesome."

Kerry glowed with pride. Destiny's attention was thankfully diverted to the girl and less on the fact that Eton didn't smell like body odor after exerting himself. Neither did she anymore.

"Where's your husband?"

She would have liked to know that herself. "He's looking for proof of our family owning the island."

"Cool. I also did a little research, and it sounds like in Iceland, squatting is kind of a thing. Like, if you've been somewhere for so many years, it's just your place. Norway has laws that protect long-term residency too."

"That means that if this island is declared a province of either country, we have a claim?" It relieved Destiny to hear this news.

"You would have a pretty solid claim, yeah. The UK has pretty low tolerance for squatters, *but*," Eton emphasized the word, "this is a pretty weird case, so I don't think they would just evict the last remaining inhabitants of the island they inherited. It would be highly frowned upon."

It was good to know that people in the new world had respect for such things. It wasn't like Nathaniel's time, when someone could be simply gifted an island. The assurance would be something Daniel could appreciate as well.

"I'm going to take a shower," Kerry announced. Before Destiny could leave, Kerry plucked a bar from her tray, picked up a bag on the floor, and left the cottage.

They had a setup of sorts outside. A cloudy screen that surrounded a metal device where water came streaming from a container. Kerry must have been preparing for it, and Destiny showed up right at the wrong time.

She stood there. Frozen in place, eyes on the floor. Destiny didn't dare look at Eton, but she imagined he was doing much of the same.

The thought of Daniel reminded her of his disapproval of Eton. What would he think about her coming here without him? There were no rules of engagement with strangers because they never dealt with strangers before.

Suddenly aware of the position she'd put herself in, Destiny muttered an excuse and fled the cottage. She made it a way up the trail only to find Eton chasing after her.

"I was just going to give you a package," he said, handing her a black shiny bag. "I'm pretty sure it's Daniel's clothes."

"Thank you," she said, bowing her head before turning and leaving.

"And hey," Eton said. "Don't worry about what people think about you or the island."

Did he know? It was a stupid thought. Even she didn't know what she was. "I imagine anything perceived strange would be on display for the world to see as well."

"Definitely," Eton said. "Which can sometimes be a good thing because it normalizes diseases and disorders that people wouldn't have known about otherwise, but the internet can be an unforgiving place. They only need one piece of the story to make their own judgments regardless of how it affects the people involved."

If people got wind of their differences, which way would that pendulum swing?

Would they be understood and accepted, or would they be ostracized and condemned? Daniel would not be willing to put himself out there to be tried and judged by strangers, nor would he be able to forgive anyone who made such judgments against her. She feared his worst tendencies would come to the surface in such a situation.

The house bore over them like a great, watchful eye. Its windows saw everything, and the two wings that extended in front of the entry reached out toward her as if to remind her of where she truly belonged. Was there a place for her in the new world? Eton stopped walking. He stared at the house as if the house was telling him he was not invited.

"Thank you," she said. "I enjoyed our talk."

"I'll bring your packages to the house when they arrive so you don't have to walk to the shore."

She considered it and decided that it was a good idea. She couldn't wait for her clothes to arrive. Daniel would be angry that she and Eton were alone together—he'd asked her explicitly not to do that. But even if Daniel didn't approve, she'd enjoyed this discussion with Eton. Maybe Daniel would join them next time.

She smiled and nodded. "I'd like that very much."

Inside the house, she was happy to find that Daniel had at last come back to the mansion. He'd left the back door open. She closed it and called out for him, but there was no answer. She checked the drawing room to find several books had been taken.

Their empty spots on the otherwise packed bookshelf were notably apparent. In her bedroom, her clothing and jewelry table was in shambles. Things tossed carelessly, and she found her mother's brooch on the floor. He'd searched for something and then left in a hurry.

Did he even notice she'd left? The idea upset her enough to make her ,remember that she was still angry with him for keeping secrets from her. This had gone on far enough. She would go to the cottage and give him a piece of her mind.

There was once a soft trail that led to the cottage, but it had long overgrown with bushes and saplings. More than once, she worried that she might have been lost.

Their terrain was wild, with bushes and new trees. If she wasn't careful, she would be liable to find a cliff instead of the cottage. She may be more durable now, but she doubted even she could survive a fall from that cliff. Wild red rose vines climbed over everything. It was an utter jungle—at least, what she imagined a jungle to be.

Lost in the overgrowth, she closed her eyes and listened for the waves crashing against the rocky bluff of the island.

The sound guided her way to the edge where the cottage sat. The winds had knocked out the windows, and the roof was patched and sparse. It made her sad to see it in such disarray. There was once a time when she wanted to live there.

Inside, the home smelled of mold and damp. The moisture from the sea and rain had infected the interior. She resisted the urge to weep. There was no way she and Daniel could live here now. It was too far gone. The only things that remained intact were the sturdy pine bookcases that protected the books her aunt left behind. Their leather spines hardened and cracked with time, but the pages themselves were preserved.

Daniel had indeed been here. He had taken some books but left others scattered about. Since when did her bookworm husband hold such blatant disregard for books?

She picked up the stories her husband had left so carelessly and put them back in their nests. She would want all these brought to the mansion where they would be safe. But then, she couldn't help but think about what Eton had said. Was anywhere safe?

The sun bowed before the forest when she returned to the mansion. It had been nearly two days since she had last seen her husband, and she had traded her boredom for anger—and an all too familiar emptiness was all that remained.

CHAPTER TEN

AS ABOVE, SO BELOW

Standing at the base of the stairs, Destiny followed the soft knocking sound. It interrupted her sweeping. There had still been no sign of Daniel, so she thought it might have been him finally coming home after several days.

Padding into the room, she found the basement door was open. With no heavy sense of dread, it occurred to her that the last time she followed an open door, it led to the same place.

With daylight fading, she lit a candelabra with her pink lighter and took it with her down the old dry steps.

The rapping noise sounded again. It was coming from the catacombs. A sour feeling simmered in her stomach, and she hesitated. Mother never liked her being down here, though she never said why. It wasn't a forbidden place, but her mother's disdain for it was enough for her to steer clear of it.

"As above, so below," was something her mother would mutter before spitting on the ground.

Fumbling in her pocket, she went back into the basement and into the kitchen, where she found a reel of twine. She tied one end to the stair railing in the basement before going back into the chasm. Destiny was not about to get lost down there.

Destiny's hand trembled as she gripped the candelabra. She tugged gently on her handy string, making certain something still tethered it to normalcy. Wading through the tunnels, some made-made, some—clearly not—Destiny understood her mother's words.

It did not take long before she recognized every room and hallway. The basement was a mirror image of the home that sat on top of it.

If only her hands could stop shaking. All this time, her family had lived on top of this bizarre copy of their home. There were no doors or furniture, and the walls were smoothed, hardened dirt instead of wood and wallpaper, but she knew it to be home.

It was her home. The monsters lived in Sallows Hall.

Standing in the entryway where the front door should be, her mind reeled at the meaning. If the monsters lived in Sallows Hall just as she did, was she a monster, too?

There was no door. In its place was a tunnel that descended downward into the pits of hell itself. Was this where the monsters came from or where they went to? Destiny wasn't certain the monsters had ever left.

Her mind shouted at her to run back up the stairs. But Daniel might be somewhere down here. He might have gotten lost or hurt. The rapping noise could have been him, but it also could have been something else. She gasped and tried to keep her frightened noises to a minimum.

The noise happened again, but it was from several stories up. She'd moved back up the stairs and into the hall when she heard it again. She fought the urge to cry or run. Stepping into the room, she realized it was where her room would have been. There was no furniture or any sign that it was her room. She just knew it to be true. There was a soft glow coming from the room, and she nearly fainted with relief.

"Daniel," she said.

He turned to her and said, "Do you realize what this is?"

She nodded. "It's the house."

He stared at the room. "This is your room. Did you see the downstairs?"

"We need to get out of here, Daniel."

"You're probably right."

The string didn't lead them back to safety. Drawn upward instinctively, as if she were buried alive and clawing her way toward the surface. The twine provided a sense of security, nothing more.

Destiny reserved her urge to yell at him until they were topside. He shut the basement door behind him, and only then could she fully breathe. "I can't believe you," she whispered.

Daniel only frowned in confusion.

"You left me all alone for days," she cried, slamming the candelabra on the kitchen table.

"What are you going on about?" Daniel said. "I've only been gone a few hours."

She could only shake her head incredulously. Had their inability to sleep confused his sense of time?

"Have you no sense of time anymore?"

He gazed out the window and shrugged. "I wasn't gone all that long."

"It was days!"

Daniel could only shake his head. "No. I went to the cottage. Found some things of interest and went to the catacombs to investigate. I didn't spend days anywhere."

She was so frustrated that she could cry. He pulled her into his arms. She tried to fight it, but his strength was beyond hers. "I believe you. I just don't understand. I wasn't in there for days. It's impossible."

Something wasn't right. Daniel wouldn't lie to her about something she could easily disprove. He lost track of time, but it wasn't something she had ever done. She allowed herself to be soothed by his embrace. In the growing calm, her eyes opened as something occurred to her.

"I wonder if it has something to do with the catacombs."

"It wouldn't surprise me," he said.

"Wait here," she said, grabbing the candelabra to relight it. Destiny went back into the basement and into the darkness of the catacombs. Though she felt no need to explore this time. Instead, she waited on the stairway. She counted to one thousand before returning to the doorway. There, she found Daniel quietly but franticly pacing the basement.

"How long was I gone?" she asked.

Daniel pointed to the cellar window, and the sun was rising.

"I counted to one thousand and came back."

This was impossible. Time was different somehow in the catacombs. Daniel hadn't intentionally avoided her. He really thought he was in there for a few hours. How anyone could be so relieved that such a thing existed in their basement, she would never understand, but it meant that Daniel had no control over the circumstances that had separated them.

"How could this be?"

It rendered Daniel speechless. Her mind went to the ghost hunters and all the people who would want to explore this place. They would find the tunnel at the bottom. The things their family protected the world from could crawl up that tunnel and cause chaos once again.

"What did you find that made you come down here in the first place?" she asked.

Daniel was frightened. He wouldn't look at her, and he shook his head as if he didn't want to tell her either. "Daniel," she said.

Reaching into his pocket, her husband pulled out a small leather-bound book. He handed it to her. "It wasn't what was in the cottage so much as was what was in my pocket this whole time."

It was the journal of Nathaniel Sallows. Daniel had put it together at last. The monsters of Sallows Island were real and probably still alive.

"The room," he whispered. "It was like the cavern in the basement. Time worked differently there. I went into the room first, but it felt like decades later that you came for me... I have green eyes."

He had some memory of the engagement party, after all. He found the room first and was trapped in there. It was only for a short time for her, but it was centuries for him. In that time, Daniel became something else.

"It's not who you are now, though."

"And what is that exactly?" he snapped. "We're not human."

"No," she shook her head. "I don't think we are, but that doesn't mean we are bad or evil. We are like this to help people."

Daniel nodded. "We must do whatever it takes to protect the world from whatever lies below."

This changed things. As much as she wanted to leave the island, it would have to wait. If Sallows were not strong enough to end the monsters, she and Daniel would be.

"I'm going to start by walling up that doorway. I'll put another wall in front of that, just in case."

Monster or not, walling off a problem was a most human solution, but what else could they do? She eyed the entryway and felt a chill all over. The more she and Daniel unraveled the secrets of the Sallows mansion, the more frightening it became. What creatures lurked in the layers below?

The stories her mother dismissed as politics and fear-mongering were real. They were real, and the Sallows were the monsters all along.

Destiny couldn't leave the island. It was a kick to the gut, but she could not leave until she knew for a fact that her family was not a threat to the world and that the world was not a danger to them.

"I'm going to find that damn decree," she said, storming up the stairs.

CHAPTER ELEVEN

THE GREEN-EYED MONSTER

That night, they sat in the drawing room together, reading. She was rereading one of her favorite poems, *Christis Kirk on the Green*. It provided a much-needed diversion from the heavy information of late. Though the ending left much to be desired.

Daniel read the diary of Nathaniel Sallows on the edge of the loveseat. Occasionally, she would glance at him from her book, hoping his eyes would meet hers. He was sitting so tensely, he didn't notice that her legs were resting across his lap. She'd give an occasional flick of her foot, hoping it would get his attention subtly, but he was too distraught to play.

"What else did you find in the cottage?" she asked.

Daniel looked up from the book and stared at the wall in front of him as if he were searching for the answer in the wallpaper. "It wasn't any one thing," he started. "More like a collection of little things that led to one big conclusion."

"About the catacombs?"

"About everything."

Her husband was struggling with something, and she wished she knew how to help. It wasn't every day that you learned you were a monster. She couldn't blame him for being shocked by it.

By now, it was apparent that time did not operate accurately in some spaces of the house, maybe the whole island. It explained Daniel's disappearance, their long sleep, the Green-eyed Monster, among many other things. Mother had once told her the island was "glitching," but she did not understand the word. Perhaps this was what she was referring to.

She couldn't change any of these things. They were in the past, where neither of them lived. They were here, in the now, on the sofa. How could she get him to understand that? "Did you try on the clothing?"

He shook his head. "No, I will later."

There would be no moving forward for Daniel until they went back.

"If you could just try to tell me," she said. "Even if it makes little sense, just try."

Daniel said nothing. He just looked at her with sad eyes. She waited for him to explain. To say something. Her feet slid off her husband's lap as he stood, "I need to get started in the basement."

***

She saw little of Daniel for the next few weeks. Sometimes, she would see him through the windows as he wandered the island, collecting boulders in a wheelbarrow before tossing them down the basement steps.

Other times, she would stand by the basement door as he returned, hoping to catch him. He kept a grueling pace, and it seemed like there was nothing she could say that would alter his course. She spent her days and nights alone and wept like some lovesick girl. This wasn't what marriage was supposed to be like.

The squeaking of the wheelbarrow signified Daniel had returned. Unable to take it anymore, she rushed down the grand stairway and into the kitchen. He was dirty and disheveled. He didn't so much as greet her when she came in.

"Daniel, please," she pleaded as she followed him into the basement. He barred her way down the stairs with his body. "Surely you can take a break. I miss you. You must have half the island down there by now."

"The sooner I get this done, the safer you'll be."

She didn't need to have a wall sealed off to feel safe. She needed her husband. Since he came out of the catacombs, he had not been himself. The entire event was disturbing on many levels, but enough was enough.

"I need you," she told him. "I need you here, with me. You can work in the basement at night, but at least spend the day with me. Or let me help you—"

"No," Daniel said roughly. "I'll not have you down there."

"Why?" she asked. "I'm just as strong as you are. If anything comes out, I can help you."

Daniel was clenching his jaw as if he were angry with her, and she didn't understand why. She practically threw herself at him and stroked his jawline and the thick cords of his neck. He barely even held her back, and it made her feel desperate.

"You haven't even seen me in my new undergarments," she said, hoping to distract him.

"I need to get more stones," he said, pushing her aside before walking away.

She could only stand there in total helplessness as her husband slipped from her fingers. Why was this happening? He was too kind a man to tell a harsh truth; maybe he thought it would be too much for her. Maybe they were just too different now, and he was trying to avoid the reality himself.

Once she was certain he was far from the house, she walked along the yards of Sallows Hall. She navigated through the overgrown hedge maze to the center. The swing that once hung from the tree had long since rotted and fallen to the ground. The fountain was dry, leaving a green stain at the bottom of the basin.

As a young girl, she had made a series of secret exits in the maze that only she knew about. Those doors had long overgrown, leaving few options for her now. She moved to the end of the maze and saw that the original path had also grown over, forcing her back the way she came.

Emerging from the hedge maze, she was startled by the sight of two men with boards in their hands and a tripod with a device on it. They seemed just as surprised to see her as she was by them.

"Hello there," a man with a yellow shiny hat said. "Didn't mean to startle you. We're just surveying the island."

She gave a nod and smiled as best she could. She would go into the house and lock the doors, and that would be the end. As she opened the door, the second man perked up and said, "Hey, are you supposed to be in there?"

She ignored the pounding of her heart and thought about how her mother would respond. "I am the only one who is supposed to be in here," she said as evenly as she could manage.

The men gave confused expressions but didn't wish to argue. They were just curious. If she told them more about herself and her life here, they might relay the information to the other countries.

"Are you a native?"

"I am."

"We would love to ask you some questions if you don't mind—"

"I mind," Daniel said. He had abandoned the wheelbarrow just outside the forest and must have run the rest of the way. His face was stony, and she moved toward him instinctively, concerned about what her husband was about to do.

The men both took a step back. "We're just surveyors, mate."

"If you guys don't want us here, we can just leave," the man with the shiny hat said.

"Will more of you come?" Daniel asked.

"Well, probably. Many people have questions. State officials for the UK plan on coming sometime this month. I don't know about the other two countries."

Daniel came at the men then. She wasn't certain of what he intended to do, but it was enough to frighten the men into abandoning their equipment and running. He was about to give chase, but she blocked him, allowing time for the men to flee.

Digging her feet into the ground, she shouted, "Daniel, no! Stop."

She could hold him off long enough for the men to run down the hill and out of sight. Only then did Daniel relax. His eyes shifted from anger to guilt. Why was he doing this?

"I need to get back to work."

"You're not the Green-eyed Monster anymore," she said. "You're Daniel, my husband."

"I'm going to do whatever it takes to keep it that way," he said, stalking off.

Why wouldn't he talk to her? Why wouldn't he let her help? She picked up a massive boulder and threw it with one arm. It missed his head by a few inches, but he didn't slow.

"What is wrong with you?" she shouted. Her fists balled, and her eyes were wet. It was probably loud enough for the men to hear. Daniel paused and turned for a moment. She could see the hurt on his face, but he resumed course for the forest.

There was nothing she could do but stand there and watch him leave. She wanted nothing more than to fall to her knees sobbing. Would he have turned around if she had? What would mother have done? Helicant Sallows would never let a man see her broken. She straightened her spine and put away her sadness the best she could.

The overcast clouds were heavy with rain. It was best to go inside before it started. There were knocks on the front door echoing through the hall, and she scrambled to meet them before Daniel came back. She hadn't thought him dangerous to others, but now she was uncertain.

"Eton," she breathed.

She pulled open the door to find Eton frowning. "I caught those guys running away from the mansion. Is everything okay?"

Everything was not okay, and she couldn't hide it. Her face contorted to stay the weeping, and he leaned forward.

She brought Eton into the drawing room. He shivered and rubbed his arms. "It's colder in here than it is outside," he commented. "Do you want a fire?"

She nodded, and Eton got to work with a lighter with paper bags and the stacked wood that had been there for hundreds of years. "Wood is super dry," he said as they blazed in the fireplace.

"Are they okay?" she asked at last.

"Oh yeah," he said. "I told them Daniel was just a little grumpy because of all the weirdoes wandering around his house. I smoothed it over. They are going to go back to the UK to report that there are natives to the island, so the procedure will be different now."

Daniel wasn't just grumpy. He was unhinged. She was certain that he meant to harm those men. "Procedure?" she asked.

"Yeah," Eton said. "I tried to ask them more, but they didn't know. They mentioned you could get an advocate to act on your behalf. Like a lawyer or something. Probably not a bad idea."

Destiny nodded. Eton huddled by the fire, and white plumes of vapor came from his mouth. "You're not cold at all?"

A lawyer was a brilliant idea. She could contact one using Eton's internet. An excuse to go to the mainland at last! A visit to the new world. "Could a lawyer stop more people from coming here?"

"I don't think it could stop everyone, but it could help you maintain control of the place. Give you authority to make people leave."

"Daniel can't deal with this anymore," she tried to say, but she began to cry instead. Eton practically leaped from his spot beside the fire and took her hands in his. "Hey," he said. "It will be okay."

She shook her head. "You didn't see him."

"You think he's going to hurt someone?" Eton asked.

"I don't know—"

"Do you think he's going to hurt you?"

"No," she said with true confidence. "He'd never try to hurt me."

That much she knew to be a fact. Never would Daniel hurt her.

"I think he's just trying to protect you," Eton said. "Guys get weird when their space is threatened."

Despite herself, she couldn't stop the tears. She tried to be more like her mother, but she wasn't made of that kind of metal.

"Hey, you know," Eton kneeled before her. "Whenever I have to go to the mainland, you know what I tell Kerry?"

His eyes were so blue, even in the firelight. His hair was capped, but the occasional strand came loose, framing his face.

"I tell her that if someone comes to the store she doesn't like, or if she at all feels uncomfortable, she should come here and find you and Daniel. Now, I wouldn't tell my baby sister to go to just any guy for protection. I know in my heart that Daniel would never hurt her. I'd like to think he'd protect her just as he is trying to protect you."

Eton's faith in Daniel's goodness made her feel better. He was right to make that assessment. Daniel would sooner cut off his own arm than lay it on Kerry. If only his temperament were so generous toward men. She smiled, though it felt stiff and awkward. "Yeah," she whispered. "I know he would too."

"Just give him a break," Eton said. "He'll come around."

She had been. How many breaks and excuses did she have to make until it was too much? Before or after he killed someone? Her mother wouldn't see that as problematic, but she was not her mother. If Helicant taught her anything about marriage, it was that it ended upon death. But that wasn't practical in a world with internet and melting glaciers.

"It's getting late," she said, regarding the low-hanging sun. "You should get back to her."

Eton swore under his breath and backpedaled down the steps. "Yeah, I got to go. I'll come back next time I get a chance. But don't hesitate to come to the store for anything, anytime."

***

Eton made his way down the steps and towards the door. He wanted to get out of the mansion as soon as he could. For one, it was warmer outside, and two, it gave him the creeps. He could see why the ghost hunters were convinced the place was haunted.

It felt as though the house was watching him. It was like that weird panic he felt as a kid. When he knew there was nothing under his bed, but when he turned the lights off, he still ran and jumped into his bed. This house was like a monster under the bed, just waiting for an ankle to grab.

"Stay away from her," Daniel said.

Eton peered over the banister to find Daniel leaning against the stairway. "I overheard your conversation. Don't think me ungrateful, but there are things you don't understand. It's for your own good."

"Dude, she's falling apart up there." Eton tried his best to hide his anger, but it was obvious. He was getting himself emotionally invested in a girl who was not available...again. This wasn't his fight, he knew that, but he couldn't stop himself.

To his credit, Daniel appeared pain-stricken by Eton's words. There was love there, but why was he holding out on Destiny like this? It was like he knew something she didn't. Eton wanted to argue the point, but he needed to step away from whatever this was.

"I'm rooting for you guys," Eton said, with his hands in the air. "I'll stay out of it the best I can. It's not my business, but if she comes to me, I will not shut her out the way you do."

Eton sensed Daniel move behind him. He turned, but Daniel was already beside him. A powerful hand clutched the hood of his sweater, and he was being lifted off the ground. Eton was on his toes, barely scraping along the floor. He was six-foot-three and was being picked up one-handed like a puppy.

Daniel opened the front door, where he dropped Eton on the porch. The door slammed behind him. Eton straightened out his sweater and the shirt underneath. Last time he got on a scale, he weighed one hundred and eighty-five pounds. He might have lost some weight since he arrived, but there's no way a man could pick him up with one hand.

He didn't overthink it; he just ran for the cottage. When Daniel said there were things at work, it probably had something to do with the freakish strength. What was he? Was Destiny the same thing? Maybe they were just heavily inbred with some mutant gene.

It was dark by the time he got back to the shop. He found Kerry furiously working on her knitting when he came in. "Hey," he said.

"What's wrong?" she asked, pausing her work.

Eton shook his head, but Kerry had already caught on to the scent. She would not let go now. "What happened?"

He told her about the guys fleeing for their lives. About the total wreck he found Destiny in. How Daniel kicked him out of the house.

"There's no way he should have been able to do that."

Kerry's eyes were wide, and she set her knitting aside. "Eton, I don't think you should go up there anymore."

"I won't," he said. "Not my circus."

"If she comes here, you need to send her on her way back."

Eton shook his head. "I can't do that. What if he—"

"No," Kerry said. "I know you. You want to be the hero, but these people are not normal. You can't get involved."

"They are fine. He just needs to relax, that's all. I'm not getting into it. I promise."

Kerry didn't believe him. She glared at him and resumed sitting on her stool.

"I'm going to wash up," he told her.

"Why did you shit yourself?"

Eton laughed, "Maybe just a little."

"Okay, I'm going to talk to Holly, then go to bed.... Eton?"

"Yeah?"

"Brie was looking for a way out of her marriage. Don't be that way out for Destiny."

Just hearing her name was enough to make him cringe. He could leave the country, start a whole new life, leave social media, even change his name, but he still couldn't get away from Brie.

He poured boiling water from the kettle into the camping shower they had outside. Using the soap his sister made, he scrubbed himself down one foot at a time in the barrel. He wasn't mad at Kerry for what she'd said. It just stung to hear it out loud. He had taken all the blame for what happened with Brie. He was the one who made the moves on her, but she was the one who kept coming back.

Ignoring the biting cold, he scrubbed all over a second time. Drips of lukewarm water fell as he relentlessly worked the washrag. Brie wanted to get out of a lagging marriage, and he was the perfect means. When her husband suspected she was cheating, he set up a camera and recorded them. Her husband made a nice little compilation video of the most humiliating, out-of-context parts and posted it on social media for everyone to see.

It went viral. He became the laughingstock of town. He became, "Hey, aren't you that guy..." and high schoolers would yell quotes from the video. Brie didn't even say goodbye. She just packed her shit and left.

Eton dried off and put on a pair of pajamas. He drank some whiskey and fell asleep thinking about Brie, but somewhere along the way, her face morphed into Destiny's. Kerry could say whatever she wanted, but Destiny was nothing like Brie. She was so much braver.

Destiny wasn't looking for a way out of her marriage. She was doing everything she could to make a crazy dude happy. When she had enough, Eton would be there. He would save her from this isolated little island and show her everything the world offered. Only if she came to him, though. Only if she came to him.

Chapter Twelve

COMING TO TERMS

Destiny stood at the platform of the basement steps with her arms folded while she stared at Daniel. It had been a week since she last saw Eton. Since Daniel had threatened the lives of those two men. Eton pleaded with her to give her husband a break, but watching him now, she was certain he had lost his mind.

Daniel had walled up the doorway into the catacombs. He was now creating a wall over the existing wall. "How many walls do you think necessary?" she asked.

He paused before smashing a boulder against another rock with his full strength. Both rocks shattered into pieces, and plumes of dust rose from the ground.

"It looks unnatural," Daniel said. "It's obvious that it's covering a door. If I create a new wall, people will be less likely to wonder where the door leads."

She honestly couldn't care less. That, and from what she had learned of current technology, humans would eventually discover the chasm. If they could find King Tutankhamun's tomb, they would notice a mansion-sized void beneath Sallows hall.

"Will you be satisfied then?" she asked. "Will you come back upstairs and be my husband again?"

Daniel winced. "I know I haven't been the most attentive lately. Trust me when I say that I do this for you."

He did this for her, but he didn't trust her enough to share his thoughts. There was no arguing the point. Daniel went on smashing his rocks, and she went back upstairs with her head bowed in defeat.

What was once her home and her sanctuary now felt more like a cage. The walls were in a state of decay, and the floor groaned beneath her feet. Decomposition was creeping toward her from every shadow and forgotten corridor, and if she didn't get out, she feared it would infect her as well.

Mists cascaded in layers across the island as she walked to the store. She had another lump of gold in her apron pocket. What she intended to do with it, she didn't know just yet. With Eton, the world was at her fingertips, and all she needed to do was tell him what she desired most, and he could make it happen with a few clicks.

The long walk gave her time to think about her future. She couldn't live like this forever. Even with the catacombs walled up, she didn't think Daniel would return to the person he once was. Something had altered his perspective of the world so profoundly that he could never return. If only he would let her in.

He was treating this cavern like a life-or-death situation. It was indeed important to fulfill the promise of their ancestors and prevent anything escaping from that Hellmouth, but a few rocks and some mortar couldn't stop the creatures the journal described. No, Daniel had another motive, but what?

The tiny little cottage appeared in the distance as the trail widened before melding into the sandy shore. Eton was chopping wood, and Kerry was chasing around a chicken. Maybe the chicken was chasing Kerry. It was hard to determine what the situation was, but whatever it was, it was a cheerful sight.

She felt a pang of jealousy. This was the sort of life Daniel had in mind for them. Once upon a time, it would have been enough for her.

"Good afternoon," she called from the hill. The siblings both looked up and waved. Unlike Daniel, they were happy to see her.

"How's it going?" Eton asked as he stacked the wood against the cottage.

She wanted to lie, but she was never good at it. It wasn't socially acceptable to tell people how you really felt when they asked that question. Even she knew that.

Eton frowned as though he already had an idea how things were going. "He's still..."

Destiny nodded as she pocketed her errant hands. "I don't know what to say to him anymore."

"Maybe you just need to leave him alone, let him work it out."

"I think he's lost his mind," she confessed.

Eton grimaced. He did not wish to speak ill of her husband, and she appreciated that. Her husband was possibly mad, but she would feel a conflicting defensiveness if anyone else were to agree with her.

"Why don't you come inside," Eton said. "Have some tea or something."

Kerry had gone inside and was sitting on a stool, working on a complex knitting pattern. Destiny was unsure of just what it was the girl was knitting, but the dyed wool was an array of pastel colors. It was unlike anything she had ever seen, and she fought the urge to touch the beautiful wool.

"It's absolutely stunning," she said.

Kerry smiled with the certainty only a young girl could possess. "I'm trying to make a coat, but it's not working out. This is the millionth time I've tried."

Destiny was never good at such things. Her mother hadn't done them, and her aunts hadn't visited often enough to teach her more. Not that she ever held an interest in crafting such things. She preferred reading and tending to the garden. "You've not had a single lesson?"

"No," Kerry admitted. "I was using videos online, but since we can hardly use the internet," Kerry said loudly while glaring at Eton, "I've had to figure out most of it on my own."

Eton sensed the hostility and ducked into his room. Destiny could only think of one thing that always brightened Kerry's mood. "How is your friend, Holly?"

"She's good. She's trying to get things lined up so that she can take a week off to come and visit."

"It's good to have friends."

Kerry paused, and her stitches came undone along several rows. "So, I know this will probably be weird for you, but we're not just friends."

Eton emerged from his room to observe the conversation. Destiny smiled at him, not understanding what the fuss was about. "A best friend is not weird."

"Yeah, she's a best friend," Kerry said. "Like the kind I kiss and stuff."

She still didn't see what was weird. Friends kissed one another all the time. Maybe affections between friends had changed in this era.

Kerry repeated the phrase "and stuff" a second time.

Destiny wished she understood what young Kerry was trying to explain. What stuff could she possibly mean?

"They are lovers," Eton said.

"Oh!" she said. It embarrassed Destiny that she even required an explanation. She felt as though this was something she should have figured out on her own somehow, but how could she? No one that she knew of preferred the same gender. It's not like they would tell her about it.

"Is that going to be weird for you?"

The only references she had were in historical accounts. "Many people throughout history took same-sex lovers. I've just never met someone who was like that before."

Kerry sighed, and her needles plopped into her lap. "The Amish woman took it better than our parents did."

"Amish?" she asked.

The siblings took turns explaining a solitary clan of people who lived without modern technology and were heavily religious. It did indeed have a lot in common with how she and Daniel once lived, minus the religion.

"We are pagan; at least, I think that is what we are," Destiny said. "Mother said that Christianity was a tool to suppress women."

"Oh," Eton said. "That's cool. Like, you're a pagan cult."

She didn't understand the admiration. They'd been told that the mainlanders would hate them. Things had indeed changed.

"Is that why your family came here?" Kerry asked.

Oh, no. This wasn't the conversation she wanted to have. "Well, no one knows for sure, but that was my mother's theory."

"Your family wouldn't be the first to escape the fucking Christian plague," Eton said. "And your mom was right. They used to burn women alive just for the hell of it."

"That's absolutely horrid!"

"They said they were witches, but really, they were just women who they couldn't control," Kerry said.

This information was a stone thrown against her windows. In her head, the new world was a fully enlightened and magical place where someone could be anyone. Sure, it had its complications, but a remote island had its drawbacks as well.

"I don't care if you and Holly are lovers," she said, changing the subject.

"Do you think Daniel would get weird?" Kerry asked. Just what was this poor girl's impression of Daniel? Kerry must have thought him a monster. She wasn't wrong.

"He used to be a rather open-minded man," she said. "He's under a lot of stress right now, and it makes him a little less so. But I don't think he would see two women in love as a threat of any sort."

Kerry didn't appear convinced but took up her knitting once again.

Destiny supposed that was a universal fear of one's friends and family rejecting their beloved. She stared at Kerry until their eyes met. "I'm sure she's lovely, and I'd be honored to meet her. Daniel will feel the same."

This made Kerry cast her gaze downward, and her cheeks blushed happily. She gave Eton a wink, and he, too, smiled. It was just as important to Kerry as it was to Eton that Holly be welcomed.

After a while, Kerry put away her knitting and went outside to care for the animals, leaving her alone with Eton. Silence fell across the cottage store as they struggled with what to say now that they were alone and unsupervised. "You're such a good big brother," she said.

"Our parents didn't take the whole lesbian thing very well," Eton explained.

"The what?" Was Kerry a type of witch or non-Christian? She knew the Christians enjoyed persecution.

"She, eh, likes women." Eton rubbed the back of her bright red neck.

Destiny didn't understand.

Eton shrugged, "That's not the person they thought she was, I guess."

She didn't understand. Kerry was still Kerry, even if the person she loved was not a man. "I admit I know little about this, but men in Roman times took male lovers all the time. Hadrian was still Hadrian. Nero was still—unfortunately—Nero."

"Society has changed a little since Roman times. Being gay isn't a big deal for most people; it's just that it surprised our parents."

"Is this perhaps a Christian principle?" she asked.

"Well, we're not religious, but yeah," Eton struggled to answer.

She could understand the parents in some ways. "Like you said about Daniel. He just needs time to think and come to terms with it."

"Yeah," Eton laughed. "It feels like I was wrong about that, though."

She hated that Eton and Kerry didn't hold faith in Daniel, but they were not wrong to do so. "I thought I knew him," she whispered.

"No offense," Eton said. "I think you just didn't know anyone else."

"What?"

Eton stood beside her and leaned his back against the counter. "Before everyone died, did you have other options?"

Destiny's mind reached into her foggy past. It didn't take long to discover the answer to that question. No," she said, shaking her head. "It was always Daniel and only him."

Eton rubbed the back of his neck with the palm of his hand. "Yesh."

Her prospects never felt limited until Eton pointed it out. Her chest puffed with defensiveness, but it quickly deflated. He was right. "I guess when an island is your entire world, your expectations are a little different."

"Did you ever think about just leaving?" Eton asked. His voice was soft, and she could feel his breath on her neck.

"Sometimes," she admitted. "I was just too afraid, I think. That and we didn't have a boat."

"You know, Bart is due for a visit. You can come with me if you like. Check things out."

The idea of leaving the island was exciting and terrifying at the same time. Her mouth fell open like an idiot, and he smiled. "Hey, it will be okay. I'll be with you the entire time. Just a short visit."

"How will I know when Bart arrives?" she stammered.

"Well, if you stay here with us, you'll already be here when he arrives."

She let out a quiet gasp. "You want me to stay?"

The idea hadn't occurred to her. Daniel wouldn't approve—no, he just didn't care anymore. The realization stung like the thick needles full of the morphine Edward once used to treat her night terrors.

"Yeah," Eton said, and Kerry nodded in agreement.

The image of the mansion staring down at her with its many eyes made her stomach curdle. He would likely be there, smashing rocks day and night. She would be all alone.

"I'd like that very much."

Even though Kerry was attracted to women, the three of them decided it would be best for her and Kerry to stay in the same room. Kerry did not want to share a room with her brother, citing that he snored too loudly.

***

That night, Destiny lay on a cot in the tiny room that once belonged to Daniel and his brother. She stared at the ceiling most of the night. While it was horribly boring, it gave her time to think about Daniel.

Even as she lay, he was probably working obsessively in the basement to seal up any evidence of the catacombs. Stacking rock after jagged rock. Unyielding and untiring, day and night. Did he even notice she was gone?

The chickens were flapping wildly, and the sheep were bleating. Frowning, Destiny peeked through the window into the pens and saw the animals were indeed frantic.

Images of the broken doe came to mind. Slipping from her cot, Destiny went outside and checked on the animals. She was immune to cold and hunger, but Destiny still struggled to see in the dark. Walking around the perimeter of the pens, the animals ran from her as much as they did the unknown assailant.

From the corner of her eye, something moved.

Destiny whirled around to behold what she thought was a tree in the dark, curling and licking like a giant tongue protruding from the earth. She gasped and clamped a hand over her mouth to keep from screaming.

She needed to get closer when all she really wanted to do was run away. Dragging her feet forward, the thing gave pause as if it could hear her footsteps. Before Destiny could move closer, the enormous worm slipped back into the earth.

Destiny stood alone in the darkness, but her husband's plight no longer felt irrational in the presence of a worm the size of a tree living in the ground.

CHAPTER THIRTEEN

ROOMMATES

Eton wasn't surprised when Destiny came to the store without the intent to buy anything, as he hoped she would. She must have been lonely in that big old house, with only Daniel doing whatever the hell he was doing in the basement.

It was Kerry's idea to ask her to stay. She cornered Eton while Destiny was playing with Chapstick. "Hey, is she okay?"

"I don't know."

"Do you think we should invite her to stay?" Kerry asked.

Wasn't she the one who said to send her home? His sister was far more softhearted than she wanted to let on. He couldn't say anything without being accused of trying to seduce her. All he could do was shrug. "I can ask."

Kerry frowned, "Okay. It's just that after what you told me, I don't think it's a good idea for her to be alone with him. He sounds unhinged."

"I'll ask," Eton said.

"Okay?"

"Okay."

He slept restlessly that night. Were things between them over, or was it going to drag out slowly and painfully as it usually did? He wasn't in any hurry to make his move. On the contrary. Eton wanted to make certain that the timing was right.

If he learned anything from Brie, it was that just because she reciprocated did not mean she was ready to be in a new relationship. Destiny was the marrying type and was worth however long the wait would be. And even if things didn't work out between them, she didn't deserve this.

The next morning, the three of them drank coffee and did the morning chores. Everything was so simple. It was like she had been there since they first opened the shop. There was no sign of Daniel, though Eton worried that at any minute, he would come bursting through the door.

While he was checking on the bills, the front door swung open. Eton reached for the handle of his baseball bat. He had been anticipating this moment since Destiny walked in. Her husband was here to collect his wife and probably kill him. He didn't want to resort to violence, but Daniel was uber strong, and he wasn't about to take any chances.

Several giggling people his age wearing beanies and wool coats from Höfn came bursting in through the door. There were seven of them, all shopping in his store. Behind them, Bart stood with a triumphant grin.

Kerry and Destiny were both equally alarmed by the swarm of tourists that shopped the store. Eton was more worried about Destiny, who probably hadn't seen that many people in years. She came up beside him behind the counter and smiled, "This is exciting."

"Bart," he laughed, shaking his hand. "What's going on, my man?"

"I'm starting my own goddamned tour," Bart said.

"I thought Iceland wasn't cool with it."

"Fuck it," Bart boasted. "These kids paid me more in one day than I would make in two weeks' fishing."

Destiny must have assumed that the rugged old man with the Icelandic accent was probably the Icelandic fisherman, but he introduced them all the same. "We should warn them about Daniel," she told both Eton and Bart.

"Right." Eton cupped his hands over his mouth and said, "Ladies and gentlemen, if I could get your attention."

"There are locals who live on the island. We ask that you steer clear of the big house. Please do not leave trash, be respectful, and if you have questions, please come to me, Kerry, or Destiny."

The visitors seemed receptive, and Kerry rang them out at the counter.

"You live here?" Bart asked Destiny.

She flushed a little and nodded.

"My dear, anytime you need a ride to shore, I would be happy to take you free of charge."

"Thank you," she replied.

"We talked about going to shore today, but..." He glanced at the group.

"I don't think we should leave Kerry alone," Destiny agreed.

He knew she was really thinking it had more to do with Daniel and less to do with Kerry. His sister was fine, but the way Daniel had reacted to the surveyors was enough to make anyone concerned.

"I think I should make my way home," Destiny said while observing the group of tourists apprehensively.

"Yeah," he agreed. "I'll walk you there."

Away from the crowd, the two of them made their way to the mansion. Destiny was wringing her hands and chewing on her lip as she watched the horizon. "Are you sure you want to go home?" he asked.

"Yes," she said before following it up with, "No."

Destiny did that thing with her fingers again. She twisted and contoured them in a way that he imagined was painful. "I don't want to go back, but I don't want him to hurt anyone. If I left him and a group of people like that were to encounter him, I don't know what he would do. I would be responsible."

Eton understood all about responsibility for things that were not his. What Daniel did was Daniel's fault, but Destiny felt like she could prevent that. Much like when he took on too much of Brie's marital problems and got way in over his head.

"I know you feel like there's something you can do to stop it," he said. "But sometimes you have to know when to draw that line." Who was he to be giving advice?

"Draw a line?"

"It's like when you feel compelled to help or control a situation that you didn't start. Know when to step back."

Destiny took his words hard. Her head hung low, and she nodded and said, "But I think I started this."

What could she possibly have started? It didn't matter how things started between them or why. What mattered was what was happening now. Telling her this wouldn't matter; someone told him the same things when he was with Brie. And look how that turned out.

They spoke little the rest of the way. Destiny was too deep into her own thoughts. When they reached the mansion, he took her hand and pulled her close.

"Just promise me you will leave if he hurts you."

Destiny nodded. "He'd never hurt me."

"You keep saying that, but I don't think you know him anymore."

She pulled away from him then. He watched her go up the steps and into that evil house and wished there was a way to make her stay. Not because he liked her, but because he really didn't want to see her go back when she hated it.

If he seduced her, professed his love, and whisked her away, Daniel would forever haunt them. Destiny needed to end this on her own before they could move forward. Even if it scared him to leave her with Daniel. She had to make her own choices, and he had to respect them.

Chapter Fourteen

SHE WAS LIKE US

Destiny found her husband sitting in the drawing room. His old clothes were ragged and torn, and his hair was dirty from toil. He sat hunched over with his arms resting on his knees. He was staring down at the floor with a defeated expression.

"Daniel," she whispered.

"Where did you go?" he asked. "Never mind. I know where you went."

The venom in his voice was poignant and ugly. She'd done nothing wrong, yet in his mind, she clearly had. "I was tired of being alone. I stayed with Kerry and Eton."

Daniel let out a bitter chuckle.

"You've done nothing but ignore me for the past month," she said. "The one night I stay over with friends, and you make me feel like the wanton adulterer."

"So not paying constant attention to you is an excuse to go running off to Eton?"

"I didn't run off to him," she said, pointing towards the cottage. "I visited them the way people used to come and visit in this house."

"That was different," he argued. "You weren't a married woman who did not inform her husband."

"I didn't plan on it. I was going to come back," she confessed. "But the thought of coming back here made me miserable."

"I make you miserable?"

"Yes!" she shouted. Daniel winced, and she felt horrible for hurting him, but she didn't regret her words. He needed the truth of where she stood.

Daniel rested his face in his hands and said nothing. She resisted the urge to comfort him and allowed him to sit in his feelings. He couldn't make her feel this way without consequences.

"It has nothing to do with Eton," she told him. "I slept in Kerry's room. I wanted to go to the mainland with them for the day, but when their ferryman arrived with a boatful of visitors, I said I had to come back. They are afraid you're going to hurt me, Daniel."

He didn't speak. Was he even listening? Daniel's eyes turned upward from his dirty hands. "I'd never—"

"I know," she mumbled. She sighed and sat beside her husband. "I know you would never hurt me, but can you say the same to other people on this island?"

"They have no business coming here."

"You have no right hurting anyone either," she said. It shocked her he would even defend such actions. Where was the sweet man she knew and loved? Her eyes welled as the suspicion came to fruition. Daniel had no qualms about hurting anyone if they got in his way. But what was his goal?

"You're right," he said. "I just want to protect us."

"I need you to promise you'll hurt no one."

Daniel's eyes flickered. "I can't promise you that."

She was chilled to her core by his answer. Her bottom lip trembled as she spoke, "I don't think you understand what that means for us."

Daniel had tears in his eyes, but he blinked them away. "At least you'll be safe, and that's all that matters."

Sounds of life came from outside. Her heart launched into her throat as she ran to the window to find that the visitors from the store were outside the mansion. They were taking pictures and frolicking the hillside. Daniel was behind her, also watching the visitors.

"Eton told them to stay clear of the mansion," she said.

"As if the new world has respect for anything."

"I'm going to go talk to them," she said. "Please stay here."

She went downstairs and around to the side where the four of them stood. When they saw her, they all shifted like children caught stealing the berry pie. Destiny folded her arms and made her best Helicant impression. "You were told to leave this place alone."

"We just wanted to take a few pictures," a blonde woman with dark sunglasses said.

"You were told to stay clear of this house," she repeated. "Now leave before we have you removed from the island."

The group backed off and made their way down the hillside. The wind blew in the opposite direction, pushing her dress and hair away from her, but she ignored it. She commanded what was hers. When she returned to the drawing room, Daniel was gone.

She checked the basement and saw that he had completely walled off the entryway to the catacombs and was now cleaning up the mess he'd made. Daniel peered up at her between chunks of brown hair. "I want to clear all the evidence."

She let out an exasperated shrug and tried to help, but Daniel blocked her at the steps. "No," he said. "Just let me handle this."

"Really, it's all right."

"I'll tell you what," Daniel said. "Once I finish up here, I'll go wash up and put on those clothes from the new world. How does that sound?"

She knew he was attempting to pacify her again, but it was working. She just couldn't help herself. It was a farce, but one she wanted to play. "Do you mean it?"

His hands slipped to her waist, where he gave a gentle squeeze that made her ache. "I'd like to see those things you bought as well."

"Okay," she whispered before going back upstairs.

They spent the next several hours rekindling their relationship. Daniel did indeed appreciate the new undergarments. He was assessing his new clothing in the mirror. They were the same fashion as Eton wore. Dark, tight pants with a crisp white shirt underneath a thick flannel one that buttoned up the front.

Destiny lay on the bed, practically drooling over him. "I don't think anyone will ever cut a better figure in those clothes."

He grinned at her and turned to view himself in the mirror. "I used to be so fat. I never thought I could look like this. I don't suppose food will ever be a concern again."

"All food and drink taste like nothing. It could be poison; it could be ambrosia. I wouldn't know the difference," she said. Now that reminded her of her mother. The woman so seldom ate, Destiny always wondered how she lived.

"Eton's shop?"

"I had to blend in," she explained. "At night, I lay on a cot and pretended to sleep while Kerry snored away. I slept in your old room, actually."

Daniel gave an impish grin. "Did you see my artwork?"

She hadn't.

"My brother threw pig shit at me one day. I got so mad, I carved "Joseph is a pig fucker" on a wooden beam along one wall."

Her laugh came unbidden then. It burst from her nose, and she made an unseemly chortle, but she didn't care. It was enough to get Daniel laughing, too. "The night we went to sleep. You told me about the story your mother told you about why she had lived for as long as she had."

Destiny remembered. "She said it was one of these potions and that she only drank half, so it only extended her life some."

"Do you think that was what happened to us?"

"I guess it could be that as well as anything. Though my mother still needed to eat and use the bathroom. She could have been faking it. It never seemed like she wanted to eat, and when she did, it was only a few bites."

"You know we are not human, then," Daniel said.

It was a conversation they had tiptoed around for months now. Perhaps Daniel was finally going to let her in. He was going to talk to her about what had him so obsessed. She put down the bottle, turned around to the bed, and faced her husband.

"Yes," she said. "I know we're not human. I don't know why or how, but the fact that we've yet to die from hunger, exhaustion, or from the cold is proof enough."

Daniel sat beside her on the bed and stroked the top of her hand. "I don't think Eton or Kerry would do anything to harm us if they learned about what we are, but that doesn't mean others won't."

"What do you mean?"

"Those people, the ones who woke us," Daniel said. "They were ghost hunters. They made it their job to seek the strange. Life that is beyond human, Destiny. We are beyond human. There are people out there who want to know how it works. People who would tear us inside out if it meant unlocking our secrets."

Destiny's mind came to a complete stop. "That can't be true."

"Eton and I had a talk about it," Daniel said. "If the government or the scientists got wind of what we are, we would become experiments. Like Uncle Edward's rats."

The poor little lab rats. She shuddered at the thought and recalled the story about Daniel setting them free while he was Beth's understudy. Mother said the rats were within an inch of their lives anyway and refused to punish him for it. Edward wasn't as upset by it as Beth was. She saw it as a breach of trust but ultimately forgave Daniel as well.

"Is that why you were so angry with the surveyors?"

He nodded. "I don't want them to take you. I won't let anyone put you in a cage and cut you apart or fill you full of venoms out of curiosity."

All this time, his fears were over how the new world would treat them. She had similar concerns, but she had never been tortured like Daniel had. She had never been locked away in a room of pain while time stood still. He knew what torture was. He had endured human cruelty on a level that she could never understand.

She leaped from the vanity seat and into her husband's arms. He pulled her into his lap, and she kissed his face all over. "Why couldn't you just tell me this?"

"Because that's not everything."

The hike to the cottage on the cliff was worse at night. Thankfully, Destiny had grabbed a mini flashlight from the store the first time they went to Eton's place. She wished her inhuman abilities gave her night vision. She would have gratefully exchanged the need for food for night vision.

Daniel found the path far better than she. He was ahead of her by several feet. She scrambled to keep up, even with the flashlight. Daniel didn't rely on light as much as she did.

"Can you see in the dark?" she called out.

"No," Daniel said somewhere in the overgrowth. "I've spent many nights this last month roaming around in the night. I'm far more familiar with the area."

When they arrived at the cottage, she could see why. Parts of the cottage were missing. Stones dislodged from corner sections, and the small cobble wall was dismantled. Her husband only shrugged.

"After I sealed up the wall, it occurred to me that the wall I built would seem more natural if I used similar materials."

"I had thought to live here with you one day," she said. "Before I saw how damaged the inside was."

"Did you bring your lighter?" he asked.

She nodded, and they entered the decrepit cottage. Once inside, her husband wasted no time in pulling several books out of their cases. He checked the titles before stacking them on the coffee table beside the moldy chair.

"This place could have been a wonderful little home for us," Daniel agreed. "It's too bad we didn't wake up sooner."

He took the framed map off the wall and set it on the books.

"What are you doing?" she asked.

Daniel pulled her close and kissed her hard. She went positively limp in his arms as his hands searched her body. His hands smoothed over her silken blouse, and she let out a gasp as he shoved his fingers roughly in her front pocket and pulled out the lighter.

"I'm going to burn the evidence."

She felt the rush of cold when Daniel let go of her. He was moving towards the back bedroom and causing a ruckus. Tossing things around. Old and rotten as they were, they still belonged to Aunt Sophie. "What about the decree?" she asked.

"It's not in here," he said. "I checked the place top to bottom."

Emerging from the bedroom, he knocked the bookshelves down behind him until the room was an impassable heap of books and wood. "I've been waiting for a dry spell for some time," Daniel said. "Tonight is finally the night."

Before she could issue a protest, Daniel lit the books lying on the ground with the lighter. It took several attempts, but once the fire started, it burned nearly as much as the rage in Daniel's eyes. He grabbed the small stack of books and the map before pushing her outside.

The cottage burned, and it felt as though she were losing a piece of her history. She once loved that cottage. Daniel looked at it as a threat that he had removed once and for all. He led her back to the mansion and to their bedroom, where they made love.

***

"Along with Nathaniel's diary," Daniel said. He was naked underneath the thin sheet. "I found a genealogy of the family from the first family all the way to us."

Her eyes followed the lines and the scrawling ink. The family arrived on the island in 1589. She noted how small the family tree was. "If this is correct, we were only four generations from Nathaniel's family."

"Look at your mother."

She found Helicant but shook her head. "This isn't right. According to this, she was Nathaniel's youngest daughter."

There were no dates apart from the one of arrival, but that would have made her mother at least four hundred years old. There was a line scratched by her name, linking her to Nathaniel's great-grandchild. "She's also tied to this part of the family."

"That asterisk is a sign of adoption," Daniel explained. "For whatever reason, your mother disappeared and then reemerged later."

It was inexplicable, and she went weak all over. There was so much her mother never told her. "The potion was real?"

"She was old when you knew her, but she could have remained young for years and years before she resumed aging again."

Her fingers trembled with the recognition. Her mother wasn't just Nathaniel's daughter—she was the witch—and the reason for banishment to the island. What was she?

"Have a look at this."

He got her out of bed and led her to the place where they first woke up. They were still naked, but their bodies no longer sensed the chill. Standing outside the broken wall that led to the hallway they'd left, Daniel held up the map.

"This isn't here on the map. Whoever drew this wanted us to forget about that place entirely."

He led the way into the hallway, toward the room they woke up in, and shined the flashlight inside. The light was enough to show chunks of rot and decay. Maggots breathed life into the padded walls. Spikes and heavy steel chains lined every corner. There was no place for respite here. No place of peace. "This was my home."

Destiny's stomach was twisting in knots. "Daniel, I want to leave."

"This is the room where they kept me and tortured me until they no longer resembled men themselves. Rather than lose their humanity, they sealed me away and left me in there for all eternity."

"I want to leave," she nearly shouted before doubling over. Her husband was too deep in thought to notice. "Daniel—"

"And that's where you found me," Daniel said, turning to her at last. "Destiny, my beautiful, gentle wife."

Kneeling, he picked her up and carried her away from the hallway.

"Please," she whined.

Daniel kissed her temple and carried her away from the hallway and back to her bedroom. The rest of the night, he held her close and whispered gentle words in her ears. She'd forgotten what it was to be afraid and vulnerable. It wasn't until they were back in that room that she was reminded. That horrid room. It reminded Daniel of what he was when she wanted him to forget.

"Please, Daniel," she pleaded. "You're not that thing anymore."

"Don't you see? Our family didn't die," he explained. "At least, not all of us."

He handed her another book, but she pushed it away. Written words tasted like the food she tried to eat and the liquids she tried to drink. They no longer held light for her, not anymore. "I can't."

"It's about a curse," Daniel explained. "I'll read it to you."

She was a witch. The fiercest and deadliest any of the witch hunters had ever encountered. I caught her indulging herself on the flesh of men and babe. I brought the cannibal low before the king. He asked her, "Does Satan's grasp hold you so dearly?"

"Burn her," the crowd chanted, but the witch only smiled. Forced to her knees before the king and defender of our Lord, she smiled and said, "Burn me, yes, but my family will live on."

"You have doomed us all!" Nathanial shouted at his daughter as her mother sobbed in his chest. The witch was unmoved. "You can't burn everyone," she said. "The time will come when the world has all but forgotten this day."

"My descendants will have spread like wildfire. Then, they will turn into monsters. Some you know from your worst nightmares, others you will know not. They will overtake your city and claim the lands you stole from my family and my future."

The king was a wise man and well-versed in the ways of witches. "This is not a spell but a prophecy, is it not?"

The witch's eyes lit with a cunning evil as though she were Lucifer himself. "Quite learned you are, my king."

"In all prophecies, there is a martyr, redemption, exile, and restoration," the king said, standing from his tall throne. If one of these is not satisfied, the prophecy cannot be fulfilled. The cannibal's tongue flickered the way the old serpents would, but she said nothing.

"I hereby banish all named Sallow to the provincial island. They may have a ship and anything they require to live on this island. This island shall henceforce be known as Sallows Island. This is their land, and this is their title. Should any monster surface, they are responsible for its death."

"Knowing she had been beaten, the witch screamed and kicked. Her near-naked body was exposed for all the court to see and—"

Destiny sat up and regarded Daniel carefully. "What does it mean?"

Her husband only stared at her, holding the small book. He clearly enjoyed reading it, but she'd had enough anxiety for one lifetime.

"The king said that in order for a prophecy to be a prophecy, four things need to happen," Daniel explained. "If those things didn't happen, the story repeated itself."

"Our family was exiled to an island, where the family members turned into monsters until a martyr gave redemption, and then, there was restoration."

She wanted to strangle him. To put her hands on his thin neck and rattle it until he finally stopped moving. Beyond frustrated, she just needed a straight answer. "Daniel…"

"Okay," he said. "Sallows were exiled to the island where, at some point, they all turned into monsters. If a martyr did not sacrifice themself for redemption, the story would repeat all over again. You were the martyr, Destiny. You saved me from an eternity of pain and finished the prophecy."

Destiny's brain hurt from all this, but it made sense in its deluded way. "I fulfilled a witch prophecy—my mother's prophecy—and that's why the island is suddenly visible to the real world?"

"That's my theory." His lips trailed her temple. "That is why time doesn't quite work in the room or in the basement."

He had put together the puzzle while she was still working on one piece. It wasn't every day that one found out their mother was a witch. She collapsed on the bed, exhausted by the weight of all the new knowledge.

"My mother would've been happy to know her son-in-law thought she was a proper witch."

"I think she's still out there," Daniel said, gazing out the window. "I think she would have been incredibly proud of you."

"That I broke her curse and freed the family from repeating the same doomed fate?" She eyed her husband. "I think you underestimate how spiteful my mother was."

"She wouldn't want you to relive it over and over again."

"It's a lot to take in."

"You understand now why I wanted to seal the catacombs as much as I did?" Daniel asked.

"I suppose it was to prevent us from getting sealed in."

"Time works strangely there," he explained. "I didn't want to risk anyone getting in there, for one, but yes, I didn't want anyone to seal us in the way the Sallows tried to seal me in."

"I don't think Mother had this in store for us."

Daniel smiled. "No, once you fulfilled the prophecy, you would be free to live however you chose. I think that is what she wanted for you."

That sounded like something her mother would have wanted for her, but Helicant wasn't here. The only person who mattered was in front of her. "But what do you want for me?"

Daniel's green eyes met hers. "I want you to be safe to make those choices."

Something inside her told her that Daniel wanted her to make choices, just so long as those decisions were the ones he deemed safe. Since he considered the rest of the world a danger, she feared that there were no safe choices from now on. If she wanted to live the life Helicant Sallows intended for her, she would need to live a little more fearlessly.

CHAPTER FIFTEEN

THE NEW WORLD

The knock on the front door made them glance up from their respective books and at one another. Of course, Daniel wasn't expecting company, but neither was she.

The scent of wood polish lingered in the freshly mopped entryway. Since Daniel's revelation and the burning of the cottage, things had returned to normal. There were unspoken conditions to this truce. There was no talk of the new world, though she desperately wanted to pay a visit. There were also no discussions of the room of pain, though sometimes, when he assumed she was too busy to notice, he would sneak off. She would find him coming down the stairs later, making one excuse or another, but she ignored it just so long as he didn't make her go up there.

At the door was a petite brunette wearing a multicolored scarf. "Kerry!" she exclaimed.

"Hey, it's been a week since we last saw you," Kerry said. Her hair was smoothed, and her makeup fully applied. Her lips were so shiny. Like a freshly polished and waxed floor. They also glittered, but Destiny didn't think she would wear something so sparkly on her lips.

"Come in," she said, opening the door wider.

"Yeah?" Kerry said as she stepped in.

"I think we've worked out at least some issues," she explained. The last time Destiny saw them, she didn't want to go home. It was only natural that Kerry worried about her. She was a good friend.

"Things have chilled out?"

"I think so. We've come to a much better understanding of one another's feelings."

"That's awesome."

She was pleased to find that Daniel had a fire going by the time she brought Kerry into the drawing room. "Hello," he greeted her. "I'm afraid it's still cold in here. I had the windows open last night to air the place out."

Kerry squished her arms to her sides, clearly from the cold. Daniel pulled out a blanket and wrapped it around her shoulders. "I know, it's ghastly cold."

Distracted by her surroundings, Kerry gazed around the room, clutching the blanket tight to her shoulders. "I've never been in here."

"We lack the manpower to maintain the house," Daniel explained. "So, we don't care for the rooms other than the ones we occupy."

"No shit. This place would take forever to clean."

Daniel smirked but said nothing.

"Hey," Kerry asked, "we saw a bunch of smoke the other night. Was that you guys?"

"No. There was an arsonist among the visitors," Daniel said woefully.

"Oh no," Kerry said.

Speechless at Daniel's bald-faced lie, Destiny nodded sadly. It was so easy for him. A bout of insecurity reminded her that her husband could lie like that to her just as easily.

"It wasn't this house, was it?" Kerry asked.

"No," Daniel said, stoking the fire. "It was one of the abandoned cottages."

"I would say you should file a report, but I don't know who you would file it with yet."

"There's still no word on what country this would be considered a part of?" Destiny asked.

"No, I don't think so. Bart has heard nothing. He told the Icelandic police you live here, and they gave him some tips. That's why I'm here, actually."

She gave Daniel a hopeful smile. Her husband was interested but remained unmoved.

"Bart said that you should talk to the city officials in Höfn. They would know better than anyone what to do. They could probably talk to Norway and the UK on your behalf."

"Do you think they would allow us to live here?" Daniel asked.

"Well, they can't make you leave," Kerry said. "There are laws against that everywhere. You're the natives of this island. They would probably declare it a province, but you'd be allowed to do whatever you've been doing."

"But we would need to go to the mainland," Destiny reiterated. Excitement bubbled over like a pot of boiling water, and she wasn't certain she could contain it for much longer.

"Yeah," Kerry said. "I know that's probably a scary thought, but while you guys are there, you could get stuff to work on the house. I'm sure there are a lot of things you need."

"If you could excuse us for a moment," Daniel said.

"Sure," Kerry said, scooting closer to the fire. Her glossy lips still trembling. They rounded the corner and stood to discuss it in the hallway.

"What do you think?" he asked.

Destiny's mouth fell open, and she gave a giggle. "You want to go?"

"If this is how we establish our hold on the island, I think we must."

She grew so excited she jumped up and down and let out a little squeal. They were finally going to the mainland! Daniel's was a reserved happiness, like a parent indulging an eager child. "Okay then."

They returned to the room to find Kerry bathing in the firelight. "When do we leave?" Daniel asked.

***

The boat was already at the dock by the time they made it to the shore. Destiny was wearing her favorite outfit she'd ordered online, a sweater and a pair of jeans with sneakers, much like the ones Aunt Coral once made for her. Daniel was striking in his black jeans and black button-up shirt. It was a silken material they didn't make on the island. They were like regular people. At least, she hoped that would be the case. In her pastel pink handbag sat another lump of gold about the same size as the one she'd given to Eton.

"Hullo," Bart greeted them with a wave.

"Hey, Bart!" Kerry called.

A few people were standing at the dock, but for once, Daniel didn't seem agitated by their presence. They had locked the door before they left, and that was good enough for him. "Isn't Eton coming?" Daniel asked.

"No," Kerry said. "Business has been picking up since Bart started his island tour. The Norwegians seem to have caught on too."

"Oh," Daniel said. "I suppose that's good for you guys."

"We still tell people to avoid the big house, but you might want to get signs."

"We'll have to do that," Destiny agreed, squeezing Daniel's arm.

Bart overheard some of the conversation and shook Daniel's hand. "I'm sorry if anyone has caused you trouble. I try to only take the ones I think will behave. Maybe I'll make them sign a waiver."

"A waiver?" Daniel asked as they filed into the boat.

"A contract that states they will follow your rules or otherwise be fined or some other penalty. If this becomes a part of Iceland, they can get involved if anyone causes you trouble."

Daniel nodded. "I appreciate that."

The men continued talking as Destiny wandered around the boat. It wasn't a large boat. Scuffed and reeking of fish, but she had never been on a boat before and found everything fascinating. Kerry tried to contain her smile.

"What?" she asked.

"You're like a little kid," she said. "Touching everything."

"I suppose I am a child in this situation."

"Daniel doesn't seem phased," Kerry said, glancing at him and Bart. They were having a rousing discussion. Despite her fears that he would be anti-social, he was quite the charming man.

"Daniel can lie," she muttered under her breath. Kerry gave her a queer expression. There she went again, dragging everyone into the fray. Today was supposed to be a fun day. She was finally leaving the island for the first time in her life. She just couldn't help but feel resentful when Daniel handled the situation so smoothly.

The boat jolted to life suddenly. If her heart still beat, it must have stopped in that moment. Bart had turned on the motor, and the boat sputtered to life. Even Daniel braced himself before his slick demeanor returned. He caught her smile and grinned back at her. For the first time in four hundred years, their lives were their own.

It was a several-hour boat ride. She and Kerry joined the men in the captain's cabin, where Bart told funny stories about his fishing trips or his children. "I imagine the two of you are thinking about little ones."

She smiled and nodded. It was true. They were thinking about children, but they could never have them. That could never be a reality for monsters like them. Daniel pulled her towards him and said, "We're taking our time. If it happens, it happens."

"Good," Bart agreed, steering his boat. "Take all the time you need. Kids made your beard grow white," he said, scratching at his own beard.

Everyone laughed at Bart's comment. It reminded her of her own childhood. She was an awful child. Her mother always told her that her children would be worse as punishment. Perhaps being barren was the most fitting curse of all for a terrible child.

"We're coming up on the city now," Bart said. "You should go up there and look."

Daniel followed her up to the deck level, and together, they saw Iceland for the first time. It was a stretch of land as far as the eye could see. Destiny was suddenly afraid. She had an urge to run back to the cabin, but Daniel squeezed her hand. "It's going to be okay."

Bart killed the engine as they came closer to the port. There were so many boats. Overwhelmed by the cords and sails that blotted out the ocean, Destiny's breath caught in her chest. Some boats were quite large. Some were little more than row boats.

"We can just hang out here if you need a minute," Kerry offered.

Daniel gave her a thin-lipped smile. "We're okay," he said.

This was the new world. They were here. Why was she so afraid? Helicant wouldn't be as afraid as she was, but she was determined to take her first steps regardless. Once her foot touched the dock, there was no going back!

"I'll take you to the city hall," Bart said, leading the way.

It was a lot to take in. The paved roads and motorized vehicles were things they'd been told about, but to see them was startling. They zoomed about so quickly that they were blurs of color. Even Daniel paused when one came around the corner.

The houses were all similar but more vivid than anything she or Daniel were accustomed to. The pigments used to paint them were unreservedly flamboyant. How strange that real life could be as colorful as a painting. The fog of the island couldn't reach them here.

Thankfully, there were things they recognized. There were homes built similarly to the cottages on the island, and there was a great deal of foliage that was native to their island as well. Mostly wildflowers in planter boxes or around people's homes. She tried to anchor herself to the familiar in order to process the unfamiliar.

"Here we are," Bart said.

They stood outside a tall, gray house with blue trim. It had a stone foundation, just like the mansion. Daniel was also drawn to the flowers, calmed by their familiarity.

"What do you think so far?" Kerry asked.

"It's different but somehow the same." She struggled to put it into words.

Daniel nodded, "There aren't as many people as I thought there would be."

"There are only a couple thousand people living here. The rest are tourists," Bart explained. "We have our busy seasons and our slow seasons."

"I see," Daniel replied.

"It's overwhelming, but not nearly as much as I imagined," she said.

Daniel nodded, but she could feel his grip stiffen. He did not agree at all. "I am anxious to speak to these people," Daniel prompted.

The lobby was in a light wood, and there hung a great map of Iceland above a series of pamphlets. Destiny picked up one of each while Bart spoke to someone in a different language. Kerry was reading the different signs on the walls.

"Hello," a small, dark-haired woman in a dark suit greeted them. "I am Helga."

They shook Helga's hand. "I am to understand you live on the island."

"Yes," Daniel said. "Our family has for generations."

"I would like to ask you some questions if that's all right."

"Sure," Daniel agreed.

The woman clutched her notepad with one hand while she wrote with the other. "What are your full names?"

"Destiny and Daniel Sallows."

"What was your maiden name?" she asked.

Destiny frowned. She didn't have a maiden name. Daniel said, "It was Sallows."

The woman paused and said. "Are you brother and sister?"

They both shook their head. "No," Daniel said. "Distant cousins, I suppose."

Were they cousins? He was one of the original monsters from before her family came, yet he was born of two Sallows. Her mother was a monster too and distantly related to the other Sallows in her generation. Daniel's mother and her father were siblings, though, so...yeah?

"Ah, everyone on the island had the same name. I see," the woman said. "Is there anyone else besides you?"

"It's just us now," Destiny said.

"I see," the woman replied. The pain in her voice did not go unnoticed.

"Do you know when your family first arrived on the island?"

"Late 1500s. We have a few books on the matter."

"You don't have a phone," the woman frowned. "How would we contact you for further information?"

Kerry stepped in. "You can email or call me," she said and wrote her information for Helga on her notepad.

"Now," Helga said. "Do you want to be part of Iceland, or are you seeking independence?"

"I just want to keep my home," Destiny said, fighting back the tears.

The emotion alarmed the woman, and Daniel said, "We want the right to determine who can come and go, we want to stay in our home, and we don't want to be bothered."

Helga came around the counter and gave Destiny a hug. It was unexpected, but she closed her eyes and accepted the embrace. If she could identify with any country, it would be this one. It was so small and perfect. So beautiful. Maybe she was naïve, but she couldn't imagine there was anywhere better than where she was now.

"We wouldn't mind being Icelandic; we just don't want our lands trespassed on."

"I can't promise anything," Helga said. "But knowing there are natives on this island changes how the UN will approach the situation. Your input will have quite a bit of sway. I can tell you that."

"What if we had documentation that proved a country gave our family the island?" Daniel asked.

"Do you have such a thing?" Helga asked, raising her thick brows.

"Well, there is mention of it in our history, but we've yet to find it."

"The process is still the same," Helga said. "It would still go before the UN, but any documentation would be in your favor. If you find it, please let me know as soon as possible so we can show it to them."

"When is this vote happening?" Kerry asked, with her hands on her hips.

"It hasn't even been decided yet."

She wiped her eyes, and Daniel pulled her close. "It's been a rather exhausting day," he said.

"Sure," Helga said.

On the way out, Kerry asked, "Where's the bathroom?"

"Right over there." Helga pointed to a door off to the side.

This reminded her she needed to pretend to be human. "I, too, need to use the bathroom," she announced, a little louder than she intended.

She waited beside the door until Kerry came out.

"So, this is a little different from an outhouse," Kerry warned.

She couldn't help but smirk. Not because she had no intention of using the toilet but because Kerry was prepared to give her a tour. "We have toilets in the mansion."

"What!"

"We have them," she explained. "But they never actually worked."

"Oh," Kerry said. "Gotcha."

Destiny shut the bathroom door and flipped a switch. A fan spun, and she stared down at the porcelain bowl. It hardly resembled what she once sat on every brisk morning on the island. It was rounder, smoother, and much smaller.

Counting to sixty, she pushed down the silver handle, and the water in the bowl whooshed into a cyclone. She jumped back before bursting into full-blown laughter. The mechanism made perfect sense. The water flushed out any human waste, but it was so loud!

Turning the knobs of the sink, she found this to work the same as the indoor plumbing should have worked in the mansion. Only there were two handles. Well, there was no reason for the suspense. She turned one knob, and cold water ran. She turned it off and tried the other knob. It took a moment, but the water turned warm, and she caught on to the modern convenience.

Bending over, her eyes followed the pipes into the wall. The new world ran hot and cold water through pipes behind the wall. They were so confident in their plumbing that they put it behind the wall. In the mansion, the plumbing climbed the walls like a sort of metallic vine. She was not as backward as they expected!

The way back to the boat was a blur. Her eyes ached from seeing so much, and her mind couldn't seem to put thoughts together anymore. Daniel sat beside her. The visit equally drained him.

"If you don't mind," Daniel said. "We need to take a bit of a rest."

"Totally get it," Kerry said. "Why don't you guys stay here until Bart gets back from lunch? I'm going to find some Wi-Fi and talk to Holly."

Destiny leaned on Daniel. He wrapped an arm around her shoulder and rested his head on the cabin wall of the boat. She closed her eyes and imagined herself back in her bedroom in the mansion. She breathed into Daniel and let her mind be blank. It wasn't sleep, but it was as close as she had come since she first woke up several months ago.

There was so much uncertainty in the new world. So many people had hands in processes that would never affect them. She couldn't believe that a group of people would vote on the fate of her island when they had never so much as set foot on it.

"It's not fair," she said. "How is it the UN gets to make such decisions?"

"I suspect they are elected officials," Daniel said. "A republic from the way it sounds."

"This doesn't bother anyone," she argued.

"I know," Daniel agreed. "When we get home, I will try to find the decree. It must be in the mansion. There are so many rooms to check."

She clung to Daniel harder. "Do you think it was a mistake? Us coming here?"

Daniel's knees spread wide, and he stared into the distance. "I don't know. I thought you would enjoy it."

"I did. It's just a lot," she admitted. "Next time will be better, I think. Less business and more fun things."

Daniel looked at her. "You really want to come back?"

"It is inevitable," she said. Daniel frowned, but he said nothing. He was trying his best to keep a positive outlook on the new world, to keep her happy. That was all. Would his attitude improve with future visits, or would it be better just to leave him at home? She doubted he would let her come without him. Daniel would endure the new world for her sake, but she didn't want him to suffer. She wanted him to be happy as well.

"Hey," Kerry called from the top deck. She came to the captain's room with something behind her back. "I've got a surprise for you."

Kerry pulled out a stack of signs that said, 'NO TRESPASSING,' and danced around with them. She laughed, and Daniel's smirk rose to the surface of his stony demeanor. He would have been a good father to a daughter.

"I figured you would want some of these."

"Thank you," Daniel said.

"How are you feeling?" Kerry asked, sitting with one booted leg crossed over the other.

"Overwhelmed, I think," Destiny said. "I think it should be a while before we visit again, but I want visitors to continue to come to the island."

"You do?" Daniel asked. She hadn't meant to announce it without speaking to him about it first, but it was something they would need to accept. The new world was at their doorstep.

Kerry was staring at the couple in silent awkwardness. It was Bart who broke the silence. "Kerry, where are you?"

"We're down here."

"Everyone ready?" asked the old man. "I want to get home to my wife before supper."

"Ready when you are, Bart," Daniel said.

They spoke little on the trip home. When the boat reached the dock, they thanked Bart, who said he would return in a few days. The morning group of visitors were waiting on the dock. They were sweaty and exhausted. Their heavy backpacks weighed them down much harder than when they first arrived.

Eton was waiting on the dock for them. He took a hand out of his light blue pants pocket and waved. "That bad, eh?"

"It was just a lot," Kerry said. "They didn't exactly get good news from the town center either."

Destiny nodded. "The UN is deciding who this island belongs to."

"Wow, okay," he said. "That sounds dramatic, doesn't it?"

"They don't even have the hearing scheduled," Kerry said.

"Bureaucracy at its finest." Eton's eyes followed the line of Destiny's body before turning to the ground.

"Well, it gives us time to find more documents that prove our ownership," Daniel said. Destiny gave him a weak smile, appreciating that he, of all people, was looking on the bright side.

"Right on," Eton said, digging his foot in the dirt. "Well, I got to get back to the store. Those guys made a mess of things."

Eton's eyes lingered on Destiny's before Kerry pulled him back to the cottage with her. Daniel and Destiny made their way up the hill to the mansion before he said, "Could he be any more desperate?"

"He was probably concerned. I must have looked a fright."

"He's made it clear to me that if you were to come to him, he would not turn you away."

"I don't think—"

"He said it to my face." Daniel's voice raised. "I'm not a jealous idiot. I know the difference."

"I'm sorry." Her lips trembled. "I didn't know he said that."

"You would if you listened to me," Daniel said.

What did he want from her? Eton's feelings were not reciprocated. "What would you have me do?" she asked. "Avoid them all together? Hide in the house every time someone comes to call?"

"No," Daniel said, shaking his head. "I didn't mean to get angry. It's been a long day for the both of us. Let's just go home."

She didn't speak another word to him for the rest of the night. Every time he tried to prompt a conversation, she would act as though it were unheard. Yes, they were tired, and it was indeed a long day. He wanted to take out his frustrations on her. He was insecure about their relationship, and rightfully so. She could leave him. One word and Eton would abandon this place and take her somewhere Daniel could never find.

She felt his arms wrap around her from behind. "I'm sorry," he said.

"I know."

Daniel tensed so hard he scarcely breathed. "I don't want you to be unhappy."

"Then stop making me unhappy."

"I just need you to tell me you have no interest in Eton," Daniel said. "Just tell me you don't care for him the way he cares for you."

It was a fair request. One that Destiny should have been able to comply with, but when she opened her mouth to say it, Destiny found it much harder to say. She certainly didn't love Eton, but he was attractive.

"I like how simple things are with him," she said. "It will never be like that with you."

He stood looming over her. "Our very existence will never allow it."

That was true. She knew it was her choice to open the door, but if she hadn't, they would still play out the same history. It was more than just their history. It was Eton's personality. He wanted to relate to and understand her. Daniel was always an opposing force. Someone she had to combat or pacify when all she wanted was to be at peace.

"You don't understand," she told him.

"Then help me understand."

She was tired of trying. For once, she just wanted someone who understood her.

"You wanted me to be more positive, and I was," he said. "You wanted me to explore the new world with you, and I did."

"You hate every minute."

"I don't hate it as long as I'm with you."

"But you do," she said. "I fear we are just too different. I don't want us to make each other miserable. We have other options."

"Options like Eton?"

This day had been long and difficult. She had a lot to think about and needed silence to think it in.

Chapter Sixteen

SILENCE

It was beyond stupid to hide in her own home. If Daniel had his way, they would still be doing that. She emerged from her mother's bedroom and marched downstairs to collect the linens. She wore the ring. She was the leader, not him.

Her mother's blankets had dried and had the most refreshing scent. She pushed the quilt to her face and inhaled deeply. Hints of lavender still lingered from the soap. She took them all down and folded them neatly before replacing them on her mother's bed.

Daniel had blessedly gone on another one of his walks. That was fine with her. They needed space, no matter how small. While he was gone, she swept up the kitchen area and made it appear as though people used it. She would buy some tea and snacks. That way, when visitors came, she could provide refreshments.

She used the water from the old well to mop the kitchen floors and wipe down the counters. Daniel left a surplus of wood at her disposal, so she created a neat little stack beside the oven and inside the oven. She thought about keeping it on to provide some amount of heat if needed.

Destiny cleaned the first story and opened all the windows she could to let in the fresh air. She hoped it would draw out the dank and foreboding feeling the house gave to everyone, including herself. With all the curtains back and the windows open, the mansion was almost welcoming.

She wanted the house to be unquestionable in the eyes of visitors. She couldn't hide or deny the broken wall that led to the room where she and Daniel first woke up, but she could alter the appearance. She shivered at the thought, but if she cleaned it out and made it presentable, it would look far less suspicious than it did now.

She also hoped that by cleaning the room, she would take the power from it. That if she could remove all the torture and decay, she would no longer be so threatened by it. Picking up the wheelbarrow with one hand and several burlap bags with the other, she made her way to the room.

Ignoring the increasing intensity of the turning in her stomach, she marched on. An explosion in the bathroom across the narrow hallway could explain the hole. What she could not explain were the chains and spikes in a padded room littered with various remains of animals or humans—she couldn't tell.

She closed her eyes and took a deep breath. If her mother were here, she would have told her it's just rubbish that needs to be thrown out. The sooner she got to work on it, the sooner she could be on her way. It was a small room. It wouldn't take long. She was so afraid that the door would shut and that she'd have no way out. Her heart raced, and she realized there was a solution to the oppressive little room.

She grabbed the door with both hands and ripped it straight from the hinges. Old wood splintered and jutted from where the hinges once were. She set the door inside the room and dusted off her hands. "There."

Picking up bones and bits of fur was gross, so she did that part first. She avoided touching the padded walls with their frequent blood stains. The chains were hooked to the ceiling. She simply pulled them down, hook and all. They fell from the wood with a solid tug of her inhuman strength.

The spikes, she found, could unscrew from the wall. Once she piled the spikes in the wheelbarrow with the chains, there was nothing left but the padded walls. The padding was mostly rotten. Some spots were so heavily saturated with blood that maggots had developed in the tears. Most of anything that once lived in the room had since dried up and moved on since they had first woken, but the evidence remained.

She pulled the fabric away from the wall and rolled it up tightly before stuffing it into the sacks. Beneath the padding, she found the wallpaper that existed in the rest of the house. Some spots were stained red from where the blood leaked all the way through, but otherwise, it looked just like any other room.

The way back down with the full wheelbarrow and sacks was trickier than going up with nothing. She dropped the sacks over the banister and walked the wheelbarrow backward down the steps. It was slow and awkward, but she didn't have another option.

If Daniel were here, he could have helped her carry it down, but he wasn't here. He was someone else now. She pushed that thought out of her mind. Still unwilling to forgive him. Her husband accused her of wanting to be with Eton, but the irony was that she didn't want to go to the store even when she needed to.

The separation between her and Daniel made her feel so isolated. Living in a giant empty house all alone with nothing but decay and silence. She hated these morbid thoughts and wanted a distraction, but there was no one. She wheeled the spikes and chains to the cliffs. It was a strenuous hike. One filled with a paranoia that she would be caught, but once she was there, she dumped all the room's remains into the ocean.

The bags floated for a while before the waves ultimately consumed them. There was little remaining of the cottage. The fire had done its job well. There was a stony outline of where the house once stood, but there was nothing but ash remaining inside. She wished there had been another way and that Daniel didn't have to burn it down. At the very least, he could have spoken to her about it first. She would never forget how crazed his eyes looked that night, watching the flames.

It was a humid afternoon by the time she returned to the house. She also noticed a man standing along the hillside. His large backpack suggested he was a hiker or nature lover. He stood at the no-trespassing sign and waved at her. Setting the wheelbarrow down, she went to say hello.

"Hello," she said at a safe distance.

"Hey, are you a local?"

She nodded. He was shorter than Daniel and Eton by several inches. He was balding but had a pleasant smile. "I'm Destiny."

"Kevin," he said, extending a hand. She complied with the custom.

"Are there any hiking trails you'd recommend?" he asked.

"I just came back from the cliffs over that way," she said, pointing.

His eyes followed the direction. "I was thinking of camping tonight so I don't have to rush back to the boat. Do you think that would be okay?"

"As long as you clean up after yourself, it's fine."

Kevin raised his ginger brows, surprised by her assured response. "You make the rules?"

"I do," she said, laughing. Who else would determine such things? Perhaps he was surprised that she was not a man. Christians had qualms with women; it was pervasive even through the centuries.

"Oh, well, in that case, thanks."

She didn't have refreshments yet. It would seem suspicious if he was in the house, knowing she lived there but had no food, and yet, she really did not want to be alone.

"I'm surprised you don't want to see the house."

Kevin pressed his lips together and pointed at the sign.

"I've been doing some cleaning there today. If you like, you can have a look around."

"Sure," Kevin said. "Might as well."

She showed him in through the back door, uncertain of what she had intended to do next. Kevin looked around, but he didn't seem all that impressed or interested. Was he indulging her to be polite, or did he hope this would lead to something else? Did she want this to lead to more?

"You can set your pack down here," she instructed.

She gave the best tour she could. "Now, we ask people to stay clear of the basement," she said, twisting her fingers together. "The steps are not good. I mean, safe."

Kevin smiled, and she felt flush all over. He wasn't attractive, but he stared at her so intently that she forgot how to use words. She took several steps backward and pushed through the double doors and into the entryway.

He followed her, only to pause and look around to say, "This is a big house."

Kevin followed her up the stairs. She skipped the drawing room, not wanting to expose just how living in the mansion was. Kevin didn't seem to have any interest in the drawing room. His eyes were on her as she walked up the steps. Hyperaware of every step she took, her words stumbled and stuttered into complete silence the closer they got to her room. Kevin steadily gained on her, and by the time they reached the third story, his hand was on the small of her back. Did she want this?

"Is there a bedroom we can see?"

She was aware of what she was doing. Where this was leading. It would irrevocably change her marriage or dissolve it entirely. Between the fights and the long walks, the lies, the basement, and the secrets he kept, she no longer felt married. She was alone all the time, and she couldn't bear another night of it.

Kevin didn't say a word as he shut the door behind him. She was jittery, and she couldn't believe what she was doing, but she started taking off her clothes. Kevin took off his before moving to the bed, where she joined him.

It was no accident that she brought him to her bedroom instead of her mother's bedroom where she was staying. She wanted Daniel to burst into the room and stop her, but he never did. He was off somewhere, doing something else and not telling her about it.

Kevin attempted to kiss her on the lips, but she would turn her head away each time. Getting the hint, he finally just got to the point. The sex was empty and disappointing. Kevin grunted and sweated all over her, and it was all she could do to lie there until he finished.

Afterward, she felt lonelier than ever. She rolled over and stared out the window, hoping Kevin would get the hint and leave on his own. It wasn't like being with Daniel at all. She didn't expect it to be, but she thought there would be some comfort in the act.

Kevin stroked her bare shoulder before kissing it. She closed her eyes and imagined it was Daniel, but her heart ached when she realized their link may have been forever severed.

"You want me to stick around?"

"I like to sleep alone," she told him.

The body beside her slid away. There was a rustle of fabric and zips before the door clicked shut. With Kevin gone, she could release the tears she had been holding back since Daniel had left the house.

***

"How do you think they're doing?" Kerry asked.

Eton could only shrug. How would he know? She wasn't here to tell them. Maybe she was happy, or maybe locked in one of the dozens of rooms in that house with meals slipped under the door. Eton was letting his imagination get the better of him.

There hadn't been a peep from the couple since the day they went to Iceland, where they had gotten some less-than-stellar news.

But with business picking up, he didn't have time to check. The counter had to be manned from open to close now. Eton had even set up a small table and chair for people who were staying to use the Wi-Fi or phone chargers.

The new generator was twice the size of the last and infinitely quieter. It was far more economical with fuel as well. Between deliveries for him and the tourists, Bart was around most of the time. Which was great. He loved the old man.

"Those girls were in the house," Eton said. Glancing at the trio of girls trying on hats. "Daniel welcomed them himself. Maybe he's chilled out a little."

Kerry eyed their guests sitting at the coffee table and said, "They said he was nice."

"He is nice." Eton wasn't certain why he was defending him. "He's just super protective of Destiny. If she's happy, he doesn't really care what happens."

"Then why get hostile with surveyors?"

"I don't think he knew what they were." Eton's voice lowered to a whisper, "I think he's got a bigger secret he's trying to protect."

Eton had seen him outside while he was chopping wood the other day. It was so early that it was still dark out. He had just gotten started when Daniel emerged from the woods. It was dark enough that Eton wasn't certain who it was, but who else would walk around in a forest at night with no gear?

Daniel hadn't seen Eton yet, so he ducked behind the chicken coop and watched him. He wasn't drunk or tired. Daniel was his usual pensive self. He was just having a casual brooding session in the dark forest.

It was hard to tell if he was more stressed than usual because he always appeared annoyed. It wasn't until Daniel kicked a tree that Eton got confirmation that his neighbor was angry. The tree abruptly uprooted from its position and was still like that now.

"What does that even mean?" Kerry asked.

"I don't know," Eton confessed. "But I think there's more to their story."

"Yeah," Kerry laughed. "But what?"

Eton leaned on his elbows on the counter, "I don't think even they know for sure."

The people at the table looked up from their phones as the door opened, and the old fisherman stepped in, flexing his suspenders. "Hello, Hello," Bart greeted.

"Hey man, what news from Iceland?"

Bart shook his head. "Ridiculousness," the old man huffed. "Evidently, the other two countries are now taking an interest in the island and want to contend with Iceland's bid."

"Why?" Kerry asked.

"Well, Scotland is claiming that it was once one of their islands and is aiming to recover it. Norway wants to be involved, just to be involved, perhaps."

Fucking Norwegians.

"But what about Destiny and Daniel?" Eton asked. Did their claim mean anything?

"Don't know," Bart said. "The UN meeting isn't until next month. Perhaps the couple should attend."

Back at Höfn, Destiny and Daniel both were massively overwhelmed by the few-hour visit. The population was around two thousand people, and they could barely handle it.

He shook his head, "I think that would be too stressful for them, but I'll tell them all the same."

"Maybe we should help them find a lawyer."

Eton nodded, thinking of the lump of gold still in his suitcase. It should be enough to get the job done. "Do you know a guy?"

Bart nodded. "Aye. Not in Höfn, but I know a guy."

"Okay," Eton said, "Here's what we'll do. You contact the lawyer; I'll talk to Destiny. Kerry—"

"Man the bridge," she said, crossing her arms. "I know."

He felt bad that he was leaving his sister to watch his store, but this was important. He regarded the two guys on their phones at the table, totally oblivious to his comings or goings. He turned around and mouthed the word "baseball bat" to his sister before heading out.

"You want me to go with you?" Bart asked.

It would probably be better, but he didn't want to invite Bart to the mansion without permission. Daniel got kind of sketchy over visitors. But before he could answer, they could see three ships coming to port, and they looked full.

"Shit," Eton said.

Bart took off his cap and wiped his brow. "Fucking Norwegians."

"Can you stay with Kerry?" he asked. The last thing he needed was for the shop to get flooded with people while his poor sister was working alone. "I'll be back as soon as I can."

"On it."

He ran toward the house, kicking up yellow dust along the trail. He was halfway up the hill before it forced him to stop by the burning in his lungs. He walked the rest of the way. He hadn't thought he could make it running as far as he did. It must be all that wood he was chopping.

He was still a little out of breath when he pounded on the door. Waiting several minutes, he knocked again before peeking through the windows. "Hello?"

"What are you doing here?"

He spun around to find Daniel standing behind him. "Jesus, dude," Eton cried. "You scared the shit out of me."

"I thought I told you not to come here."

"Well, you also told me to come and tell you of any updates on the status of the island. So, what do you want, man?"

Daniel stepped onto the porch and a few inches from his face. The utter contempt in the guy's eyes had him tense all over. "Tell me," Daniel growled.

He told him what Bart had said, and he also gave him a heads-up about the Norwegians bringing people to the island. Daniel shook his head. "I don't want boatloads of people coming here, but I suppose I have no say in the matter."

"I don't know," Eton said. "We can try to say they don't have permission to dock and hope they listen. It's worth a try."

Daniel stewed about the situation for a few minutes before shaking his head. "No, I don't want to use false authority. I can't control the situation. I'd rather she learn the hard way."

Eton heard the last sentence, but he wasn't certain he heard it correctly. "Learn the hard way?"

Daniel's green eyes flared, and he took a step back with his hands up. He did not want to anger the guy with inhuman strength. If Daniel could uproot a tree with a single kick and pick him up one-handed, he could turn Eton into compost.

"Don't tell me she hasn't come running to tell you her every woe."

"Oh, that's awkward," Eton said. "We haven't seen or heard from Destiny since you guys went to Iceland. I just wanted to see if you guys wanted to hire Bart's lawyer to represent you in the UN meeting."

Daniel's mouth dropped a little, and he bowed his head and sighed. "I've been a complete ass."

Eton felt bad for the guy. "I like Destiny. You're not crazy. I like her a lot," he said. "But I've already learned this lesson. I won't have anything to do with her unless she is over you. Like really over."

"I appreciate your honesty," Daniel muttered, sliding his fingers through his long brown hair.

"I get it," Eton said. "I can totally see how losing the only home you've ever known would be a stressor."

"I don't know what's worse. The island situation, or the wife."

"Hey," Eton said, "If you ever want to come and talk about it, you know where I'm at."

"Thank you, and sorry again for—"

"No problem," Eton said. "But I got to get back to the situation with the Norwegians. You should probably stick around the house just in case things get out of hand."

Please don't kill anyone.

Daniel waved him off, and he sped down the hill. He had finally made a breakthrough. It mostly explained the tree incident. He and Destiny still had issues, and he must have been trying to avoid the house. Still, it didn't explain how his neighbor could take out a tree with a single kick.

When he got back to the store, Kerry and Bart had their hands full. Some dude was trying to argue with his sister over a bottle of bottom-shelf vodka and was holding up the line. He pushed past the line and cut to the front counter. Bart's face was bright red, clearly frustrated with the guy.

"Hey, what's the problem?" he asked.

"This is way overpriced," the guy said. His waxed mustache didn't move despite how hard his lips flapped.

"If you don't like the price," he said, "Don't buy it. Next!"

He motioned to the next person in line and helped them while the guy fumed at him. He slammed down his money and left with the bottle. Kerry tried to give him his change, but he was already gone. Her lip quivered. She was new to the world of customer service. He gave her a nod. "It's all right."

With the guy gone, he and Kerry could work through the rest of the line that was damn near the door when he first walked in. It seemed like a good time to issue a friendly reminder about the rules of the island.

"Please remember to throw your trash in the garbage," he said. "Also, there are places on the island where people are still living. Please be respectful."

The woman in front of him rolled her eyes as she took her fried pork skins and sauntered out. The couple behind her looked no more impressed. "No one owns the island. You realize that, don't you?"

Eton didn't like where this was going. "Just because it's not a part of any country doesn't mean human decency doesn't apply."

"Well, yeah, but—"

"Last month, someone burned down one of the cottages. So yeah, there is no official law, but we keep track of everyone who comes here. Next."

Most of them just wanted snacks and carbonated water. Eton also noticed that the guys who had been in the seats when he left were still there. "Have they bought anything since I left?" he asked.

Kerry shrugged, and they had roped poor Bart into carrying things back to the boat. He shook his head, turned around to the extension outlet, and unplugged the cable box. A few minutes later, the crowd had disbursed, and Kerry let out a groan. Busy was good for his business, but Eton was worried about crowd control. The larger the group, the less interested they were in following rules or being respectful. Then there was that baldheaded hiker with the mustache.

The door slammed open, and he was ready to yell that they were closed, but it was just Bart. "Fucking Norwegians."

Chapter Seventeen

FALLOUT

The morning light paced across the room from the wall, making its way down to the dry floorboards. Destiny remained motionless. She'd rather indulge in self-loathing for the rest of her life than spend another second in productivity.

"How are you holding up?" Daniel said as he sat beside her on the bed.

Destiny didn't want to see him. Well, she did, but she didn't want to tell him what had happened. She couldn't even form the words. She wasn't even certain what her motivations were to begin with. What did she possibly think she would gain by such an action? She wanted to make him hurt, but it only came back threefold.

"I thought I wanted us to be done," she said. "So I did something I can't take back to make you leave."

She couldn't see his face, but she didn't need to look to know how broken he would be. His hand went stiff on her hip, and it took several minutes before he spoke. "It wasn't with Eton, though, was it?"

Sobs strangled her. Why was he so stupid? This had nothing to do with Eton! She couldn't reply without sounding hysterical, so she shook her head. It was a mistake, but it wasn't something she could take back. Even if they could move past it, they would still face the same problems, but with an addition of betrayal.

"A visitor?" Daniel's voice held a bitter edge.

"He was a short, ugly, bald man with a strange mustache."

"Here?" he growled.

Her sobs broke free, and she buried her face in her pillow.

"Here?" he shouted as he forced her to roll over. One hand was on her inner thigh and the other between her legs. She didn't want him to touch her. His fingers violated her and worked her labia to further shame her. She didn't fight as he felt her, weakened by her guilt. He felt the residue and flicked his hand with a curse.

"I'm sorry," she said before shoving her face back into her pillow.

Daniel stormed out of the room. He was leaving her alone again, only this time, she deserved it. She cried for a while. When her tears ran dry, she was motivated to get up, solely because she resented the bed where both crimes took place.

Trusting Daniel was long gone from the house. She sat in the drawing room. She read through a few poems before settling on the works of Gwerful Mechain. She took solace in the poet's words.

Tiborea, the mother of Judas the traitor,
She was a loving wife, don't hate her,

Yes, she'd done something bad, and she regretted that decision, but she'd struck the blow for a reason, and he refused to see it. She had lost all will to clean the house. Her limbs were too heavy to lift a broom, and her heart ached with each step up the stairs.

Perhaps being in her mother's bedroom would ease the lowness she felt. As if she could somehow commune with her mother and tap into Helicant Sallows' strength, she would find her own. She sat at the vanity and toyed with her mother's belongings.

What would her mother think of all this? A part of her worried that her mother would find her as disgusting as her husband did. It nagged in the back of her mind, and she heard her mother's cutting words and scratchy voice, but they said nothing of importance. Her mother was gone. Helicant may still have been alive out there somewhere—a version of her anyway—but her mother was not here.

She was born and destined to break a curse. It was broken now, so what happened next? All conversations regarding the future had always ended with "When you get married."

Well, she got married. Now what?

There was no place in the house where she felt peace. It was her haven no longer. She braved the heat and walked down to the cottage by the shore. As she walked, she couldn't help but notice there were a lot more people around. They stood in pairs or small groups by fires. They all wore enormous hats and sunglasses as they basked in the sun, taking turns applying lotion on one another. Tiny bits of garbage littered the once immaculate countryside.

The closer she got to the cottage, the more populated the place became. People were hovering around the cottage the most, though no one noticed one another. They were all staring at their phones. It reminded her of staying with her great aunt and uncle as a child. They always read together. At the dinner table, with or without company present. It was like they wanted to escape the world altogether. Mother said reading so much would ruin them, but she said nothing about Destiny's reading habits.

Her great aunt and uncle had nowhere to go and nothing to do. It only made sense that they constantly read, but why come to an island just to do the same thing you would anywhere else?

Bart was at the dock, clearly annoyed with the trio of boats just on the other side. A few men of various ages, each with pale blond hair, manned the new boats. They all looked so similar they had to be related. They stood around with mocking smiles. It seemed they were intentionally antagonizing Bart.

He saw her and waved. "Hullo!"

Destiny forced a smile and greeted him. "Hello."

"Can you believe this shit?" he asked.

She frowned from the daylight but also the new company. "What happened?"

"The fucking Norwegians learned this island had no jurisdiction, so they brought all their tourists over."

"No jurisdiction?"

"Yeah," Bart explained. "They spoke with the Coast Guard. Since this island has no country, we have no say on who can visit it. Not even the people native to the island."

Destiny bit her tongue. This was her island.

The old fisherman walked her to the cottage. "But don't worry, I spoke to a lawyer. His office is going to contact Kerry and schedule an appointment."

A person fluent in law would be most helpful. Still, she was uncertain, and the grinning jackals at the dock soured her already bitter mood.

"What if something happens in the meantime?" she asked.

"I honestly don't know, miss. I'm too old to keep the peace, but if anything gets out of hand, I'll show them what Icelanders are made of!"

She giggled at his good-natured demeanor. "How is your wife?"

They pushed past the throngs of visitors to get through the front door of the cottage. They weren't as busy as she would have expected. There were people sitting in a new lounge area, and the shelves were thin, but it was otherwise vacant.

"She is happy with the added income," Bart said. "We sent some of the money to our children. One of them has a baby on the way."

"Your first grandchild?" she asked. Eton was at the counter. His eyes met hers.

"My fourth!" he said. "I only had two children, but my daughter is productive. She had three, and my son is having his first."

"Destiny!" Eton shouted as he came around the counter. "Long time, no see."

He moved to embrace her, but she took a step back, and he lowered his arms. His face fell, and Eton saw that something was wrong.

"I was a grocer in my time," Bart said. "I'll take over."

Eton gave a thanks before he led her out the door and away from the crowd. "What's going on?"

Her face broke into a miserable pout.

"You can tell me," he assured her.

"You're going to think me a terrible person."

"Never," he said. "Not unless you kicked a puppy or something. Did you kick a puppy?"

She couldn't think of anything more horrible. "No!" she cried. "Why would I ever do such a thing?"

Eton laughed. "I'm kidding, it's a... Never mind. Homeschooled."

It took her a moment to register that he was joking. Too upset to catch the jest, but in hindsight, it was quite funny. She gave a brief grin.

Eton snickered and said, "See, well, guess you're not that bad then."

She supposed he'd feel different when she told him the truth. "I took another man to bed," she said.

He said nothing for a few minutes as they walked along a small cobblestone fence. "Recently, I'm guessing?"

She nodded and said, "A day or two ago." She hoped it didn't seem weird to him; she couldn't pinpoint the exact date. Time had a funny way of slipping away when you didn't sleep or eat.

Eton had his hands in his pockets. Waiting for him to say something was nearly as painful as it was when she told Daniel, only her husband didn't give such a long pause. He chewed at his bottom lip as he looked up at the clouded sky.

"I've been there," he said.

"You've cheated on a spouse?"

"Well, not quite. I was sleeping with a married woman for several months."

"I see." Daniel was an able judge of character. He'd said as much about Eton when she dismissed it as jealousy.

"It ended badly," Eton said.

It made her feel better to know that she wasn't the only adulterer. "Why did you do it?" she asked.

"It's complicated," he said, scratching the back of his neck. "At first, I thought it was because she and I had a connection. As time went on, I knew she wasn't going to leave her husband, but I stayed anyway."

Eton turned away and stared off at the ocean. She wanted him to tell her the rest. She got between him and the ocean. Not that he couldn't simply look over the top of her head if he wanted to. "Why did you stay?" she asked.

He looked down at her and smiled. "Because I had nothing else to do. I dropped out of college—school. I was working with my dad. Going nowhere. Everyone I knew was in school or getting married. I was lost, and I wanted to feel like I wasn't lost on my own."

They were kindred spirits, she and Eton. They sought happiness in others without knowing themselves. Finding the room vanquished the phobia. Why would Daniel eradicate her loneliness?

The isolation in Eton's voice was tangible. It resonated with her own feelings that Daniel couldn't ever understand. He could be on his own. He loved it. Growing up with two parents and two other siblings in a small cottage, she didn't blame him, but it created a canyon of expectations in their marriage.

"I was often alone as a child," she said. "My mother was old, and I was...sick. I thought if I were married, that feeling would be banished forever."

"No," Eton said. "You can stand in a room full of people and feel like that." He waved his hand up and down between them. "It's like a pane of glass that separates you from everything. Being with people doesn't solve it. Be with yourself. That doesn't really make sense, I guess."

She disagreed. "No, it makes sense."

"I'm just glad it wasn't me," Eton said with a laugh. "I think I finally got Daniel to understand that I won't steal his wife."

"I can't be stolen from someone who never wholly had me to begin with."

"You just got married," Eton said. "That shit takes time."

Her breath seized in her chest. Was it too late? She feared the damage was done. "I suppose now we'll never know." Her voice trembled.

"We make mistakes," Eton said wistfully. "We're human."

But I'm not.

They made their way back to the cottage to find the crowd had dispersed. She squinted and noted two figures in matching outfits, and Eton muttered under his breath. Officials were here. They wore black vests and utility belts that held things she had never seen before.

"Hey," Eton greeted them. "How can we help you?"

"We're looking for a man named Kevin Greene," one officer said. His English held a heavy accent. Her heart stopped. Was it the same Kevin she had slept with?

"I don't know the name. What does he look like?" Eton asked.

"About one-seventy centimeters, seventy-four kilos, bald, with one of those curly mustaches."

She steeled her legs as they threatened to buckle. The man they were describing was indeed the Kevin she had slept with. She turned to Eton, who was frowning.

"A guy by that description caused a bit of a disruption a few nights ago. I can't confirm it was the same guy. Our guy paid cash."

"What kind of currency do you take out where?" the second officer asked.

"We take Kronas and pounds as long as they are smaller bills. Otherwise, it's card only."

"Did the man pay with pounds?" the second officer asked.

"He did," Eton said. "He threw a fit because he didn't like the price of vodka, slammed down some notes, and left before we could give him his change."

Both officers nodded slowly. "But you haven't seen him since?"

"No."

The first officer handed Eton a card and said, "If you see him again, call us. We have some questions for him."

"Is he dangerous?" Destiny asked. She knew nothing about him when she took him to bed. The pit of regret in her gut only widened. The consequences of her transgression only got worse.

Both officers' faces were stony and unreadable. "If you see him, don't engage. Just call us."

"If he is still here, chances are he will need to come back to the store for something or another."

"He's still here as far as we know," the second officer answered. "Unless the boatmen are lying."

Murder.

A howling chill took hold of her, and she struggled to maintain her composure as the worst-case scenario came to her mind. What if Daniel had found the man? What if her husband had killed him? Daniel was right about this age. People did not simply go unnoticed. The technology was too superior, and the people too entwined with it. Just as she and Daniel could not move freely without proper documentation, people could not vanish without questions being asked.

Eton eyed the dock and said, "Bart is a good guy. He wouldn't lie, especially if he thought people were in danger. I can't say the same for the other ships."

"Noted," the first officer said.

"We have a few more questions for them," the second officer added. "We'll be on our way."

Destiny could barely contain her trembling lower lip. "I should go," she told Eton.

She tripped on the uneven ground as she made her way to the trail. Before she could get too far, Eton took her hand, forcing her to turn around and face him.

"Destiny," he said. "I don't know what the two of you are hiding, but whatever it is, you can tell me. No matter how weird it is."

Just how much did Eton know? She turned around and marched back to the mansion without looking back. She liked Eton, but it was rude of him to make such implications. Their secrets were their own, and he had no right to question them.

What was it that tipped him off? She had gone to such lengths to maintain a human appearance. She had given nothing to Eton that would alert him to a *weird* secret, and her husband was far too intelligent for such oversights. Was it possible that he'd crossed paths with another member of the Sallows family?

CHAPTER EIGHTEEN

WHERE THE GREEN GRASS GREW

I t did not surprise her that the mansion was empty. Daniel was still stewing about her confession. She did not blame him for being angry and hurt, but there were more important matters at hand to discuss. Mainly, she wanted to know if he had something to do with Kevin Greene's disappearance. She also needed to talk to him about the suspicious store clerk.

She couldn't wait for Daniel to come to her. These were urgent matters that could not wait. She left the house while there was still daylight and went to the cliffs to see if her husband was there. She saw an unfamiliar motorboat cruise away from the island, but there was no sign of Daniel. He wouldn't have come here. From here, she could see moving stars, fast boats, and planes overhead. It would have been too upsetting for him.

Much of the island was forest. It was full of animals and wild berries that had sustained her family since Nathaniel Sallows first arrived on its shores. It was a dense and wild mass that had taken more ground since she was last awake. No one was here to hunt or deforest it anymore. It was free to set across the earth and absorb the green landscapes and stone fences that stood in its way.

The evening's twilight was emerging when Destiny stood at the edge of the forest. She had never gone inside before. Nerves frayed as she shook her head. It was stupid to be afraid. She couldn't die from cold or starvation. She was stronger than any animal living in that forest. What could be in this place that she would need to be afraid of?

The only thing that came to mind was her husband. She was afraid of what he had done and how far he was going to go. The admonition made her take a step back and put a hand on her unsettled stomach. She was afraid of Daniel. Not just what he would say but what he would do. What would he do to Eton if he thought Eton knew of their secret? The same thing he did to Kevin?

She didn't know for certain that Daniel had killed anyone, but the timing was not likely a coincidence. The new world made her husband erratic and highly agitated. Combined with her betrayal, Destiny wondered if she'd pushed him beyond sanity.

Taking a deep breath, Destiny went further. Her little flashlight and the moon served as the only lighting she had in the forest. Wading through dead bramble, she tripped on lifted tree roots while she called out to her husband. She could feel the forest watching her in silence.

There was a sudden, inexplicable feeling of panic and pain—something she hadn't felt since she had woken. It brought her to her knees. It was cold. She was freezing all over, and her jaw tremored so hard she thought her teeth would break. Forced to crawl away from the fallen tree, she crouched on hands and knees when the pain suddenly abated.

Gasping for air, she steadied herself and dried her eyes. She shined the flashlight on the area and saw nothing unusual. A fallen log beside a tree and a small patch of grass. Only, she hadn't seen a single patch of grass like this in the forest. It was green and lush, but only in an area large enough for a single person to sit.

It was familiar, this spot, but she was unsure of why. She stood up and walked towards it again and felt the sensation again. The unrelenting cold returned as she stood on the patch of grass. She had visions of herself lying propped up against the log, her lips blue with dark circles around her eyes. She was wearing the dress she wore when she first woke up. She couldn't explain it, but she felt as though—in another life perhaps—she had died in this spot where the green grass grew.

Stepping back out, humanity vanished within her. From her chest to her fingertips, the pain and fear trickled away. It was strange, but she didn't have time to dwell on this, though she would show Daniel one of these days. If he would still speak to her after what she had done.

Despite her feelings of hopelessness, she pressed on. The least she could do was allow Daniel to plead his case. If he had indeed killed that man, she didn't know what she would do. Leave the island, perhaps. Never see him again.

She came upon curious things all around. They were once traps of some sort. The ones that were not already sprung had been broken. Ropes and elaborate knots that once hung from tree limbs and little stakes in the ground. She almost stepped into what appeared to be a pit with sharpened sticks in the bottom. She would have walked right into it if it were not for the large branches stuffed into the opening.

Daniel had done this. He intentionally set off the traps and pits in case a person or animal happened upon them. He didn't do it for himself—he already knew where they were. She felt a pang of remorse for thinking him a murderous beast. How could she think Daniel capable of murder when he took such care?

There was nothing left for her in the forest. Even if he was in the forest, she would not find him. Careful to avoid the patch of green grass, she made her way out of the forest in what felt like less time than she used traversing in. She came out downhill of the mansion, but her aim was otherwise true.

Lighting a candelabra she had in the kitchen, she went upstairs. She nearly dropped it at the sight of Daniel sitting on her bed waiting for her.

CHAPTER NINETEEN

Monsters After All

"Daniel," she stammered.

He said nothing. Her poor, sweet Daniel appeared tired and broken, and it was all her fault. She moved to sit beside him, but her husband flinched. She hated this. How badly she'd hurt him. Destiny did not believe for one moment that she had done the right thing. She just didn't think it would hurt so much.

"Guess I deserve that," she said, sitting further away.

Destiny sat with him in the stillness. Discomfort raged in her chest, but she forced herself to endure it. It was the least she could do.

"I'm just getting some things," he said.

"Where are you going?"

"The old doctor's cottage," he said. She was always forgetting about that cottage. It was bigger than the other two and not too far from the mansion. It was also the only remaining unoccupied building on the island.

"I tried to find you," she said. "I went to the forest. The strangest thing—"

"I don't care," Daniel interrupted. But he cared. He cared very much but refused to let her in. She thought about what Eton had said, about how trust takes time. Maybe she wanted too much from Daniel too soon.

"Can we talk about it?"

"For your sake or mine?" he asked.

She shrugged. "For ours."

Daniel's throat bobbed, and he said, "I understand why you did it. I just wish you hadn't."

"I'm uncertain myself why I did it."

"I kept accusing you of wanting Eton," he said. "I can see now that you didn't want him. I pushed you without cause."

"And I wanted too much from you," she said, twisting her fingers in her lap. "I am so lonely, and I thought you were to blame. I see now that it's me. It's my fault I feel this way, and no one can fix it for me."

Daniel looked at her then. "You don't blame me for leaving you alone?"

"I should have given us more time," she said. "But I must admit, you frighten me."

His head bowed, and he said, "Sometimes I frighten myself."

"What happened to the man?" she asked.

"I didn't do it if that's what you're asking."

It was as if the room had run out of air. The man, Kevin Greene, was dead, and her husband knew how. What if the officials came back to look for him? When all their other leads went cold? People didn't disappear in this world. Their names floated in systems, and their images appeared on the internet.

"Officials are looking for him," she said. "Eton knows something is different about us. Why?"

Daniel gave a weak laugh. "I don't know."

"You don't know, or you don't care?" she said through gritted teeth.

Her husband only shook his head. Daniel was done with the conversation, and so was she. Getting off the bed, she picked up the candelabra and went to the door. Before leaving, she turned around and said something she could no longer contain.

"If you no longer care about protecting our secrets because I made a mistake, it means you never truly cared about our safety or well-being to begin with. It just means you wanted to control me with them."

The green in Daniel's eyes flickered even in the dim lighting. "I suppose that is true. Perhaps I am just a monster after all."

She fled the room, taking all the light with her. Up the stairs to her mother's room where she shut and locked the door. There would be no coming out until he was gone. She would wait for days if that's what it took. Daniel was not the person she once thought him to be. The man she married was teetering on madness and willing to take anyone along for the ride.

***

With the last of the customers out, Eton could finally lock the door and flip the sign over, but his day was far from done. He had made a bank deposit a few days ago but wasn't able to even look at the bills or do any bookkeeping until tonight.

Kerry vanished to her bedroom. Knowing full well that it took him all his concentration to do the bookkeeping, she didn't want to distract him. He imagined she wanted to talk to her girlfriend as well. They were hurtling through the winter, and spring quarter was just around the corner.

It was nearly two in the morning by the time he organized and reconciled all his expenses. By the time everything was said and done, not only was he in the positive, but he had gotten out of the red without Destiny's surplus funding, and that was after they paid everything up for the month. His eyes ached, and he rubbed his brow. Perhaps it would have been a greater victory had he not been so exhausted.

The shop needed to be reopened in a few hours. He thought about just drinking some coffee and pulling an all-nighter, but he knew better than to do that. Eton was in the best shape of his life, thanks to all the wood-chopping and heavy lifting. He was seeing muscles in places he only saw on the cover of magazines. When he went to bed at night, there was no fretting about the unknown, about what he read on the internet, or the exam he had already taken. Nowadays, when he hit the bed, he ceased to exist until awoken—not by the alarm, but by the light of dawn and the chickens.

This life was far from perfect. He would kill for a real, honest-to-god shower. Hot, clean water he didn't have to dredge from a well and carry three miles. He would need to thank Daniel for that tip about the well, but he wasn't certain it was worth the trip. He'd much rather carry ten-gallon bottles from Bart's ship.

As much as he enjoyed being away from the rest of the world, he was alone. Not the isolation he and Destiny had talked about. Not the kind that made a person do desperate things for affection while convincing themselves it was okay just to get by.

It was literal loneliness. The kind that made him and his sister try to socialize despite having nothing to talk about. He just wanted to talk. Open his mouth and speak even if no one was listening. He wanted someone to talk to him, even if it was about makeup or a girlfriend.

Kerry had it easier. Yeah, she was stuck in the shop, but it was only for the winter. She had a future ahead of her. He did, too. Just because he didn't get through college didn't mean he couldn't go back later or that this was the end all be all. This adventure would be a great conversation starter on a resume. It didn't have to be his entire life to prove a point. He was successful; that was enough.

How he felt now must have been how Destiny felt most of the time. He often chatted too long with customers. They gave him polite nods and frantic eye shifting that made him flush. Had he really become *that guy* who worked at every grocery store?

He slept in the next morning. The sun had been up, and Kerry was shouting his name from the other room. He stumbled out, still in his pajamas, rubbing his eyes, to find customers were filtering in.

"Could really use an outhouse break about now," Kerry said.

"Shit," he said, "Yeah, I'll stand here. You go."

It was ten in the morning. He normally woke up around six before the sun came up. He would need to thank his sister for covering his ass whenever she returned from the outhouse—yet another inconvenience of living the Amish life. He longed for a toilet. A real, flushing toilet. One he could sit on without creaking, awful smells, or the fear of splinters.

On her way back in, Kerry brought in another armful of wood. It was something they'd made a habit of doing ever since he figured out how to chop wood. It kept the fire burning and the store warm enough to only need space heaters in their rooms at night.

"Thanks for letting me sleep in," he said.

Kerry set the wood on the stack beside the oven. "I figured you needed it. You were up late. How did everything work out?" she asked.

"Hm?"

"The bookkeeping," Kerry reminded him.

He had just woken up. His mind was still hazy, and he was standing behind the counter in his pajamas. "I need some coffee and some pants."

After he dressed, he helped himself to a large cup. He drank about half before he finally spoke. "We're doing really well," he said. "Like, even without Destiny's money, we broke even."

"That's great!" Kerry said.

"It will probably fluctuate with the tourist seasons, but I am happy with where we're at."

"Have you considered telling our parents?"

"Hadn't occurred to me." It honestly hadn't. After the last conversation with their dad, he didn't imagine a whole lot could recover his image in their eyes. They had seen the video Brie's husband posted. It was probably the reason they allowed him to cash out his college fund and bail the way he did.

Kerry was leaning on the counter, her fingers drumming on the countertop. It seemed she was nervous about something.

"Something on your mind?" he asked.

His sister cringed and gave him a look. "I want to go to New York. I know they won't like that."

"Art school doesn't exactly scream lucrative career," he said. "I want you to follow your dreams, but if there's anything I learned from college, it is that your perspective changes as you become an adult."

Kerry chewed on her lip and said nothing.

"Don't get me wrong, I think what Holly is doing is super cool, but her family is loaded, and that woman is bound for NASA with her math skills."

"I don't want to go to school in New York," Kerry confessed. "I just want to live with Holly."

Kerry's admission floored him. He understood why she was so nervous about telling their parents. She didn't want to go to college with her girlfriend; she just wanted to live with her girlfriend.

The condition for cashing out his college fund was to take Kerry with him for the term. They had to have known he would stumble, and they probably expected him to fail. It was supposed to be a lesson for her on why college was so important to attend. They didn't like her being a lesbian, but at the very least, they appreciated Kerry's motivation to go to college to chase after Holly. But now, here she was, just wanting to play housewife.

"And...do what?" he asked.

Kerry shrugged. "Make soap."

His mouth fell open, and she laughed. "I can't wait to see how our parents are going to take it."

He was fumbling hard. She was asking him for support, and he was at a loss. What could he say without sounding like an asshole? Kerry wanted to make soap. In New York. At eighteen. It was quite a shock for him because he always assumed he was the family fuck up.

"Kerry," he started but didn't have the heart to finish.

"No, no," she said. "I want to hear your real opinion. I'm a big girl. I can take it."

"You want to make soap?"

"Yes," she said, laughing.

"Help me out here," he said. "Like your own business or..."

"Yeah, I want to run my natural line of bath products that are eco-friendly, sustainable, and fair trade. Holly said I can live with her rent-free. I'm going to work part-time and use the money I make to launch my line, and I'll either sell it online or in department stores."

"Okay." Eton had to give her that. "Now you're talking. You got to work on that pitch a little more."

Kerry laughed and brushed her hair behind her ear. "Are you going to tell mom and dad?"

"I can talk to them if you want me to."

Kerry cringed.

"Well, I'll keep it between you and me," he promised. "If you want me to talk to them, I will. Work on your business pitch and model when you can. I'll vouch for you when the time comes."

"There's something else," Kerry's awkward, cringy smile meant she had already done something and hadn't told him.

"What?"

"Holly is coming to stay a week."

He wasn't too perturbed by that. While he had never met her, he'd heard a lot about her. Kerry usually drove to New York on weekends to see her so that their parents didn't make things weird. They still argued about whether Kerry and Holly should be allowed to sleep in the same bedroom under their roof.

"Cool. When?" he asked.

"Today."

Oh.

CHAPTER TWENTY

INNS AND OUTS

I t had been three long days since Daniel left. She had weighed all her options, and each time, she found herself at a crossroads. Provided things legally went her way, she could stay and use all her resources to preserve the mansion, turn it into a business of some sort. She could charge for admittance and hire help to care for the home.

Then again, she could ask the lawyer to help her with citizenship papers. She could take anything worth value and leave the island forever and let the country decide what to do with it. Perhaps she could petition on Daniel's behalf so that he became the sole owner.

She fiddled with the ruby ring on her finger so hard that her finger developed a red line from where she had been continuously spinning it. It surprised her she didn't wear a groove in the floor, pacing as hard as she had been. Though she wore the tread down on her heels.

Daniel didn't have any interest in resolving things between them, and perhaps that was for the best. She wished she had decided before acting, but it had happened and was now over. Her mind wavered like a reed in a pond. One minute, she wanted Daniel to leave her, and the next, she was hoping there was something to salvage.

Something had gone wrong with Daniel. He might have had a part in that murder. Her husband was a wounded animal who was liable to lash out at anyone. She didn't want to tip him over the edge, but she did not know where that edge was. She did not want to spend the rest of her life walking on an ice-covered pond. Those waters would grow warm no matter what she did, and she was afraid of what he would do when the days grew too warm.

Opening the chest in her mother's room, she found the treasures her family had brought with them when they first settled. As strong as she was, there was no way she could lift this. She didn't know if Daniel knew just how much they had or if he even cared. Still, she felt insecure and wanted to hide it, just in case he got vindictive.

She felt splitting it was the proper thing to do. Even if he hated the new world, he would need money. She would need to talk to him about his preferences. She found herself torn between staying and going because, in either case, she would face the same dilemma. At some point, it would occur to those around her that she was not human.

There would be no other husband. None that could remain close enough to her without discovering her secret. Eton lived miles away and already knew something was amiss. She couldn't be with anyone for long before they discovered her secret. Daniel was the only one who would understand.

The new world held intrigues and fancies for her to explore, but her island housed the only person she could be entirely safe with. Even if their marriage was over, he would still understand her more than any other person could. She counted out the treasure. They each would get an equal amount. She put her stash into several sacks, and she walked down to the cottage with her funds.

Bart wasn't at the docks when the dirt sifted from her shoes, giving way to the sandy shore. She worried that her timing was poor and that she would need to come back another day. It was something she did not wish to delay. Eton and Bart had contacted a lawyer. She would need funds to be available in the common day fashion in order to pay him.

She opened the cottage door to find Eton and Kerry at the counter with a small line of customers. He glanced up from his tablet and smiled at her. For a moment, her problems were gone. Eton would make certain that she had all she required to separate from Daniel.

Once the customers were out of the way, Eton ran over to her. Kerry made herself scarce. She was grateful for how sensitive his sister was in these matters.

"Hey," he greeted her. "What's all this?"

"Gold and gems," she said. "I was hoping Bart would be here today. I'd like to go to a bank on the mainland and set up an account."

There was an element of sadness in his eyes. Sympathy perhaps. "You're really going through this."

She couldn't look at him all of a sudden. What a mess she was. Daniel would've been loyal to her no matter how miserable he was, but she didn't want to force him to live that way. She loved him too much for that.

"We are separating," she said. "He is living in the cottage by the forest. Once I get my funds squared away, I will give half to him."

"What about the island?"

She nodded. "I suppose we figure that out when the UN makes their decision."

"That reminds me," Eton said. "Bart said his lawyer friend doesn't deal with this kind of thing but referred me to someone else. They should call me pretty soon."

"Is Bart coming today?"

"Yeah," Eton said, tucking his hands into his back pockets. "He comes every day now. If you just want to stick around, he should be back. You want to stick all that into a bank?"

She did indeed. There, someone could assess the value and give her one of those cards that carried all her money. It was all so frightening. She wanted to run back to Daniel and promise to never leave the island again, but that just wasn't the right thing to do for either of them.

Eton extended his hand to take the sacks from her. Without a second thought, she handed them over, only to realize her error. Eton's arms dropped to the floor from the weight of the sacks. His eyes were wide and mouth agape.

"Jesus," he whispered. "I'll just drag these into my room for now."

She moved to help, but he motioned for her to stay.

"No," he said. "You carried this for miles; I got it."

She watched Eton pull the sacks away. They scraped against the floor, leaving heavy lines, and she winced. "I... Your floor."

"Oh, that's just stick-on vinyl, no worries. What the hell do you do?"

"Life is hard here. We have to be strong."

"Well," Eton said, rubbing his belly. "The wood chopping has been giving results."

No wonder Eton suspected something was different about her and Daniel. Their facades were slipping. It was just another reminder that she could never be with Eton or anyone else. The new world wasn't hers. She would need to abide by their rules to go unnoticed in the crowd.

Eton reemerged from his bedroom. "What about Daniel?"

Guilt and loss weighed on her like stones in her pockets. Would there ever be a thought in her mind that did not lead to Daniel? "I don't know," she said. "We haven't been on speaking terms."

"He took it pretty hard."

She nodded and wiped the moisture from the corners of her eyes. "I'm afraid that I've made a mess of things."

"Do you still want to be with him?"

Before she could answer, the door behind her creaked open. A familiar old man stood in the doorway. He was wearing new suspenders, and his hair no longer stuck out from under his cap. Bart got a haircut.

"Hullo, kids," he greeted them.

"Just the man we wanted to see," Eton said. "Destiny here wants to open a bank account."

"Oh," Bart said. "Can you do that without an IIN?"

Eton's face fell.

"What does that mean?" she asked.

"It's an Icelandic Identification Number," Eton explained.

Bart nodded. "You need one to have a bank account."

"Oh, well, I suppose I won't be requiring your services today after all," she said. Disappointment weighted her limbs, but she was also somewhat relieved. Daniel had one more day to come and forgive her, but that wasn't right, either. She supposed this was the gods' way of punishing her for her infidelity.

"Maybe that's something the lawyer can help with as well," Eton said. "You'll probably become a citizen of whatever country this becomes."

She nodded and put on a brave smile. She didn't feel optimistic, but what else could she do?

"Just as well," Bart said. "Today is not the day to be traveling to the mainland. The seas were choppy, and the Coast Guard issued warnings of turbulent weather. I think we're docked for the night."

She didn't understand. "But it's nice out."

"Yeah, but the sea has its own weather. I warned the missus; she knows I'm docked."

A few hours later, Eton, Bart, and she stood on the dock and watched the horizon. Bart pointed at the dark clouds ahead. "See those? They came down from the north. They will probably miss this island entirely on their way south."

They were indeed ominous-looking clouds, but that wasn't what caught her eye. Along the east, three tiny specks were moving towards them. "There are boats out there," she said.

"What? Where?" Eton asked, straining to see.

"There's no one stupid enough to be out there right now," Bart laughed.

They couldn't see as well as she could. They were only human. She waited and watched as the boats came closer before saying, "I'm sure."

"I don't doubt you," Eton said. "We just can't see what you can."

She shot him a look, and Eton stared back. The implications were lost on Bart, who was intent on finding what she was talking about, but Eton knew something was different about her.

"I see them now," Bart said. "Three boats coming in. Oh, no..."

"What?" Eton asked.

Bart muttered a curse in Icelandic, and Eton squinted harder to see just what had the old fisher so upset.

"It's the fucking Norwegians!" Eton said.

"The mother fucking Norwegians."

CHAPTER TWENTY-ONE

THE STORM

The hostility was seething in the salty air. She stood with arms crossed and her jaw squarely set. Bart and Eton stood a few paces in front of her as if they were shielding her from the onslaught. Eton was digging the pad of his shoe into the sand while Bart made disapproving noises.

The boats floated to the dock, and ropes were thrown and tied off. They'd filled each of the three schooners with people. All the guests had to stand, there were so many people. The boatmen got off first and made ginger appeals to the three standing at the base of the dock. They were tall and blond, with ruddy faces.

"The storm forced us to dock," an older man said with a gentle accent.

"Awfully large groups for a day like today," Bart said.

Destiny could only grit her teeth. There was no reason to say they couldn't be here, and she had even less right to ask them to leave, considering the circumstances. She didn't want any of those young, beautiful people to get lost at sea.

"They need to leave the occupants alone," Eton said. "I think that is understandable, right?"

"They don't get to say who stays," the youngest of the men shouted while staring pointedly at her. The blond man waved him off, and she bit her tongue. Making a fuss would only make this worse. Don't give them what they want.

"Of course, we wouldn't want to irritate the hosts of an island without law," the older of the three said.

"No consequences, you mean," she said despite herself. "Just because you don't follow our laws doesn't mean they don't exist."

The watchful eyes of the people on the boats made her blush, but she wouldn't back down. "Well, it's not like we're going to jail," the man insisted.

"No," she glowered. "But that does not mean that there are no consequences."

The man tilted his head as if he found her threat appealing. She wished he'd try. He would be in for a nasty surprise if he tried to hurt her.

"What she means is that there are laws," Eton smoothed. "Until the UN makes an official ruling, this island is under the Coast Guard's jurisdiction."

Eton said it loud enough for all the passengers to hear. "If you cause any problems, we will not hesitate to call them."

"Fine," the older man said as he waved. "We will camp out around here tonight. There will be no trouble. We will have them all back out at sea in the morning."

The man who spoke to her still had his eyes all over her. He was trying to intimidate her. They expected her to be proper and modest like the Amish, but the woman who raised her was anything but. Destiny liked to think she was like her mother, and in times like this, she thought as her mother would. What would Helicant do? On impulse, she gave a slight smile and winked at the man. He blinked in surprise.

"You want to sleep in the cottage tonight, Bart?" Eton asked.

"Nope," Bart said. "I got a cozy little bed waiting for me in the boat."

"How about you, Destiny?"

"I don't know," she said. "I'll stay here at least until the store closes if that's alright."

"Totally fine," he said. "We will need all the help we can get."

She spent much of the day helping Kerry and Eton run the store. Restocking the dwindling shelves while the pair checked out the customers. There were many other things they needed help with. The wood beside the fireplace was dwindling, but the wood stacked along the outside of the house fared little better.

Between the surge in sales and helping her, Eton had nearly forgotten his own needs. She navigated the clusters of young adults around the cottage and took the ax out of the chopping block. She had put a wood round on the block and raised her ax to chop when a young man came to stop her. He had closely cut dark hair and was strangely and most uniformly tanned.

"Oh," he said. "Little lady with an axe."

She frowned at his patronizing. There wasn't any time for boasting. People could freeze tonight.

"You should hold that axe like this," he said as he came up behind her.

His insistence and familiarity with her was enraging. The gall he had to assume she couldn't chop wood before she even swung the axe! His minute adjustments of her handling only proved he had never held an axe in his life and was merely hoping to bother her.

"I think I'm capable enough, thank you," she said as she shrugged him off.

"Okay, okay," he said.

She only rolled her eyes before slashing the axe into the wood round. The edge of the ax bit into the cutting block, and the wood round was now split into thirds. The man was rendered speechless.

"As you can see, I can get on well enough. If I needed help from a man without calloused hands, I'd alert you."

A group of men laughed at her new friend, and he walked away with a sulking expression. She smiled a bitter smile and cut the wood into more manageable chunks. She didn't stop until the woodshed was full, and the amassing crowd of people became a distraction.

She wasn't tired, nor was she sweaty or overheated. Destiny stopped because she wanted to, not because her body begged her to quit. She feared the crowd made similar observations. Back in the store, she found Eton and Kerry were not so fortunate. Both were fatigued. Their shoulders slumped as they drooped over the counter.

She stood between them at the counter and whispered in Kerry's ear, "Would you like me to take over?"

Kerry looked at her brother for permission. Eton gave a nod. "Yeah, I'll ring stuff up and you can bag it," he told her.

"Okay, everyone, down to one line," he called. "Stay where you are, and we will point at you when we're ready."

There was a deaf murmur, but the customers remained compliant all the same. Kerry dodged out the door and presumably to the out-house. It quite suited Destiny. Maybe the new world wouldn't be so bad.

"It's amazing how nearly sixty people can maintain a line like this," she said. Though it was the same people in line when she had arrived this morning.

"That's because they want to use the Wi-Fi," Eton explained as he briskly ran a shiny card through the square attached to his tablet. "I allow them to stay for a half hour per purchased item. So, they stay until their time expires and then buy another carbonated water."

The girl he was ringing out looked up at them from her phone, annoyed that her behavior was being called out but opted to say nothing about it.

"That one is going to give me a bad review," Eton said.

Destiny could only shake her head. While there was social networking and vast information on the internet, another form of exchange was for people to tell other customers about a store or other such business.

"It can be really useful for small businesses to grow, but since people are more likely to complain than leave a positive review, the results are often skewed and can hinder a business."

"And since that woman heard you explain to me about the Wi-Fi, she will leave a bad review?" It made sense to her. She wouldn't like it if the shop keeper spoke unkindly of her either.

"She probably does it to everyone. Trolls are going to troll."

"What a horrible thing to say!" she laughed. "She was perfectly adequate in appearance."

"No, I'm not saying she's ugly. I mean, I think she is the type of person who goes on the internet and comments solely to make others miserable."

Once again, while technology changed, people never really did. "I had a great aunt who was incapable of saying anything kind."

"Oh yeah?"

"Come to think of it, she looked like a troll," she said. "She had this mean old cane with a handle carved into a fox. She used to hit us with it if we came too close. One night, my cousins and I thought her to be asleep, and we approached her. We meant no harm. We were daring one another to get closer. The first person to run away was a frightened field mouse."

"Who won?" Eton asked.

"The fox that got a cane right alongside the backside."

"It was you, wasn't it?"

Destiny gave him a wicked smile. "My mother used the cane to beat the old woman out of our house and let her hobble home."

Eton's brows raised. "Don't piss off your mom. Noted."

No indeed. "She is quite a woman."

"Is she still around?"

"I don't know." If her mother was around, she would have revealed herself by now. Daniel said Helicant was long gone. He might have been right, but what about the others? The Worm and whatever mangled the doe corpse?

Kerry charged back into the room. "All right, your turn."

"Yes!" Eton dashed out the door so quickly he tripped on the way, making her laugh.

She and Kerry went about their work for some time. Most preferred the debit card. It was a simple method of paying. It would be vastly superior to lugging around gold and gems. She couldn't wait until she had one as well.

"That card?" she asked. "It is connected to their bank accounts somehow."

"Yup," Kerry confirmed. "Our system runs the card and sends the money that is in their bank account to our bank account."

"What if they don't have enough money?"

"It will decline," Kerry said as she showed her how it worked. "I slide this card through the card reader, and the customer can either use debit or credit. If debit, the customer uses a pin number, if credit, they sign for it."

"What is the difference?" she asked.

"Credit means that it's money owed. It takes a little longer to transfer the funds, but the customer doesn't need to use a pin number. Debit happens instantly. If there isn't enough money in the bank, it gets declined."

The conversation died off again rather quickly. She couldn't help but wonder if she'd upset Kerry somehow. She was a little standoffish to begin with, but she felt a deliberate chill, as if Kerry didn't want to be near her.

The line had finally waned, and they had a few minutes of reprieve. She realized it was because Kerry wasn't as strict with the Wi-Fi policing as her brother, and the customers were all on their phones.

"Are you upset with me?" Her words were staggered as she didn't want a customer to overhear.

Kerry's eyes darted around as if she thought about fleeing the conflict, but she regrouped. "It's just that Eton really likes you," she said.

Destiny wasn't certain why that should cause tension between them.

"He doesn't always know when it's the right time to get involved," Kerry clarified. "I know you are having trouble with Daniel."

Kerry was most likely referring to the situation Eton had told her about. His sister was afraid that he would fall into the same trap again. Falling in love with a married woman only to get his heart stepped on. If she was in Kerry's position, she'd have the same concern.

"Eton and I are just friends," she said. "He and I talked about the woman he was involved with, as you say. He knows it was a mistake even when his heart doesn't always agree."

Kerry's face softened. "I'm glad we met you."

She smiled, genuinely happy to have reconciled the conflict as soon as she had. Kerry was a friend, and so was Eton. For the first time, she had real friends who were not relatives. "And I'm so glad I met you. The both of you."

There was something else that concerned Kerry's round little face. "They still haven't found that guy. Do you think that Daniel...?" she struggled to finish the sentence.

"That he had something to do with it?"

Kerry nodded and swallowed hard.

"I don't know," she whispered. It was the worst thing to imagine, but she couldn't help but wonder the same.

From the diary, the family tree, and the story about the witch, for the first time in Sallows history, there were several correlating sources that confirmed the mythology surrounding their island. Everything lined up, but it could be coincidence. The stories corroborated one another, but that could be because one inspired the others. And her mother had lived through four generations? Why didn't mother warn her? If there was ever a time she needed her mother, it was now. She would know what to do.

"Hey," Eton's voice ripped her back into the present. "Are you okay?"

She nodded, but her face probably gave her away. Eton wasn't convinced. He stared at her for several long moments, but she wouldn't burst into tears today.

Eton checked the time. "We'll be closing in an hour. How about I walk you home?"

She liked the idea of Eton walking her home, but Kerry made her feel so self-aware. After their last private conversation, she didn't want his sister thinking she was a liar. There was also the fear that Daniel would spot them walking together by some unfortunate chance.

"No," she said. "I'm fine, but I'd like to go home now if that's okay."

"Sure," he said. "Of course."

She gave a nod and mouthed a silent thanks before clumsily working her way around the counter. The nice thing about the new world was that the surrounding people were blessedly oblivious as they stared down at their phones. She knew that if it were not a phone, it would be a book or something else. It was human nature to crave a departure from the mundane and predictable until the more exciting points of life could begin.

An unusual warmth struck her as she stepped out. The blackened horizon confirmed her fears. A storm was closing in on her tiny island. The skies were so dark that they made the island feel as though it were already night. Rain threatened to break the stale, muggy air at any moment.

They littered the trail to the mansion, the stranded visitors hovering around little fires. She feared that when the rain came, the visitors would be unsheltered. Daniel would have said to leave them, but even he wouldn't abandon them come the rains. Nowhere else but the mansion could house this many people. It was the right thing to do.

Clutching her hands together, she turned around and went back into the store. Eton and Kerry both looked up at the same time. Their faces truly were similar. She never noticed it until now. It was in the shape of their eyes and lips. If they had been the same sex, they would have been difficult to tell apart.

"It looks as though it's about to rain," she announced, playing with her fingers.

Eton shrugged. "They should have thought about that before coming over here the way they did."

"The tourists couldn't have known the storm was coming in the way it was," she argued. The Norwegian sailors did not have the purest of motivations, to be sure, but these were young people who didn't ask to be left out in a storm all night. It was a mistake on their part.

"Well," Eton said, "I have some tents, and I guess we can squeeze as many in here that we can—"

"Send them to the mansion," she interrupted. Untangling her fingers, she forced her hands down at her sides. "They can stay in the mansion. I have plenty of firewood."

"Are you sure you want to do that?" Kerry asked. "That's a lot of people."

She wasn't certain. In fact, she had a terrible feeling about it, but it was wrong to leave those people out in a storm. Kerry and Eton were also new to the woes of the island. Storms here were treacherous.

Rain came at all angles, if you were fortunate; otherwise, it would be ice pellets that shattered glass. The waves would come several miles ashore, dragging anything in its path back out to sea. The ocean would crash so hard against the cliffs it felt like earthquakes. This wasn't an act of goodwill; it was an act of conscience. She couldn't sit up there in her mansion while a potentially fatal storm took the lives of young, stupid fools.

"You'll want to bring your animals inside," she said. Straightening her back, she tried her best to use her Helicant Sallows voice. If they needed a leader, it was now. "When it storms on the island, leave nothing outside. This cottage is vulnerable to flooding. Do you have ropes?"

Kerry's shiny lips made a big O as her mouth gaped like a fish. Eton's head bobbed in a shocked nod. "Yeah, we got some."

"If it does flood, you'll need to lead the sheep up the hill. You'll either need to bag the chickens in a sack, release them, and hope for the best, or let them drown."

Both siblings still stared at her as if they didn't know who she was. It wasn't often that she took on such responsibilities, but this was a matter of life and death. "Come along," she clapped her hands. "Let's get to work."

She took a deep breath and walked the trail towards the mansion. The first cluster of people was shivering beside a pathetic fire. Scantly clad girls in shirts that exposed their midriff. The summers here were tepid, and the winters glacial. What were they thinking? They must have mistaken the storm's warm winds for normal weather. Unaware of what was to follow.

"If you promise to be respectful and follow the rules of my house, I will invite you to stay in the mansion for the night."

Their eyes lit up and the three girls nodded eagerly as they followed behind her, working her way up to the mansion like some *hipster* messiah, collecting wayward tourists. Sometimes the girls went to the dimming lights along the trail to tell the others, other times, it was her who approached. More and more people were following behind, and the daylight was all but extinguished by the time they reached the top.

She turned to face what was now a large crowd, and she cleared her throat. "I realize many of you did not know the fishermen were bringing you here despite the storm warnings. Storms on this island can be awful and even deadly.

"Under these circumstances, I am inviting you to stay in the mansion. Please be aware that this mansion is old, and most of the rooms are in disrepair. No one has lived here in a long time. We've been doing our best to restore it, but we are few and have limited resources.

"Please stay in the rooms I provide for you during the night. In the daytime, if you like, I shall let you roam the house. If a hallway is locked, it's because of severe water damage and mold, so please stay clear of those areas."

Some were nodding, others looked unimpressed and even bored. One young man raised his hand. "Yes?" she asked.

"What's the Wi-Fi password?"

That terrible feeling radiated into her ribcage. She was in for a long night, and she was in for it alone.

With the furniture moved, she could put many people in the drawing room. She stoked a fire to life while the visitors sulked as close as they could to the warmth.

"It's dreadfully cold, I know," she said. They were all too awkward or cold to speak. She knew they were anxious, much in the ways she felt when she was human. Uncertainty was an awful plague on the mind.

The dining room could house the rest of visitors. She had several men to lift and pull the table to one side of the room and people scrambled to sit on the chairs beside the fireplace. "I'll bring blankets," she promised as she backed out the double-doors.

"Is that a fox?" someone asked, pointing at the stained glass on the doors.

It was the same picture as on her mother's bedpost, a fox on a hillside. She always knew it to be the same, but never stopped to think of the connection and wondered if it meant anything. There was probably a story here, but it was one of the many stories her mother had failed to tell her.

"Yes," she said. "I'll be back momentarily. You'll want some more firewood."

"We can help," a man with long blond hair in a bun offered.

Oh, a gentleman! She led them to the woodpile, and they began hauling bundles up to the rooms while she went to the linen closet and pulled down as many blankets as she could hand out. A few muttered thanks and asked her questions about the house. Like chicks emerging from their eggs, they were recovering from the ordeal, and Destiny was glad for it.

A man with a spikey hairstyle and bronzed skin approached her. He was nearly as short as she was. It was a marvel how people varied in the new world. They were all different colors and sizes. Their hair ranged not just in the natural colors but in a full spectrum. They had markings on their skin and piercings. Both she found jarring, but she came to understand that this was self-expression. Could she ever blend in with these people?

"Hey, a few of us still want to party. Do you mind if we do that outside?"

She supposed if they wanted to drink and be wild, they could do so outside. "Please keep the noise to a minimum."

"Do you have any plug-ins?" a girl asked.

"I'm sorry, no, they built this house before electricity."

Another girl came to her and said, "Are there bathrooms?"

Goodness, she had nearly forgotten about that. She led several girls outside the kitchen to the outhouse.

The rain had not hit yet, but there was electricity in the air that suggested thunder and lightning were only a few miles off the shore. It was going to be worse than she initially thought.

People were lying on the ground in her linen sheets, and her bottom lip trembled. They were children all bundled up amid a storm. What would have happened if lightning struck? She wanted to throttle those sailors for being so irresponsible.

She was standing at the top of the stairs when Eton came in. "Did you tell those guys they could do that?" he asked, pointing outside.

"They wanted to drink and be merry. I said it was fine, just so long as they were quiet."

"Ah..."

She didn't wait for Eton to utter a description. She went down the stairs to have a look for herself. A red-hot glow came from the windows. Their fire was so massive that she could see nothing else from her front windows.

Pulling the front door open, a wave of heat poured into the chilly house and pulled at her hair. Eton stood beside her, wide-eyed. Six men were each holding a bottle of their choice and were dancing wildly.

"You need to stop selling alcohol, Eton."

"Yup."

It wasn't so much the dancing to their wrenched music or even consuming alcohol while chanting loudly with the song. It was that they had stacked wooden pallets stolen from the store disposal site and stacked them dangerously high.

The fire blazed along the wood and threatened to make the whole bonfire collapse from the instability. To make matters worse, they were throwing garbage all around the front lawn. She gasped at the stupidity of it all. Where did they get such an idea to begin with? On the other side of the bonfire, there was a familiar face, and she put together what had happened.

Chapter Twenty-Two
WHEN THE PARTY IS OVER

The youngest of the Norwegian sailors was no doubt the instigator of the bonfire. By his foot was a box of alcohol and metal cans. Eton didn't sell the libations; this man brought them and the pallets to deliberately rabble rouse.

He pointed at two of the visitors. "You there, grab that pallet and toss it on the fire."

"The lady said—"

"I don't give a fuck what the lady said. She doesn't own this island. We can do whatever we want."

Her fists balled, and before she could think of what to say, she stomped off the porch and right up to the smirking, insolent child.

"Come to join us for the party?" he asked. His pale hair and face reflected the fire, giving him an orange complexion. His blue eyes pierced through the dark.

"I told them they could drink and have themselves a quiet party," she shouted over the music. "But I did not say they could create a massive fire and trash my home."

The young man lifted his hands and said, "I don't make the rules, and neither do you."

"Hey bud, this isn't about rules," Eton joined in, placing a well-meaning hand on the boy's shoulder. "This is a safety issue. This thing can come down on someone and really hurt them."

"Don't you patronize me," he spat before shoving Eton away. "Just because you got here first means nothing."

"You don't destroy what you love." Gods, how that statement hurt.

There was no reaching this boy. He was of wanton disrespect and chaos without a place to dispose of his energy. It reminded her of Cousin Drew, especially in the firelight.

"No one cares about which country the island belongs to," Eton said. "We are just trying to keep the place from being trashed. You don't litter in Norway, do you?"

The boy was inebriated. He was rowdy to begin with, but he swayed as the firelight confused his step. "This is our America," the boy laughed. "We come to rape and pillage!" he shouted, and the other men cheered.

The threat was enough to set her into motion. It may have been a part of a current-day phrase, but she had had enough of this. There would be no raping anything or anyone. She wasn't the drugged and frightened girl Drew once chased around in the maze. In some of those memories, he raped her and left her in the woods to die of exposure. That version of her was long dead.

In that moment, her sights went red as the Norwegian boy transformed into Drew before her eyes. He had no regard for the island or for his fellow humans. Getting beaten up by a girl in front of his friends would provide ample humility.

"Destiny, no." Eton tried to stop her, but he couldn't stop the back of her hand connecting with the boy's face. A loud slap clapped over the droning music, and the boy's face was hit with enough force to send the rest of his body spinning to a fall.

It was quite comical. She sputtered into a giggle and tried to stop herself with her hand. All the men around the fire were staring, and the music came to a pause. The entire island, even the storm itself, came to a halt before it sprung into life all at once.

Eton was being pushed into her from the side by one of the boy's friends. She didn't remember him standing beside her to begin with. The boy got up and sneered as he wiped the blood from his lip.

His expression was one that said he was intent on killing her. He roared at her, and something inside her roared back. A part of her she didn't know existed.

She hissed at him, "Do your worst."

He broke the end of his bottle and pointed it at her, but the absurdity of his threat made her laugh wildly. If he knew what she was, would he have dared? She doubted it. The rain released from the sky in large, fat droplets that rolled down her head and face. The storm had reached them at last.

"Who are you?" Eton asked, but his opponent punched at his face, forcing him to give the fat, swarthy man his full attention.

I am Destiny Sallows. Heiress to Sallows Island. A monster.

She pursued the boy with full intent. He stepped away but continued to threaten her with his pathetic weapon. Along with the increased downpour, stones were being thrown. Who they were aiming at was uncertain as some stones hit the boy and some hit her, though they did as much harm as the water did. Most crashed through the flame and landed ineffectively around the yard.

She charged and swiped at the boy and he flinched as the clouds let loose a booming thunder. He was afraid of the storm. It struck her with such a cruel delight.

"You're just a boy," she told him. "A sad, frightened little boy who thinks that authority holds him back."

She didn't know where this was coming from. Her rage and spite roiled within her and spilled from her mouth. Something about him enraged her. It had to do with how smug and fearless he had become when he thought of himself as the stronger being. He thought it entitled him to everything her island had, just as Drew once thought himself entitled to her. He was only just realizing how wrong he was.

Eton was on the ground. He was being kicked by two men now. She lost interest in the stupid boy and flew to her friend's aid. She shoved one man away and swung wildly at the other but missed.

She wasn't exactly one for rowdy behavior. It was enough to get the two assailants to back off but not enough to stop the projectiles from the other side of the fire. Her feet betrayed her on a wet rock. She fell flat on her back, laughing. Her neck cracked so loud that she felt it crunch between her ears.

Destiny had landed wrongly on a rock, and her head was not sitting quite right. A swift jerk of her head and another, more subtle crack tickled the back of her throat. She laughed at the absurdity of it all.

Eton's eyes were wide on his wet face. The others may not have noticed, but he did. "You okay there, Rocky?"

She did not know this Rocky, but she was wonderful. Her laughter was full-bellied and cathartic. A monster living on top of a Hellmouth with her estranged and possibly murderous husband while the rest of the world decided the fate of the only home she ever knew. How could she not be okay?

They were being circled by several men. Fear was creeping into her mind as she calculated how many she could handle. She didn't know the first thing about fighting, but she was far stronger than they were. Her only problem was that they outnumbered her, and Eton was a weak point.

"You can't die, can you?" Eton asked.

"I don't know," she said. "I've never tried."

That made Eton chuckle. "What I mean is—"

He didn't have time to finish his question. A rubber boot kicked him in the stomach and sent him into a curled position, gasping for air. They kicked her, too, but it hurt no more than the rocks did. It was hurting Eton, however. She tried to cover him the best she could while the attacks increased, but it wasn't enough. If she didn't stop them, they would kill Eton.

Catching a foot mid-kick. With the twist of her hand, the bone snapped, and the owner cried out in pain. She tried to get up, but they kicked her leg out from under her. The rain had made the grass slick and the dirt muddied.

She fell to her knees as someone grabbed a handful of her hair. She reached up and grabbed the hands. She squeezed with all her might as the assailant cried out. Several fragile bones snapped under pressure. Other men were screaming then, but it had nothing to do with her.

A man flew and landed nearly ten feet away before a dark figure moved through the fire's shadows. One man was punched so hard she swore his skull would split in two. Eton groaned and opened his eyes to see the fat sailor's feet go out from beneath him before landing on his back beside Eton.

"Hey man," Eton said.

The dejected sailor said nothing. His eyes full of questions. Several tried to flee, but it was too late. The one she caught was howling loud enough to be heard all the way to shore. People were emerging from the mansion now. Staring and judging the group of men. Angry shouts and curses were being uttered and the blond man who helped her with the wood gave chase along with several others down the hill.

"You should lie down," Eton mouthed silently. She had been under attack by six or nine men. She should at least pretend they'd hurt her. Destiny gave a cry and flopped down beside Eton.

"That was dramatic," he whispered.

The fat sailor was crying beside Eton.

People were surrounding them, touching and talking to them all at once, wanting to know if she was okay. Daniel's face was among them. He picked her up and carried her into the house. Her strong facade fell, and she wept as she rested her head on her husband's chest.

Eton would be okay. She could hear people on their phones calling for help. He was making jokes about his current state. Eton would be a giant bruise tomorrow, but he wasn't dead.

"You came out of nowhere," she said. Daniel navigated the throngs of people who were near tears, asking if she was okay.

"She's all right," he said several times. "Everything is okay now, thank you."

"What in bloody hell did you do?" he muttered.

"How I've missed you and your grumpiness."

"I'm serious. What's with all the people?" he asked before nodding to another group. "She's all right, I'm just taking her upstairs."

She told him of the Norwegian fisherman who had been the source of most of their visitor problem. How they brought over tourists even when the Coast Guard warned them about the storm. "I couldn't just leave all those people out there," she said.

Lightning and thunder were directly overhead. Daniel looked out the window and watched the spectacle in the skyline. "No," he agreed. "When I saw the fire, I thought perhaps lightning had struck the house and caught it on fire."

"That too was the Norwegian fishermen and his friends."

Destiny had so much to say to him. She wanted to hear his words and his thoughts, even when she already knew what he would say. Forgetting all about the man he may have murdered. She didn't know what had happened, and he said it wasn't him. Would he lie to her as easily as he did to everyone else?

"What have you been up to these days?" she asked.

The lightning occasionally illuminated Daniel's face. "Lots of long walks," he said. "Exploring the forest. Tidying up the old doctor's cottage."

The mood was slipping away from them. The witty banter and the sudden intimacy had faded, and they were back to the resounding canyon that separated them even in the close quarters of her bedroom.

"I've missed you," she said. It felt like a whimper, and she hated how desperate she sounded. She was the one who'd pushed him away. Why did she feel this way again? Daniel didn't answer. He continued to watch the commotion outside.

"People are coming to the house," he said.

Three official men and one woman met them halfway down the stairs. They introduced themselves most informally. "Hello, ma'am," the first one greeted her.

"We got the story. Just want to ask a few questions...make sure you're all right."

"I was so frightened," she said with an intentional weepy voice. "Is Eton okay?"

"He's fine, just a little banged up," the officer assured her.

"We caught all eight of the men involved. They've been arrested, and we're issuing several hefty fines on the Norwegian fellows."

"Yes, they put all these people in great danger," she gestured to the litters of people lined along the stairs. "We're trying our best to house them, but this house isn't in any shape to be lived in."

"Well, your fisherman friend had called us about them several hours ago. Said their boats were over capacity. They're lucky they didn't capsize and drown all these kids," the main officer said loud enough for everyone to hear. "We came once it was safe enough."

"It was a kind thing to take them in," the female officer said. "Even if it's more of a museum than anything."

"Thank you," Destiny said. "We couldn't leave them out there; it could have killed them."

The female officer looked around and said, "As for the rest of you lot, you can come along with us."

After seemingly endless questions and several hours later, Destiny was escorting the Coast Guard out the front door of the home. Daniel kept his distance mostly. He blended in as he assisted the visitors out of the house. It wasn't until the very end that the police caught up to him.

"You gave those boys a hell of a wallop," the leading officer said.

He shook his head in dismay. "I came up the hill and saw them surrounding my wife. He had her by the hair..." Daniel showed with his own hand. "The poor shop boy was on the ground, and they just kept kicking him, kicking my wife."

"Enough to make a man go mad," the officer said, nodding. "We pulled that boy's file. It was as long as my arm."

"No surprise there," Daniel said.

They chatted a little about the status of the island. If she didn't suspect her husband of murder, Destiny would have loved for them to stay longer. "How did you manage in the storm?" she asked.

"We would have been here much sooner if it weren't for the storm," the principal officer explained. "Usually, the big ones like this blow right through. It's still on the western side, but it's well on its way out. You should have clear skies come the morning."

She was holding the front door as the last officer lingered. The other three had made their way down to the shore with the group, but he seemed to be waiting for something. She chewed on her fingernails while he lingered in the doorway.

"You, eh, hear anything about that guy from Scotland?" he asked.

"The one that is supposedly missing?" Daniel said from behind her. She felt his hand on her shoulder, and he gave her a gentle squeeze.

"Yeah," the officer said. "He gave the store clerk a bit of grief, and that's the last we heard of him."

Her mind went vacant as she felt Daniel press in. She had no reason to feel threatened, she told herself. Daniel would never hurt her. The officer's eyes were unreadable. What did he see when he looked at them?

"Someone burned down one of the cottages around that same time," Daniel said. "I didn't see signs of a body, but he may have been the arsonist."

The officer's ears perked. "Fire?"

She nodded along with Daniel's lies. "Oh, I don't know. About a month ago? We honestly didn't notice. We live further down the hill."

"Would you mind if we have a look later this week?"

"We'd be grateful," Daniel said. "Wouldn't we?"

She forced herself to smile at the officer. It hurt, but she wanted to protect Daniel. Protect the island and its secrets. This must have been Daniel's way of punishing her for her adultery.

"Right," the officer said. "I'll see you then."

"Goodnight."

Destiny closed the door and leaned her back against it. She let out a sigh. This was too much for her to handle. She parted her lips to tell Daniel as much, but before she could speak the words, his mouth was on hers. His hands brushed against her face before tangling in her hair. She was breathless and pinned against the door.

"Did you do it?" she asked, breaking free of his kiss. "Did you kill him?"

"No," he muttered as he nibbled her ear. It felt wonderful, but Destiny couldn't allow herself to become distracted like this.

"Could you lie to me the way you did to that policeman?"

He kissed her throat and gently unbuttoned the pearl buttons on her silky blouse. She missed him, but could she accept him if he killed that man? If he had lied to her several times about it?

His hands roamed her chest before he pulled her close. Kissing her on the mouth as if to stop her from asking further questions, his hands slid her pants down.

"This is a mistake," she breathed out before his mouth found hers once more. He didn't care if it was wrong, and in that moment, neither did she.

***

The drawing room was a mess of sheets and blankets. Destiny emerged from the room, exasperated by the amount of folding she would need to do. Most of these hadn't been washed in a rather long time and smelled musty. The visitors were probably grateful to be free of them. She had an industrial-sized laundry room and a lot of time on her hands. There would be a great deal of washing in her future.

Daniel stood at the base of the stairs as if he were uncertain of what to do. She wanted him to stay, but he still refused to answer her about Kevin. "What happened to him?" she asked, descending the stairs.

He frowned. "You don't want to know."

This was no lie. Whatever happened disturbed him on some level. No doubt it was one reason the accusation upset him so. She stroked his face. "Just tell me the best you can."

"He was hiking throughout the woods," Daniel started. "He cleaned up after himself even if he was drunk half the time. He even freed a doe from a trap I missed. Still, I was angry about you and him. The bastard," he turned away from her then.

"He found Drew's old cave of horrors, only it was occupied. It resembled one of the taxidermy creatures my mother created. It had hoofs, horns, talons, a beak..."

It was another of the island's monsters. "The Chimera," she said breathlessly.

Daniel had his back turned to her, but when he spoke, his voice broke and took her heart with it. "It had bits of clothing still. I'd know that tattered fabric anywhere."

Oh no...

How stupid she was. If Daniel was the Green-Eyed Monster, and her mother was the Cannibal Witch depicted in the journal... the other Sallows must have been monsters from the diary, too. "Who was it?"

He bowed his head. "My mother."

Bracing him from behind. She pressed her face between Daniel's shoulder blades and held him tight. "I'm so sorry."

Several minutes passed before Daniel resumed his story. "The man went into the cave, and the Chimera tore him apart. I'd be lying if I said I tried to stop it or that I didn't enjoy the spectacle," Daniel chuckled. "The wails he let out."

What a horrible thing to say! She let go of him then. "You frighten me, Daniel."

He bowed his head. "Do you want me to leave?"

"No," she admitted, bowing her head in defeat. "But I can't go down this path with you. I just can't. And I'm so tired of being alone."

"You wouldn't be alone if you just stopped fucking other people."

The statement stung, and Destiny flinched from the anger in his voice. He had every right to be angry, but this was too far. He would never recover from it. It didn't matter what she did. She straightened her spine and put on her bravest Helicant Sallows expression as she fingered the ruby ring on her finger.

"What's done is done," she said. "And you do not have the right to shout at me."

Daniel's eyes searched the room as if he no longer recognized it. There was nothing here for him if he couldn't forgive and be honest with her. She wanted to hold him, but she gripped the stair railing instead and prayed to her mother for strength.

"Just tell me what you want me to do," she said.

He snickered, turning around to face her. "All right. Never see or speak to anyone but me, forever."

Surely, he wasn't serious. That was impossible. Maybe that was the point. It wasn't possible for them to make this right. Not in the new world or the old. Unless it could be just the two of them forever, it was over. Might as well ask her to set the sun forever, knowing that only they would survive.

"Goodbye, Destiny."

Chapter Twenty-Three

HÖFN

There was a knock on his door, and Eton let out a weak groan. It didn't stop his bedroom door from opening. His sister bustled into the room with a glass of water and his painkillers.

"It's you—again," he said. Not that he was ungrateful to his sister, he just wished it was Destiny.

"I'm just giving you your pills."

He rolled over and took the pills and a few sips of the water. Kerry glared at him, and he drank a bit more. "What time is Holly coming?"

"She said she would text me when she got on Bart's boat."

His bruised ribs made him wince when he sat up, but he would be fine once the painkillers set in.

"Why are you getting up?" Kerry asked.

"I want Bart to take me to shore today to meet that attorney."

"I think that can wait." Kerry crossed her arms and acted like a barrier between him and the door.

"I'm fine," he said. "I'm not driving, and I'll just be sitting on a boat."

She couldn't stop him. The UN meeting was coming up, and this whole incident only cemented the fact that people were in danger without there being an authority out here. By people, Eton meant himself. Destiny may not have gotten hurt, but he would have been killed if Daniel hadn't intervened.

"You never gave me the full story," Kerry said.

He owed her an explanation.

"I don't think Daniel and Destiny are normal people," he started. "Sit down."

He told her about Daniel in the forest. How he thought it was just his eyes playing tricks on him, but Destiny's strength was crazy, too. "I'm not sure exactly what they are, but I don't think they are human."

Kerry's face scrunched into an awkward smile. "Maybe you should go back to bed—"

"Last night, I would have died if Destiny hadn't shielded my body with her own. She took kick after kick and didn't feel it. She was lying on top of me. If she flinched or cried out, I would have heard it."

"Dude—"

"She grabbed a guy's foot and snapped it like a candy cane. She broke that guy's fingers with her bare hands."

"I thought Daniel was the one who did all that?"

"No, I only told the police that so they wouldn't suspect Destiny, but he threw a guy ten feet. The time he kicked me out of their house, he picked me up with one hand, Kerry."

He got the sense she was believing him. "I've tried to ask Destiny about it. The thing is, I don't think she knows what they are. She won't deny it, but she just kind of avoids the question."

"Destiny isn't very good at lying," Kerry admitted.

"I think that's why Daniel is so crazy protective. I think he's afraid of people finding out about them. He doesn't want Destiny getting hurt."

"Do you think he killed that guy?" Kerry asked.

"I think he did. He's crazy when it comes to her."

"So, what are we going to do about this?"

He shrugged. He wanted to help them. They were like an extinct species. Something magical had taken place in a world full of science. What would happen to them and the island if anyone else figured it out? But he wasn't certain that Kerry would agree.

"I sort of want to help," he hedged.

His sister nodded. "I do, too."

It could have been the painkillers, but his shoulders went slack, and he felt the tension in his chest ease. He only hoped that the couple would trust them enough to share their secret. It might have been part of the reason Destiny and Daniel's relationship was on the fritz. It had to be hard, pretending to be something they weren't in a world that they didn't know. She wanted to explore, and he wanted to protect her.

The front door opened, and Kerry yelled, "I'll be right there!"

"I should man the counter so you can get ready," he told his sister.

"No, I'll be fine."

The counter bell rang, and he dragged himself to his feet.

"No, Eton, I got this."

The bell rang several times. "Damn, someone is impatient," he said. "Hey, buddy, just give us a minute, okay?"

The bell rang over and over. They forgot all about their argument about who was going to do what, and together, they charged into the store front to find Bart and a curvy girl with dark, spiraling hair and a septum piercing.

Bart beamed as Holly smiled, and Kerry clapped her hands over her mouth. Her oversized orange sweater nearly covered her face, and Eton couldn't help but get a little teary-eyed when he saw his sister crying.

"Oh, my God!" she squealed as she danced in place.

"Kerry, come here!" Holly cried.

The couple hugged and kissed. Kerry's face was blotchy from crying and he smiled while leaning against the cottage wall and spaced off a few minutes to give the couple some space. Bart was wiping tears from his eyes like the old sap he was.

"Is he okay?" Holly asked when she saw him.

Kerry started laughing at him, but he didn't see why. "Eton, go back to bed."

Bed sounded pretty good, but he had things to do. "I got to go," he said. "You know, for Destiny."

"Are you high?" Holly laughed.

"No, no," Eton lied.

"You certain we need to go today?" Bart sided with the women. "Another day wouldn't be so much of a delay."

Eton shook his head and limped toward the fisherman. Destiny and Daniel didn't have another day. "If you don't take me, I'm going to call the Norwegians."

That was enough to get Bart all fired up. "Fuck the Norwegians!"

There was absolutely no sign of the storm from the previous night. Eton was wearing a neon orange life-vest—a condition to him getting on the boat. They also banned him from being within seven feet of the railing. The salty air hit his face and his hair got that awesome beach texture.

"Eton." He heard a gruff voice.

"Eton…" a slightly less gruff voice said. It was Destiny, and she was smiling at him in that white cotton dress, her blonde hair blowing in the wind. She was Wifey material, for sure.

"Eton!" she yelled in a gargled old voice while she shook him.

He opened his eyes and came face to face with Bart's red and parched skin. "Bart," he said. "You need a breath mint, man."

"You fell asleep against the top house."

He didn't see what the problem was.

"We're here."

Bart's car was waiting at the dock. It was a tiny blue car that Eton couldn't imagine the sailor fitting in. "Do you always drive to work?"

"Nah," Bart said, unlocking the car. "The missus parked it here for us while she does some shopping."

The unfortunate little car could house Bart. He cringed as the air pressure in the tires relented to Bart's weight before he squeezed in as well. He felt around clumsily for the lever that would roll the seat back, but his hand was too big to reach, which was unfortunate because his knees were wedged against the glovebox.

"Here, you fucking dumbass," Bart said as he poked a button on the dash. The seat rolled back several inches. He stared at Bart with his glassy eyes, and the fisherman let out a roar of laughter. "You look like a clown in a clown car."

Bart pulled the car into reverse and drove down the village road.

"Better than being an old fat man in a tiny car."

"Fuck off."

Like most elderly people, Bart liked to jack the heat in the car. Somewhere between the sweltering heat and his position that could only be explained as a new Yoga pose, Eton began experiencing a sharp stabbing pain every time he took a breath. He tried to adjust to the cramped position, but there was no wiggle room in the toy car.

"How much longer?" he asked.

"About forty-five more minutes."

He wouldn't last that long. He wasn't supposed to take his pills for another two hours, but the pains were moving throughout his ribcage, and he was on the verge of tears. He popped the cap and took a few more with a swig of bottled water. Bart said nothing as he was too busy singing loudly in Icelandic. He had a nice voice in all truth. It was a folk song, and Bart's voice suited it.

Eton fell asleep and dreamed of inclines and declines. Occasionally, he would open his eyes to see lush green lands with herds of sheep and Bart cursing the tiny little cars in front of him. His ears popped a few times, jarring him awake momentarily.

"You okay, bud?" Bart asked.

Did he answer? He wasn't sure if he answered.

"Hullo?"

He was being shaken, and he forced his eyes open wide as if it could somehow keep him awake.

"You better not die in my car, motherfucker."

"I can't die in here," he agreed as he hit his funny bone, trying to find the car door. He tried to use his other hand but couldn't quite get his fingers around the stupid handle. Bart opened the passenger door, and he almost fell out—if not for the seatbelt around his neck. He made an awful choking noise and regretted being alive at that moment.

Bart tilted his head. "If you're not feeling up to it, we can try again another day."

"No," he said. "I don't want to ride in this car more than I have to."

"I don't mind," Bart said. "I'll come back to the island tomorrow."

"No. I'm fine."

He untangled himself from the seatbelt. Using his legs to push himself up reminded him of the bruises going up his legs. He winced a little, but it was fine. He made it up a ramp to a small house and pulled the door open a little harder than he intended. He could hear Bart mutter a curse as the door flew open, and he struggled to catch it before it smacked against his hand.

Inside, he found a man sitting by himself at a desk. "Hullo," the man said. "Can I help you?"

"I'm Eton. We talked on the phone."

The man's hair was the same color as his suit. He stood up and shook Eton's hand. It was clear the attorney didn't remember talking to him at all. Was he that unmemorable?

"I'm Eton."

"Yes," the man said. "You mentioned that. My name is Egill Jónsson. Welcome to my practice."

"I'm the one on the island." Eton jarred his memory.

Egill's eyes went wide, and he said, "Oh, oh, I remember. You said you were uncertain if you could make an appointment because of the boat ride."

"Yeah." He slumped into the chair opposite the lawyer. "So, we want someone to represent the indigenous people's interest in the UN meeting." The word *indigenous* got stuck in his mouth for longer than what seemed natural. He hoped the lawyer didn't notice.

"Are you one of the natives?"

"No, I'm just here on their behalf."

"I see," the lawyer said.

He picked up a notepad and began jotting notes—in his tan suit. Was the suit color intentional? Or was it just on the clearance rack? Maybe he bought it without trying it on or never looked in a mirror. "Do you have power of attorney?"

"No. They are just not used to people, so it frightens them to come to the city."

"I see. What are their names?"

"Destiny and Daniel Sallows," he said. "They want to become citizens of whatever country the island becomes a part of. That's why we were referred to you."

"I do immigration, so I might help them in that regard."

"Great!" After months, they'd finally made some headway. "Do you think it would naturalize them or that they would need to apply? How would that work?"

"Well," the lawyer said, with the tip of his pen pressed to his lip. "That really depends on what the UN rules. They may want them to go through the motions, they may not. Then there is the country's decision as well. The UN doesn't decide on a county's behalf."

"Sure," Eton nodded. "Sure."

"If I am to take on this case, I'll need to meet the couple, and I'll require a retainer. This process could be quite expensive as I'll need to travel to the meeting."

He waved his hand. "We have the funds; that is not a problem."

"Okay," the lawyer said. "If you could provide me with your contact information, I will get back to you on my availability."

"So, you'll take the case."

"Potentially," the lawyer said. "I have other clients."

"We can pay a fifty percent retainer fee," Eton said.

There was a pause, and the attorney's brows rose. "You are qualified to make that type of negotiation?"

"These guys are desperate for answers," Eton explained. "I know. I probably seem a little weird, but the night before last, a group of people got drunk on the island and attacked Destiny and me. I'm on painkillers from the ordeal. They don't feel safe; that's why they need you."

"I see..." The lawyer's brows knit, and he nodded. "I'll do what I can."

Eton remembered little of the car ride home. Bart had to help him get in, but he didn't remember getting out. He didn't remember getting on the boat either, but he opened his eyes and saw the pale-clouded sky rushing past him while the boat engine rumbled even in his dreams.

***

Jeremy didn't answer the random Icelandic number when he saw it ringing. If it was important, they would leave a message. He got a lot of calls these days. Mostly advertisers and influencers looking to promote his documentary series. He had been editing a recent expedition ever since he left, though. His eyeballs ached and he more than once he fell asleep while watching hours of empty footage.

Ryan and Tiff were on a couple's retreat on his dime. It was the least he could do. His best friend had been having nightmares ever since. Something about that place really messed with Ryan's head, and it pissed Jeremy off to know that. He appreciated the way Tiff stuck with Ryan.

The message notification popped up, and he was eager to see what it was. It might have been Tiff giving him an update. Even if it was a junk call, he might have tried to hold a conversation if it meant a few minutes away from this most recent disaster of an episode. He'd have to plant sound effects or something to punch it up, but he hated doing that. This show was supposed to be an authentic and scientific exploration of the paranormal, but the more popular he became, the more pressured he felt to produce results.

"Hello, Mr. Sands. My name is Egill Jónsson. I am an attorney here in Iceland. I just had an interesting conversation with a young man on the new island. I know you led an expedition there recently, so I'd like your input. Thank you."

He leaned back in his chair and stared at the can-lit ceiling. He had thought of nothing but the mansion since he left. Between the damage to his wallet, his friend, and his understanding of the world, it had developed into an outright obsession.

This was the single best episode on his show. It was the clearest proof of paranormal activity. It had also come under fire. They forced him to take it down after some fans debunked the episode, calling him a fraud. He expected controversy with a video like that, but so many claimed people lived on the island. They had videos and everything.

He was not a fraud; he was a scientist. The show only started because no one in the scientific community would hear him out. It was Ryan's idea, really. After being turned down by several colleges and studies for lacking the right credentials or the right "fit" for their studies, it was his best friend who suggested he upload the videos online and let the internet decide.

They decided he was the real deal, and he even believed it himself for a while. It made him wealthy, and it gave him the entire world to travel and explore. Nothing came close to what he experienced in that mansion. Not that his machinery reacted much or that anything outright happened, but it was when he got back to his studio that he heard thousands of voices in the EVP all at once.

Jeremy stared at his phone and resisted the urge to pick it up. The so-called owners of the mansion had made him look like a total asshole. If he'd known people lived there, he wouldn't have just walked in. How was he to know anyone was there? He went into his kitchen and poured himself a glass of whiskey.

There was zero intention to return after being confronted by the store clerk. When those girls ran around the house with their live feed, calling him out as a liar and a trespasser, it caused a major backlash with fans. Since then, Jeremy had struggled with his audience and the network put his TV series on "development" which was a nice way of saying they scrapped it.

He wanted to go back, but not at the risk of being called a trespasser. The last thing he needed was to lose any more credibility than he already had, but those voices on the EVP machine had him obsessed. He had transcribed thousands of lines of dialogue. All of it spanned one night but on repeat. Usually, the conversations were the same; sometimes, they varied a little. Other times, the conversations differed wildly, and there were other noises, things he didn't think were human, and the screams kept him up at night. They must have been the things Ryan had sensed; he was too afraid to ask.

Picking up the phone, he dialed the number. A soft-spoken gentleman answered, "Hello, Jeremy?"

"Hi, this is Jeremy."

"Hullo, this is Egill. I am calling from Iceland—"

"Yeah," he stopped him. "I got your message. What is it exactly that you want to know?"

"Are you familiar with the situation with the UN deliberations on the island?"

"Yeah, they are going to decide which country it belongs to."

"I have been asked to represent some natives to the island. I was hoping to talk to you about them."

"All right." He leaned against his counter and took a sip of his whiskey.

"They are the couple in the video that calls you a trespasser, correct?"

"I thought it was abandoned. If I knew—"

"That is not my concern," Egill said. "My concern is that they want representation without even meeting me. Their friend Eton came to my office wanting to represent on their behalf, stating that they were nearly illiterate with technology or the modern world."

"Well, they understood how a cell phone works."

"I thought it strange that a person without power of attorney would ask to represent a couple and be willing to supply such a large deposit. I did some research when he left, and I found your video and the subsequent video.

"This is a situation of ethics, you see. I cannot relay any further information, especially if I agree to take them as clients, but I had hoped you would have some insight about the appearing island."

Jeremy smiled. He was going to get back at those people without hurting his public persona. He told the attorney his side of the story between sips of whiskey. They spoke for nearly an hour, during which he elaborated on Eton's involvement. By the end, he was wasted but gratified.

"So, you think these people are, in fact, Eton's friends who are posing as natives of the island. Is that correct?"

"I think so. Eton wants total control of the island so he can control the business that goes through there. Hey, out of curiosity, what happens if you help them become naturalized if they are American citizens?" Jeremy had a lawyer. He knew exactly what could happen, but he wanted to hear it.

"I could be disbarred, Mr. Sands."

He smiled. "So, was I trespassing?"

The attorney was quiet for a moment. "I suppose that is debatable. If you can prove they are not native to the island, which seems highly improbable, then no, you are not. If they are indeed the natives of the island, most courts would side with them."

"I'm glad we had this talk, Egill."

"As am I, Mr. Sands. As Am I."

Jeremy got off the phone with the attorney and sat back in his studio chair. He clicked a few things, and a warning came up on his screen. *Are you sure you want to delete?*

He hit 'yes' and watched countless hours of his life disappear in a blink. It didn't matter anymore. None of that mattered now. He had an idea that would clear his name and put things right. He pulled up the audio files from the mansion and printed out the transcripts. Jeremy labeled the voices with the names they called each other.

Helicant: "Let's get on with it. I think we're all ready for dinner."

Daniel: "Are you sure we shouldn't—"

Helicant: "You have the ring. Let's be done with all of this."

Daniel: "Destiny, I know you're frightened. I am, too. Just look at my hand. Go on."

Destiny: "Daniel—"

Daniel: "It's scary business, getting married. I don't know what's going to happen any more than you do. I know you're afraid of my eyes, but I also know that you don't like that about yourself. I can't promise you'll never be afraid, but what I can promise is that you'll be the one to decide what you need, and I will support you. I've read a lot about phobias, and I think I can work through it with you. Worst-case scenario, I can just wear a blindfold for the rest of my life. It will be worth it if it makes you happy."

Destiny: *Crying* "I...I... Yes (No)."

Jeremy stared at that last line. Most of the time she said no, but there was just one time where Destiny said yes during the same event. It was a strange overlap in the audio. He only caught the girl saying yes because of all the cheering. Not that he knew much about proposals, but usually people didn't celebrate when the girl said no. He had to put on several filters before he could hear her say it through all the other times she said no.

These voices were repeating the same day. He had a theory that if he used his EVP device in the house again, he would hear them doing the same thing again. People couldn't accuse him of doctoring the evidence from two different days and times. He would bring someone else in on it if they weren't afraid of their reputation being ruined. There was a good chance he could get someone to verify him despite the hiccup. It was the least he could do for Ryan.

He would go back to the mansion, confirm his EVP readings, and reveal the couple as the frauds they were. He could once again be on the fast track to becoming a respected member of the ghost-hunting community.

While he was at it, Jeremy called Tiff.

"Hey," she answered.

"How is he?"

"I don't know. He is still having the nightmare. Jeremy, I don't know what to do. The meds are not working. He says they make it worse."

Ryan was the real deal. He could sense what Jeremy was hearing on the EVP. They could call him a fraud. He could take it. But Ryan didn't deserve the abuse. If he proved that this was real, it would also confirm his friend was a real psychic. Maybe it wouldn't make the nightmares stop, but it would make sure he could always afford the help he needed.

"I'm going back, Tiff." He expected her to be upset, but she said nothing. "You saw the episode, didn't you?"

"Of course I did." She broke down crying.

The whiskey was churning in his stomach. "Did he?"

"How could I stop him?"

"I'm going to prove everything."

"Thank you."

He had a few more calls to make that night, but before he did, he made a vague post on social media about returning to the mansion to clear the *Sallow* air. It received enough attention to be mentioned on *The Tonight Show*.

Chapter Twenty-Four

ACCUSATIONS

Destiny wished she had a gift to bring Eton. Had she still needed food, she would have made him a pie or a batch of bread, perhaps. The police officers said he was okay, but he must have been in a great deal of pain from the storm incident.

The island had been much quieter these last few days. She doubted Bart would bring people over after what happened, and the other ships were told to stay away. The island almost looked as it had before it became visible to the rest of the world. If Destiny ignored the specks of trash on the countryside and animals that now inhabited the shore, it would look exactly how it had before.

Destiny opened the cottage door to find Kerry standing beside a strange-looking woman. She was tall and shapely. She wore no under-clothes, and Destiny could see the natural form of her breasts under her thin and short shirt. Her pants hugged her hips, exposing her midriff. That was not what shocked Destiny. What took her breath away was the woman's skin color.

The woman was black. Destiny had read about African people, but she had never seen one in person. Her flawless skin reflected the sun and her coiled hair looked like a black lion's mane. She had a piece of metal in her nose, but Destiny assumed that was a new world style, but otherwise, this woman was one of the most beautiful women Destiny had ever seen.

"Hi," Destiny said.

"Oh, Destiny," Kerry looked at her and then back at the woman. "Remember how I told you about my girlfriend?"

The woman's eyes fell on Destiny, and she felt herself blush far harder than she would normally. She tried to pull her thoughts together, but her mind was irrevocably scattered. Just because she understood gay women in theory did not mean she was as prepared to meet one.

"This is Holly," Kerry said.

"Hello," she said with a little curtsey. There was instant regret, as she knew it to be an outdated custom.

"You're one of the locals?" the woman asked.

"Yes."

"You're so lovely," she said before becoming thoroughly embarrassed. Her face must have been hotter than a stove fire. Holly had one of those piercings in her nose. It was a masculine piercing, but it was attractive all the same.

"Thank you!" Holly flashed striking white teeth. She had never seen hair that curled in such a way. Abigail's hair curled, but it was more frizz than anything. Perhaps if her cousin had all the benefits of the new world, her hair would have been equally stunning.

Reminded of her purpose, she broke her gaze from Holly and turned to Kerry. "How is he?"

Kerry knocked on Eton's bedroom door and he bade them to come in. He was laying in his cot reading a book. She could see the fading colors on his arms. His face was unblemished. Eton glanced from his book and smiled. He'd endured so much pain, but still smiled like a naughty boy skipping his studies.

"How are you feeling?" she asked.

"A little sore," he said. "Mostly stir crazy. Kerry won't let me stay out of bed for longer than a few minutes."

"That little boat ride was enough," Kerry said.

"Boat ride?" Destiny asked.

Kerry crossed her arms and glared at Eton, "He made Bart take him to the mainland to talk to a lawyer."

His sister was right. Destiny scowled at him. "In this condition?"

"It was fine."

"Bart said you slept most of the time and nearly strangled yourself on a seatbelt."

She didn't know what a seatbelt was, but it sounded as though Eton was in no condition to leave when he did. "When was this?" she asked.

"The day before yesterday," Eton said. "But does anyone want to know about what the attorney said?"

Of course, she wanted to know, but she wished he'd taken her with him, preferring to deal with these things firsthand. "What did he say?"

"He said he had to check his schedule but that he wanted to represent you before the UN."

The news elated her. "I can't thank you enough, Eton."

"We will probably need to go back soon," he said.

"Of course."

Eton pulled the blankets off and sat up. "I can't be in this cot any longer. I think it's doing more damage than the bruises did. Any customers?"

"Just the usual," Kerry said.

Eton rubbed his face in his hands. "When was the last time you made them buy something to use the Wi-Fi?"

"Holly has a tight leash on them."

Eton nodded and stood up. "Come on, Destiny," he said. "I need to walk outside."

She gave Kerry a knowing nod. A silent promise that she would keep an eye on him and bring him back home if he got too tired. Kerry's protectiveness over her older brother was touching. Destiny desperately wished she had a sibling. Abigail was her dearest cousin, but her night terrors made it difficult to have sleepovers and eventually, her anxieties made it difficult for her to see visitors of any kind. If only she knew then what she knew now, how different her world could have been.

She stole a few more glimpses at Holly, who smiled and waved at her. It wasn't just Destiny who found Holly captivating. There were other people in the room—she hadn't noticed them before—but it was because they had become a part of the establishment. Two young men in dark wool were always seated in those chairs, staring at their phones, except today, they were staring at Holly.

This didn't go unnoticed by Eton either. "Guys," he said. "Can you give it a rest?"

"It's fine," Holly said.

Eton motioned to the table where the two men sat. "I can't tell if that's a puddle of drool or a soda spill."

"They can stare at my gay ass all they want," Holly said while she gave a provocative wiggle of her hips. "They can't help it."

The men didn't seem to hear a word Eton said. Holly was confident and so unafraid. Kerry watched her in admiration from beside the fireplace. Those men could overpower her if they wanted to. She gave Eton a worried look, and Eton only smiled.

"If one of you even looks at Holly wrong—"

The woman's demeanor went from hot to cold in an instant. "Then I'll fuck them up so bad their mommies won't be able to identify the bodies."

Both men's eyes went wide, and they shook their heads. Holly's threat startled even her, and Destiny wasn't the one Holly intended it for.

Holly smiled. "You're good boys, I can tell. Now get up here and buy something. Your Wi-Fi time is about to end."

Eton nodded. "She's fine on her own."

He shut the door behind him, and together, they walked around the cottage. Eton had questions, and Destiny feared she would indeed need to provide him with answers. After what happened during the storm, it was the least she could do.

"I'm sorry," she started.

Eton shook his head. "It wasn't your fault."

"I could have waited for the Coast Guard. I shouldn't have antagonized them."

He only shrugged while he slipped his hands in his pockets. They rounded the corner, avoiding the outhouse, but unfortunately, that brought them within feet of the chicken coop and sheep pen. The animals sensed her and fled in terror. The chickens cowered in their coops and the sheep ran to the opposite corner and wailed in terror.

Eton frowned as he watched the spectacle. "It's just me, guys."

She gave a close-lipped smile. It didn't take long for the Eton to put it together.

"Is it you they're afraid of?" he asked.

"Probably."

She and Eton walked around the animal pens. It became more apparent by the moment that the animals hated her, and they rotated to the furthest side of their pens. Eton frowned in disgust, and she cringed. She was a monster, just like Daniel said. The animals could sense it and ran from danger the way they ran from storms or predators.

They'd made their way from the cottage towards the shore when he said, "Those guys kicked you over and over...and your neck. You didn't get hurt."

"I don't feel pain anymore," she admitted.

"You're not a ghost, right?"

She chuckled. "I don't think so. Ghosts are dead. I am very much alive." She took his hand in hers. "See, I'm warm. I get goosebumps, and my heart beats. I breathe."

"But you can't get hurt?"

She thought back to the storm. Their kicks were not pleasant, but they left no damage to her body. "I can be hurt. I think I just heal quicker, or perhaps I am more resistant to injury now."

"So, you weren't always this way?" Eton asked.

She told him about how they woke up. "It was only then that we found we did not need to eat or sleep. Before then, we were just ordinary people."

Eton scratched his head as he tried to process the information. She trusted him enough to believe that he would never tell her secret. It was probably foolish thinking, and Daniel would be furious if he found out, but it was a heavy weight lifted from her shoulders. It was so freeing to not have to hide it. She could be herself around Eton and everything would be okay.

In the distance, two figures emerged from the hill. She let go of Eton's hand. It was two of the policemen from the other day. The Coast Guard, they called themselves. Eton tensed a little, and she had to remind herself that he was not Daniel.

The men waved, and Eton waved back. "Hello," they shouted.

She smiled and gave a friendly wave. Daniel had told them they could come and investigate the cottage that he burned down. That was probably why they were here. Still, she felt twitchy and uncertain of herself. They made her nervous.

"Good morning," she said as they got close enough for a conversation.

"Morning," the leader said. "We were hoping to have a look at that cottage that burned down."

She nodded. "The far end cottage. I'm afraid you're in for a bit of a hike."

Their faces went grim. They were not so keen on going too far out. "If you follow the path to the mansion, you'll have to walk around the house. There is a thin trail that leads to the cliffs. That's where the cottage was."

"No one lived there, then," the secondary officer asked.

"No, it was badly damaged. It had been abandoned for a long time."

They both nodded. "The winds from the ocean probably did a number on it."

"Oh, the roof was nearly torn off, and everything was covered in mold," she agreed.

"Then you're not looking to press charges?" the primary officer asked.

Destiny shook her head. "No, I don't see a point in it."

"It would be nice if that guy turned up, though," Eton said. "I hate leaving my sister by herself for anything."

"It's strange," the leading officer said. "You were the last person to see him. None of the fishermen have seen him. No sign of him on the shores."

Nervous pinpricks tickled her fingers. Destiny didn't like what the officer was insinuating.

"You two got into a bit of a fight, from what we heard," the second officer added.

"I'd hardly call it a fight," Eton said. "He was angry at the price of alcohol, and I told him to take it or leave it. He left with it."

"You sell alcohol?" the lead policeman asked with raised eyebrows.

"Not anymore," Eton said.

"No, I suppose not after the fight with the fisherman boy."

She didn't like how they were framing their conversations. They made it sound as though Eton was brawling with everyone.

"I was grateful for Eton's defense," she said. "That boy and his friends were threatening to *rape and pillage* everything on the island."

The secondary officer ruffled. "You know, where we come from, that is a threat."

"That's how I took it," Eton said. "Seven or eight men against one small woman."

The secondary cop shook his head. "If that were my kid—"

"That's the trouble with this place," the primary officer said. "People think there are no laws, and they can get away with whatever, but it's under Coast Guard jurisdiction. It's not the wild west."

"Thank you!" Eton said. "I've had so many people say this place is lawless, but some laws are universal."

"Right," the secondary officer chimed.

"What's your universal law then, mate?" the primary officer asked.

The officer's tone took her back. Eton was set on his heels and stumbled on the delivery of his otherwise eloquent manifesto. "You know, just don't hurt others."

"Unless, of course, they are hurting someone else," the officer said.

"Even then."

She scowled, and both officers ignored her displeasure. This wasn't going very well at all. Perhaps she should have taken them to the cottage to exhaust them before they could ask all these questions.

"The thing is, your friend Daniel claimed he was the one who came to the lady's aid, but none of the seven men had even seen the guy. So, I'm thinking you were the one who did most of the damage."

"Am I in some kind of trouble?" Eton asked.

Both officers stood firm, and the secondary officer had a hand on his belt.

"We'd ask that you not leave the island until we find the missing suspect."

"Fine with me. I hope you find him," Eton said.

The secondary officer handed him a card. "If you see any sign of him, give us a call."

She and Eton watched the Coast Guard head for the shore. The wind pushed at their hair and faces, but neither cared. Eton was suspected of murder. They thought Eton was capable of murder. Or at the very least, they wanted to pin it on him.

"Eton..." She placed a hand on his arm, unsure of what to say.

"Did Daniel tell you anything? Anything at all?"

Could she tell him? He proved to be much stronger than she could have ever predicted, but some things, people would be better off not knowing. If the Chimera was still around, the others could be as well. The least she could do was warn him.

"There are things here, Eton," she warned. "Things even we don't fully understand. Stay clear of the woods."

"Like hell I am," Eton said. "I need proof that I didn't kill that guy, or I'm trapped here."

Is being trapped with me so bad?

Eton turned to the cottage while taking his phone out of his pocket. "I didn't tell Kerry, but the thing that killed Peabody wasn't…natural."

"Peabody?"

"Her chicken," he explained as he pulled up a video. "I have surveillance, but I told her it wasn't hooked up yet because of the internet fiasco."

Eton handed her the phone, and she watched as a creature came scuttling from the forest. It limped and crawled on its knuckles in a broken heap toward the cottage. Its long hair dragged along the grass, and its fingers were a zigzag of knobs and bends.

Her breath caught in her throat as she watched the poor monstrosity drag itself to the chicken coop and out of view. The chickens cried and fluttered before the creature emerged once more. The poor chicken flapped and cried as the creature slammed it into the ground. She prayed to the gods that the animal was dead before the monster sat on its side and broke every bone it could find.

She was speechless and wanted to throw the phone into the ocean. If she could have been sick, the lawn would have been covered. This was her charge, her responsibility. If she had been the Sallows leader her mother had been, this poor animal wouldn't have suffered. Therefore, she made herself watch as the broken creature mutilated the fowl. At least the doe was dead first.

When her eyes were too watery to see the screen, Eton snatched the phone away. "That's why I didn't show anyone. Kerry would need therapy for the rest of her life if she saw that."

That was why he was so ready to believe her. Eton had seen the monsters even before she had woken. That poor animal. Blinking back her tears, she nodded. "According to island lore, that is the Bone-Breaker. I didn't know she was still here."

Eton stared at her hard, and his expression reminded her of Daniel's. The intensity and the motivation for the greater good that her husband once possessed, though it was what ultimately drove him insane.

"Where are they?" he asked.

"The only place they could be is in the woods," she said.

"I saw Daniel stumble out of there around the time you..." Eton paused. "You know."

"Around the time I slept with Kevin."

"We can't let this continue to happen," he said. "It's not safe, and then there's Daniel—"

"I have thought about that a great deal lately," she interrupted, knowing full well what he meant. There needed to be resolution with her estranged husband. She just wasn't ready. "I love Daniel, but he seems incapable of opening up to me. He refuses to tell me the truth until he's forced to do so. I feel he wouldn't be driven to behave this way if it were not for me."

Eton came around and hugged her. It was a hug of friendship, and she desperately needed a friend. It was as though her own home was pushing her out as if it didn't want her anymore. The monsters were crawling out of their holes and making everything worse.

"I still want to protect him, even when I know I shouldn't. I still want to be with him even when I know it's over."

"What does he want?" Eton asked.

He wants the impossible.

"If we find signs of Kevin and show it to the Coast Guard, they will leave you alone. If I find any of the monsters, I will take care of them."

Eton let go of her and faced her. He had a scar on his brow. When did that happen? "What do you say we look?"

Taking a half-dead human into the woods with her while she fought potentially dangerous monsters? She should have said no, but Destiny was selfish and so tired of being alone.

Walking through the forest helped soothe her troubled mind. The terrain was so rough with exposed roots and rocks that she needed to focus on her footing more than anything else. Eton had an even harder time. She was worried that he was tiring. He stumbled often, and more than once, he nearly fell.

"We can go back," she told him.

"Please don't make me go back there," Eton pleaded. She remembered that Kerry and Holly were running the store and realized that he probably wanted to get away from the lovebirds. "I'm not tired; I'm just high."

"High?"

"I'm on painkillers," he said, with one hand on a tree while he stepped over a wide root. "They make you...loopy."

"They gave me opium as a child. I remember how strange it felt."

Eton looked up at her, eyes wide. "That's hardcore. Did you break your arm or something?"

She walked ahead of Eton, hoping to find a better path for him to follow. "No, I had terrible nightmares. I also once had a fever that nearly killed me."

"I guess they had to work with what they had."

Indeed. The Sallows worked with what they had. They endured or perished. She was perhaps the most coddled of the Sallows in her great big mansion, but it didn't mean she didn't have her share of scars.

The forest was active and chipper in the early afternoon air. The birds chirped in the trees and the wind made the bushes shuffle. In the light of day, it all appeared so serene and magical. Like a fairy tale, like something in Straparola's *Piacevoli notti*.

"I used to be so afraid of this place before."

Eton turned around and said with no small amount of sarcasm, "Oh yeah, totally no reason to be afraid of this place."

"You don't like it?" she asked. She thought the forest was quite magical. The birch trees were like great fingers emerging from the earth. Tall grasses and ferns covered the ground in a feathery green. Bogs and shallow marshes spotted the terrain and hosted bursts of purple heather.

"Well, it's not like there's an angry husband or fucked up chicken killer crawling around. The best thing we hope to find today is a body—not something I'm all that excited about either."

Agree to disagree, she supposed.

The forest was on an incline. It explained why so many roots were exposed. The forest had hills like the rest of the island. She didn't want to stray too far from Eton, but he was so slow, and she wanted to see what was atop this hill.

Digging her boots into the earth, Destiny scaled up the steep hill and came to another level of forest. "I know this place," she shouted down to Eton. "I came upon this part of the forest searching for Daniel one evening. There is a cave here."

She didn't check to see if Eton was behind her, she just assumed that he was. There was nowhere else he could be. The forest wasn't that large to begin with. She noted the trap that Daniel had broken with a tree trunk. In the daylight, the traps were much easier to avoid. "Eton?"

"Yeah," he said from the bottom of the hill.

"There are broken traps up here, so please be careful."

"Okay," he grunted. There was no reason to wait for Eton to work his way up that hill. It would take him awhile, and she did not wish to hurry him.

"Take your time," she said. "Go slow."

"No problem there," he said from below.

Navigating the old hanging ropes and broken traps, she went inside the cave. It was more of a rock formation than a cave, really, but it appeared as though something had changed. There was a great large hole torn from the ground. It reminded her of the hole in the mansion's wall, as well as the hole she found in the catacombs. As if something within the island had burrowed its way to the surface. The Worm. Could it have been the one carving through the island?

She stared into the blackness of that hole and bit her lip until she winced from the pain. Destiny picked up a rock and threw it into the void, waiting to hear it hit the bottom, but the rock never did.

"Well," Eton's voice startled Destiny. She spun around to find him nudging a broken bottle with his toe. "Kevin was here, but then what?"

"Yes," Destiny said. She ignored the cramps in her stomach and nodded. "What happened to Kevin, indeed."

Using the phone for light, they went deeper into the cave. All her bravery had melted away, and she longed for Daniel to be by her side. The hair on the back of her neck stood on end, and Eton was uncharacteristically silent.

A backpack was propped against the backside of the cave wall, right beside the giant hole. There was rope staked into the ground as if someone had used it to go into the cavern.

She moved to grab the rope, but Eton stopped her. "We can't touch it. It's evidence."

"What?"

"These days, police use science to solve crimes. They pick up hair, skin, anything that leaves a trace of human DNA and use it to determine what happened."

What would have happened if they were to find her DNA? Did she have any? She didn't want it to appear as though she or Eton had anything to do with this. Peering over the hole, she shouted, "Hello?"

There was no answer.

"We should call the cops," Eton said.

She nodded. They would clear his name. He moved his phone, and she caught a flicker of something. "Wait, what was that?"

Taking Eton's hand, she guided it back to a large square of fresh dirt. It was the size of a grave. Daniel had been here. He came back to hide the evidence of Kevin and the Chimera, the monster his mother had become.

"What is it?" Eton asked. His human eyes could not detect the slight difference in the dirt. Daniel went to great lengths to conceal it, but the dirt was too deliberately scattered, too fresh to her sense of smell.

"Never mind," she said. "I thought I saw something."

They left the forest. She had her bearings now and led him toward the mansion, as it was a less strenuous way out. Poor Eton swayed with every step as though he were about to collapse. "We're closer to the mansion than we are to the cottage," she said. "Why don't we rest there for a minute?"

"You're just saying that," Eton slurred. "You don't need rest at all, do you?"

"I've got some tea in the kitchen," she said.

"Tea would actually be pretty good right now."

Eton nearly didn't make it to the drawing room. She helped him the rest of the way and he now lay with his legs hanging over the loveseat. Really, he was much too big for the sofa, but she couldn't convince him to lie on the larger one.

"This is good," he said. "This is fine."

Destiny tried to contain her smirk. He was such an overgrown child. Draping a clean sheet over him, she started a fire. She clutched her hands together while she stared down at the monster in the relief on the mantlepiece. Whatever it was, she was one of them. Daniel might let her go, but the island never would.

Chapter Twenty-Five

REVENGE

She came into the kitchen to start the tea and found Daniel standing there waiting. His eyes shone brighter than ever as he leaned against the plaster walls facing the window. The afternoon was waning. He belonged in the dusk.

"I'm not surprised to see you here," she said dryly. "You always seem to know when I bring another man around."

"It looked like he was having a hard time."

"He is in a great deal of pain from the fight," she said. "The doctors prescribed opium, but I'm afraid he's rather sensitive to it."

"What were you doing in the woods?"

"Looking for answers." Destiny didn't want to look at him. She began rummaging through the cupboards for teacups.

"I take it you found them."

She found the teacups. Destiny held one in her hand. They would only need one as she no longer drank tea. The words stuck in her mouth, but they needed to be said. "Thank you for making it look like an accident. The police suspect Eton."

"I didn't do it for him," Daniel said. "If I had known he was a suspect, I would have smeared your lover's remains all over his bedroom. Pity."

Her husband's derangement was at full peak. He was intentionally trying to scare her, but for what purpose? "What do you want, Daniel?"

He just stared out the window. "I was going to do it," he said. "I was going to snap his neck and drop him into the ocean."

"You don't mean that." She clutched the cup as if it were her last remaining salvation. The remaining bit of humanity she clung to. She suspected Daniel wanted to preserve her innocence, but it was an impossible feat. Nothing could remain of what she once was.

"Don't I?" Daniel asked. He was behind her now, his breath soft against her neck. "You think I'd let that disgusting little man live? Eton loves you, and I don't blame him for that, but that man—"

"I am to understand Eton is safe?"

"Nothing is safe," Daniel growled. "Nothing matters anymore."

She spun around to face him, but Daniel had already left the kitchen. Her stomach lurched into her throat when she saw the double doors swinging. "Eton," she breathed.

The teacup shattered as she rushed out the side door to beat Daniel to the stairway. He was fast, but she knew which way was shorter. She cut him off at the foot of the steps and blocked his path.

"You're not to touch him," she said. "You're not to harm anyone!"

"You don't get to tell me what to do."

"What are you doing?" she cried.

Her husband gave a callous shrug. "Whatever I want."

"You can't do that, you know you can't."

"And why not?" he snapped. "You can. You brought Eton into this. You were talking to those police officers. You're the one sleeping with random men. How is it you can do whatever you want, but I can't?"

"Because I'm not hurting anyone."

"You're hurting me."

Her sob caught in her throat. "I'm not trying to. I'm sorry, Daniel. I still love you, you know that, don't you?"

There was a moment where Daniel was himself again. He couldn't look at her and how she was guarding the stairs in order to protect an innocent man. The man she loved was still in there. He was twisted and maimed by the magic at work on this island, but he was still there.

"Aw," an unfamiliar voice said from the back hallway. "Lover's quarrel?"

"Who are you?" Destiny whispered.

He had a receding hairline and was overtly muscular. He wore a blue shirt and jean trousers and an expensive gold watch around his wrist. In his hand was a device of some sort. It was bigger than a phone, and he pointed it at them. She assumed it was a recording device of some sort.

"Oh, you don't recognize me. My name is Jeremy Sands. I am a ghost hunter. I came here at the beginning of the summer. Got some really strange readings last time I was here. I was hoping you could explain that, Daniel."

Daniel turned and gave the man a scathing look.

"You need to leave," she warned. "Please—"

"Wait, your voice sounds familiar," the man said, peering out from his camera. "I should know. I listened to your voice for thousands of hours. I heard it in my dreams sometimes. You are Destiny? Destiny and Daniel! Holy shit!"

Daniel moved toward the man, and she screamed at him to stop, but it was no use. This man had a death wish.

"How do you know her voice?" Daniel demanded.

Jeremy Sands was smart enough to dodge from Daniel's grasp but not enough to stop talking. "When I was here, my EVP machine picked up hundreds of conversations. Many of them involved you two. At first, I thought you were posing as natives, but now I get it. You guys were here when it happened!"

His rambling piqued Daniel's curiosity enough to keep him alive, but if she didn't stop this, her husband would kill him. There was also the matter of Eton fast asleep upstairs. If she failed to stop Daniel, who knew how many more it would take to stop him.

"I thought Eton put you up to this, but now, holy shit. You guys are like the undead or something. How are you still here after all these years?"

Daniel lunged at Jeremy. He caught him this time, and with one arm clasped hard on the man's shoulder, Daniel squeezed his fingers until the man fell to his knees, screaming in pain. With his other hand, Daniel grabbed the device and smashed it against the wall. Several bones cracked before Destiny was able to use her whole body to knock Daniel off the man.

He slammed into the wall and she with him. Decayed wood shattered into fragments and rose dust all around them. There was no pain. Just a lover's embrace for what might be the last time.

"Run," she yelled, but he just lay on the floor laughing. "I've been here for hours," Jeremy said. "I set up cameras at several points in the house thinking you were imposters. I just wanted to clear my name, but the two of you—"

"I smashed your camera," Daniel said stupidly.

"You don't even know what a camera is, do you?" Jeremy said. "What about a cloud? Do you know what a cloud server is?"

The couple could only stare at him as Jeremy patronized them.

"You can break every camera in this house, but all the footage is being sent to a place where you can't destroy it. Come Monday, my assistant will check that place, and it will all be over for the two of you. Everyone will know I am right. There are things in this world beyond human comprehension, and here you are," Jeremy said, pointing at them.

Daniel pushed Denysti aside with a gentle calm before standing up and grabbing Jeremy by his shirt collar. "No!" she shouted as she got up and tried to fight him off. "Daniel, stop, please!"

Her husband ignored her and dragged the injured man. She threw herself against Daniel, but he was impervious to her strength. Jeremy screamed in pain as his shirt was being ripped off his body. Between her attacks on Daniel and the tearing shirt, Jeremy slipped out of the garment and made a run for the front door.

Daniel gave chase, but she leaped for him, grabbing his leg and allowing time for the man to run away. "Stop it!" she screamed.

"Don't you see now?" he shouted in the direction Jeremy had run. "It's over now. Everyone will know about us—you're not safe."

"Killing them won't change that."

"No, but it makes me feel better," he snarled. "If I don't have you, what is the point of being in this awful world?"

Daniel jerked his leg free and ran after Jeremy. She stood to give chase, but he was already out the door. He was desperate and cruel. Had they been human—his actions would not have been hers. She could have freely left him and never looked back, but she was not human. She held the hand with the ruby ring and nodded. It was her duty to stop the monsters. Even the monsters she loved.

"Des?" Eton called from the drawing room.

She'd forgotten for a moment that he was still up there. She couldn't stay to help him back to the cottage and stop Daniel from killing Jeremy at the same time. "Eton, get back to the cottage if you can," she shouted. "You need to get off this island."

Before he could ask questions, she ran out the door but stopped short at the sight in the distance. Daniel had caught up to Jeremy and had him by the neck. "No!" she shouted.

The man's face was battered. Daniel had hit him or knocked him to the ground before he picked Jeremy up by the neck and was now staring into his eyes. Destiny ran, but she knew she wouldn't get to them in time. Daniel slowly squeezed Jeremy's neck while he watched the man's eyes bulge from their sockets.

Jeremy's face was purple, and the veins in his neck protruded. Daniel watched with the most loving expression. He was enjoying this. She fell to her knees. Her stomach lurched in her throat. The man's neck cracked, followed by a horrid gushing sound.

CHAPTER TWENTY-SIX

THE REUNION

Two worn leather boots stepped into her line of sight. Enraged and crying, she lifted her head to glare at him. How could he do this? This wasn't the man she once knew. Had the room of pain changed Daniel, or was he always like this?

"You're a monster!"

He smiled as if she'd given him a compliment. "The others will come out," he said. "The smell of human blood has that effect."

The murder wasn't just cruel. It was calculated. That was why he went for Eton initially. Daniel wanted to summon the other monsters from hiding, and what better way than a human sacrifice.

She couldn't stop the tears from falling. "Are you going to kill me too now?" she cried.

Daniel's expression of remorse felt like a betrayal because she knew it to be a lie. She saw his face when he killed that man. He didn't feel the least bit sorry. "I'd never lay a hand against you," he said, stroking her cheek. "You are the purest, most perfect light in this world."

"But you'll murder everyone I come into contact with."

"That is probably true," he said with a chuckle, his green eyes glowing with a gleeful menace. "But at least now you know the truth!"

She slapped him as hard as she could. His face jerked violently to the right, and he let out a moan, almost sensual. Of course, he enjoyed pain.

"You said that I didn't open up to you. That I was hiding things from you. Well, now you have it. I am a murderer." He bowed. "I enjoy a good bit of torture, too," he said in a sickeningly sweet tone.

Eton was limping down the coastline. At any moment, Daniel would turn around and see her friend, and he would end him. She needed to distract him. "Are all the monsters still here?"

"Some," Daniel said, scanning the forest behind her. "Oh, here comes one now!"

She turned to face the forest and the creature that crawled out. Like Daniel, she recognized what remained of the gown the pitiful creature was wearing. The broken thing was once her Aunt Sophie, her most beloved aunt. She was once the island historian who lived in the cottage by the cliffs. How awful to find such a fate! Destiny would have wept had she any tears left.

"The Bone-Breaker, I presume." Daniel slipped his hands into his pockets and smiled. "I'm certain the Jaw-Maul isn't far behind."

What was she going to do? She couldn't kill her aunt the way Daniel killed his mother. If there was ever a time for her mother to show up, it was now. Surely, this couldn't be what she had intended.

The loathsome creature dragged its deformed body on twisted arms toward the fresh body. Grunting and smelling of spoiled meat. Her white hair was stained brown on the ends from the mud she had to pull herself through. They watched as the creature approached the corpse of Jeremy Sands. She picked up his arm and held it up, wiggling it as if assessing the quality before letting out a gargled wail. She snapped the bone in half and shook the arm again as if to admire her handiwork.

Destiny's knees wobbled. Daniel smiled as if he were watching a child play with a beloved toy. She glanced toward the coast and found that Eton was also watching.

Stupid boy! You should have run when you had the chance!

This caught Daniel's full attention. He turned to see Eton and moved toward him.

"Please, Daniel. No, not Eton." She grabbed his hand. When he kept walking, she slipped on the grass, and he pulled her like a dead weight. Eton limped away as fast as he could, but there was no escaping the island. The Bone-Breaker was oblivious to what was happening. It was too consumed by the dead body.

Daniel tried to shake free of her, but both hands were firmly clasped onto his hand. She wouldn't let go. The ruby ring glittered in dwindling daylight, and she had an idea. It was a long shot, but perhaps...

"Bone-Breaker!" she called. "It's me! Destiny! Please, if you have any love for me, stop him!"

The monster paused, holding the head of Jeremy Sands—now facing the wrong direction. It dropped the head and began shambling in their direction. It was working! The ring denoted the ruler of the island. She was the ruler of the island, and the monsters would obey her just as her family would have.

The Bone-Breaker was slow and wouldn't reach them in time. Daniel was so consumed with his hunt that he wasn't paying attention. She couldn't see where Eton was, but Daniel's pace remained slow yet deliberate. Letting go of him, her husband flicked his wrist with annoyance and kept walking.

What were all their names?

"Jaw-Maul, the Gargoyle," she screamed into the air, "I beseech you! Stop the Green-Eyed Monster!"

Daniel turned and gave her a patronizing smile. "You're so precious."

He stopped to shake his head at the Bone-Breaker. He noticed she was following him. With his hands on his hips, he said, "Just what are you going to do? I'm still angry about what you did to that doe."

Of all the things to bring up at a time like this. He truly was unhinged.

Destiny needed more names. "The worm and the Zombie," she cried out. "Stop the Green-Eyed Monster! Do not harm him nor anyone else on this island!"

He was laughing at her now, and she felt foolish. At least she had given Eton a head start to nowhere.

"We can still fix this," she said. "You're my husband. We can resolve this without hurting anyone."

Daniel shook his head. "No, we can't. The humans will never leave us alone. They will want to open you up, learn what makes you tick. I will not let them."

Of all the reasons to kill, this was by far the most irrational reasoning. He didn't want to kill people to protect her; he wanted to kill people in her name. He wanted to murder whomever he liked while keeping her in his pocket. "Your desires have nothing to do with me."

He turned toward Eton before saying, "All right, say I let them go. I let all of them go and they spread the word to never step foot on this island again. Will you stay?"

"You're making me choose Eton's life or a life with you."

"I suppose that's the gist of it, yes," Daniel said without turning back.

It was a cruel bargain and one she would easily make. But before she could accept, the earth resonated beneath the ground. It grumbled up her arms and legs while she lay on all fours in the grass. She smiled her own evil smile at Daniel, who was now looking toward the sky behind her.

A gray, scaly thing hovered in the air for a moment. It flapped its heavy wings rapidly but still fell to the ground with a thud. It was the Gargoyle, and they had aptly named it. It was a stout thing with horns and talons. Its fat lips protruded with tusks. On the edges of its brow and in the youth of its eyes, the thing resembled her cousin and Daniel's brother.

The Gargoyle hesitated to act. Daniel hissed and made like he was going to kick the monster, and the poor beast flinched. "He killed your mother," she said.

That sort of emotional blackmail was contemptible, but so was doing nothing while Daniel went on a murder spree. The Gargoyle screeched at Daniel; its wings raised in anger. As if her husband had determined that the little monster was serious, he stepped away, only to stumble as a giant purple tentacle split the ground beneath him.

Daniel let out a scream, as did the Gargoyle, who fluttered to safety. Her husband was not so fortunate. The extremity wrapped around Daniel. He fought against it, but it could hold him, at least for the time being.

Another tentacle shot from the ground. It was smooth but ribbed, extending nearly ten feet in the air. It was waving at her. Still in shock from her newfound powers and all the monsters, Destiny was at a loss as to who this could be. The squat little Gargoyle waddled up to the limb and petted it gently.

"Abigail?"

The tentacle gave her a pat on the head. She expected it to be slimy, but the Worm was just shiny, like a snake. None of these creatures could speak. She pitied them. They felt the need to hide, and she didn't blame them, but this was her family.

"Where are the Jaw-Maul and the Zombie?" she asked.

The Gargoyle pointed at the house.

If anyone knew, it would be Daniel. "Where are they?" she asked him.

He was resisting the Worm with all his might. Her limb was tearing in a corner where he had scratched with his bare hands. "Like I would tell you?"

"You're a monster just like them," she argued. "You should be compelled to follow my orders as well."

"They're not compelled; they're just stupid," he said, ripping at the tentacle. It bled purple ooze, and the ground rattled. Her mind raced as she tried to recall the stories found in Nathanial Sallow's diary. Who else could she call? The image of the beast on the mantle. Of course!

"Beast!" she shouted. "I beseech you! Attack the Green-Eyed Monster!"

A howl echoed from the forest. So elated with the reunion, Destiny let out a howl herself. This was her island. These were her monsters, even if Daniel wasn't. Her husband dropped to the ground. In that moment, she could have sworn he would kill her. He said he wouldn't, but she didn't doubt that he wanted to.

He gave her a cheeky grin before turning and sprinting for the cottage shop. Toward Eton, Holly, Kerry, Bart—who just became a grandfather for the fourth time. There were young people still in the shop. Daniel was going to slaughter every one of them.

"Everyone go after him!" she said. "Keep the humans safe!"

The ground shook once more as if something were tunneling toward the shore. The Worm was on the move, as were the Gargoyle and the Bone-Breaker. A massive, hairy beast darted from the woods. He was much quicker than the others, but would he be in time?

There was only one other monster left. She hesitated to call for her. All this time, she had been praying for her mother's strength and wishing for her guidance when she might have been just a call away. "Cannibal!" her voice trembled. "I beseech you, come to me!"

She stood there for several minutes, twisting her fingers into knots. It took the others time to respond. It only made sense that her mother was slow to approach. Maybe she had to travel some distance. "Cannibal, come to me!"

The sun had set, but the sky was lit with a rainbow of colors! Destiny gasped as she stared at the sky. Shades of purples and greens made a lazy trail across the sky. She had seen nothing like it. It must have been the work of her mother. Helicant was telling her to put an end to this once and for all.

***

The last Eton saw was the chicken killer before he had to start running from the resident island psycho. He didn't want to leave Destiny behind, but she was doing everything she could to help him. She wasn't the least bit frightened by the creatures. Only of him getting hurt.

He was dripping in sweat, and his ribs ached so hard, he couldn't breathe, but he got to the cottage. Falling through the front door, he shouted, "Bart! Time to go, man!"

"Oh my God, Eton!" Kerry screamed before she rushed to his side. "I told Destiny to make sure you didn't overdo it!"

"We got to go," he repeated. "Where's Bart?"

"He went back to shore. His wife wants to throw a family dinner for everyone."

Everything hurt. He didn't think he could get back up, but he had to. Destiny was still out there with her crazy husband and that thing. "Call the Coast Guard," he said. "Get everyone to the dock. Now!"

"What's going on?" Holly asked, handing him a bottle of water and some painkillers. He sat up and took them. The two customers were still sitting there as if nothing was unusual about all this. They were still staring at their phones.

We're a doomed species, aren't we?

Since it was apparent no one was going to do anything until he explained, he told them. "Daniel has lost his mind. He's coming to kill me, probably kill everyone here. There's some fucking monsters on this island, we need to go."

Kerry and Holly exchanged glances, and he scowled. "And no, I'm not high. Call the Coast Guard—let's go!"

Holly reluctantly called the Coast Guard and Kerry called Bart. A few more customers wandered in and he sighed. He was going to die in front of an audience. "In the meantime, we need to get to the dock."

"Hey, there's some guy running down the hill," a customer said.

His heart stopped in his throat, and he staggered to get up. "Now!"

Kerry was still on the phone with Bart. She motioned for him to be quiet! He could have slapped the phone out of her hand at that moment. Holly at least had the sense to grab the baseball bat from behind the counter.

Holly let out a scream and everyone—except the guys on their phones—turned to see a half-rotting dude shambling through the back door. The thing reminded him of a baseball, the way the stitches pulled his skin together, only there wasn't enough of a shell. It had no eyelids or lips and its mouth was full of teeth.

Holly held the bat out in front of her, and Kerry stood between the monster and the tourists. Its eyes shifted around the room, watching all of them. This was it. This was how he was going to die. The thing shuffled past Holly and through the room towards him.

He couldn't breathe. His brain screamed at him to bolt, but his legs just couldn't do it. Pressing himself against the wall, he wanted to close his eyes. The creature was a few feet away, reeking of dirt and rot. There was a maggot wiggling in its nose cavity. Those bulging eyes stared at him, and screams echoed in his ears. Only, they were his own screams.

Just then, the front door swung open. He never expected to be so happy to see Daniel in all his life. True, he wanted to kill him, but Daniel would have to get through the monster first! "Everyone, get out!" he shouted.

"Eton..." Kerry sobbed.

"Just go. Go out the back door. This doesn't concern you."

Holly took Kerry's hand and pulled her toward the back door. The customers carefully followed. If he was going to die, at least he could keep everyone else safe. It was enough for him.

Except he realized the trio of guys on their phones were still there. What the fuck? What part of this did they not understand? "Goddammit, guys!"

Daniel and the creature were having some sort of stare off. Daniel's expression was sad, as if he were about to cry. The monster opened its nasty mouth and a rotted black tongue waggled and the scent of decay filled the air. "Coral," it said with a gargled voice.

Daniel swallowed and took a step back. Eton took his only opportunity to slide along the walls toward the back door. "I'm sorry, father," Daniel said. "But it's time to go back to sleep!" He punched the thing he called father, and it fell to the ground before he stepped over its writhing body toward him.

"I thought we had an understanding," he said. "You know I'm no threat."

"Nothing personal," Daniel said. "I'm punishing her the only way I can."

His heart may have stopped beating. Maybe this was all too much for him; he didn't know. All he knew was that Daniel was about to murder him when a flash of something black, big, and sharp came crashing through the doorframe. The whole cottage shook, and the walls threatened to crumble.

Daniel didn't turn. Instead, he rolled his eyes before the monster clamped onto the back of Daniel's leg and dragged him out.

Was this real? He felt his chest to make sure he wasn't dead. He stared at the hole where the door used to be and took several breaths. Destiny and Daniel were not human, and they were not the only non-human things on this island. The rotting guy on the floor struggled to get up, but when it did, it followed in Daniel's direction.

They were after Daniel. That was why Destiny wasn't afraid of them.

"Was that a werewolf?" one of the phone guys asked.

He couldn't believe these guys. He just stared at them.

"Well, the other guy was a zombie, so—maybe," another one answered. The third one just scrolled on as though nothing had happened. Fucking unbelievable.

There was a yelp in the distance, and he feared for the worst. Daniel winning against the werewolf and the zombie. Eton should have tucked tail and ran, but he couldn't just leave Destiny with Sir Psychopath. Limping out the back door, he unplugged the modem and took it with him.

CHAPTER TWENTY-SEVEN

NOTHING LEFT TO HOLD

Destiny waited on the front porch of the mansion. She had instructed the monsters to bring Daniel to her. "To me," she said. "All of you must come to me."

Her nerves were raw with anticipation. What was taking so long? Had Daniel bested them all? There was no way. The ground rolled underfoot. The Worm was still alive and well. When a black figure came running up the hillside, Destiny knew it was Daniel. As he got closer, she could see the panicked expression on his face.

It wasn't until several figures followed behind that she understood why he was coming to the mansion. Humans had come to the island to protect their own. Daniel was coming to warn her, to protect her. She swallowed her guilt and doubt. She could afford neither. If he read them on her face, her plan would be ruined.

It's for the best.

Daniel came charging up the path, "Destiny, get inside. I'll deal with them."

"To what end?" she asked.

He gave her an incredulous look. "I've been a poor husband, and I am a rotten soul, but I won't ever stop protecting you."

She wanted to shout at him. This was all his fault. If he hadn't threatened to kill the man for all the internet to see, they wouldn't have sent those people in their strange black uniforms and glossy helms. If Daniel hadn't lost his mind, this wouldn't have happened.

It was no use yelling at him. He was doing what came naturally to him. It was an instinct driven by jealousy, and Daniel was the embodiment of that emotion. Biting her lip, she unclenched her fists and said, "Oh, Daniel…"

He was walking to her now, the more confident swagger of a man who felt needed. "Don't worry," he said, embracing her. "I'll keep you safe."

The men in black were still several miles down the hill, but their cries echoed in the darkness. They were frightened. No doubt the monsters were also making their way to the house. Everything was going to plan. She needed to bide her time just a little longer.

"Do you think we can hide in the house?" she asked.

Daniel raised his head to the mansion as if he were asking the house for its opinion. "For a time, I suppose, but we would do better to hide in the forest."

In the corner of her eye, she saw someone in a red flannel shirt coming up the side trail. It was Eton. Stupid boy! He was going to ruin everything. Daniel shifted as if he sensed her wandering thoughts and almost spotted the shopkeep.

"I mean below," she said, pulling him close. "The time loop could confuse things for a while."

He shook his head. "It's all bricked up, and besides, the way time works in there, it wouldn't be to our advantage."

Daniel was right. Time slowed there, not the other way around. She rested her head on his chest. It got him focused on her once again. The Zombie and the Bone-Breaker were approaching. She didn't see the Gargoyle or the Beast, but they were likely nearby. The Worm and the Jaw-Maul were underneath them.

She took Daniel's hand. "They're distracted. Let's go collect our books from the drawing room and decide what to do there."

***

In the drawing room, the fire roared, and its flames lashed against the stone chimney. She clutched Daniel's hand so hard that he pulled her in for a hug. "Hey, it's okay. No one is going to hurt you."

She was afraid, but not for the reasons he thought. The floor squeaked from downstairs, and Daniel's keen ears pricked. "Daniel," she said. "Let's run away. Just you and I."

Still in his embrace, he nuzzled against the side of her face with his, "Where would we go?"

Destiny shook her head. "I don't know. Anywhere." In the corner of her eye, she focused on Daniel, but her eyes deceived her.

"Where is he, Destiny?"

"I...I don't know," she stammered. There was a glimpse of red fabric in the hallway. She held her husband close and hoped Eton would take the hint and run. Of course, the old floors creaked under Eton's foot, and the gig was up.

Daniel tore from her embrace and threw her to the ground before tearing the doors off the wardrobe to find Eton cowering inside.

"There you are!" he said, forgetting Destiny entirely as he went after Eton, who was now running up the stairs. Why in bloody hell would he run up instead of down and out? "Daniel, please," she cried. "Don't make things worse. Let's just leave this place!"

He wasn't giving up. And unlike Eton, he wasn't injured. She charged him and knocked Daniel into the railing. Together, they plummeted through the banister and onto the marble floor. Splinters of wood rained everywhere. Eton scuttled away and out of sight, though she wished he hadn't come at all. Daniel only turned to her and smiled. "It's a shame we didn't do this much damage during other activities."

He wanted a reaction out of her, and Destiny couldn't help but give him one. "You really are mad."

He tried to get up, but she pinned him down the best she could. This only excited him more. "You could give Eton all the time you want doing it this way."

She was half inclined to use her persuasions against him, but there was a fierce pounding at the door followed by shouts. The noise reminded Daniel of whatever his goal was. He pulled her off like a rag doll before standing up. "Sorry, love," he said. "We can come back to that in a minute."

She got up and chased after Daniel, who was running up the stairs after Eton. The men in black had gotten here faster than she would have liked. Searching the entryway, she picked up the solid wood armoire like a bundle of firewood and blocked the entrance.

There, that would slow them down.

Destiny ran after Daniel and Eton up the stairs as fast as she could. Praying that Eton would survive long enough for her to reach them. There was only one thing she could do, and she hoped it was enough to put an end to this forever.

"Daniel, stop," she shouted. She came into the room to find Eton prone on the ground and Daniel standing over him. Eton was still moving. He was alive. He was just dazed. Daniel wasn't listening, he was too busy watching Eton struggle to get up. Savoring it. The pounding at the door became silent, but that only meant they were searching for a way in.

Destiny grabbed hold of Daniel and pulled him away from Eton. "You win, okay?" she said.

Daniel rolled his eyes, and she pulled him into her again, edging up against the fire. "I know there's no one else for me. I've discovered that much myself."

This made her husband look at her. "You're a shit liar. You always have been," he said, touching her lips. "You wouldn't suddenly develop a knack for it."

She shook her head. Eton was standing and at the doorway of the drawing room. She felt the heat against her skin and knew she had caught fire. "No Daniel, I'm not lying. I'm going to stay with you forever. Just you and I."

"Even if I am a monster?" Daniel asked. His eyes searched hers for a trick, but there was none. She couldn't deceive him, even if she wanted to. There was only one way they could be together in the way he wanted. There was only one way to keep the world safe from the monsters—or rather, keep the monsters safe from the world.

She gave a weak laugh. "We're both monsters, aren't we?"

Daniel's green eyes were reflecting red, and he gasped in terror. He realized she had caught fire. She clutched him close as the flames engulfed her body. Daniel did not push her away, nor did he fight it. He simply held her close as the flames took hold.

She heard shouts from the stairway. Eton would be safe. The carpet beneath their feet blazed, and the sofas swelled in flames. There were people standing at the door watching before the smoke and the fire made it impossible to see anything anymore. They held one another as the fire raged on. Until there was nothing left to hold.

Chapter Twenty-Eight

THE AFTERMATH

Several officers carried Eton out of the house and took him to a medic. They strapped things to his arms to check his vitals and pressed a plastic mask to his mouth. Oxygen forced its way into his lungs, expelling the smoke he had inhaled. "I'm fine!" His voice was muffled through the mask.

It wasn't until he saw the body bag beside him that he got why everyone was up in arms.

"Is that Jeremy?" Eton asked the woman as she checked his blood pressure.

"Mr. Sands' assistant notified police that his life was being threatened by a man on this island."

He learned Jeremy had been recording inside the house while the fight was going on. Someone must have been watching the footage remotely and alerted the authorities. That also meant that everyone would soon know Destiny and Daniel's secret. He wasn't even certain what that was.

The fire in the mansion spread fast. He tried to get off the gurney but was stopped by several medics.

"What are you doing?" the medic asked.

"Destiny is still in there," he said. The medic pushed him back down and strapped him into the gurney with quick precision. "They've got to get her out of there."

Men were being pushed out of the house by the smoke—billows of smoke bursting through every nook and cranny. "I'm sorry, mate," the medic said. "I don't think there's anything to be done."

The mansion was burning, and there was nothing that could stop it. Destiny had sacrificed herself to save him. She had sacrificed her life for his, and he couldn't do shit for her in return.

Screams and panic circulated the lawn. Groups of people ran like herds away from two figures limping toward the house. Everyone watched in silent awe as the zombie guy and the other thing entered the mansion engulfed by flames.

"What the fuck?" the medic uttered, just as enthralled as everyone else. The zombie caught fire before it could even get through the door. The police had broken that down. The shriveled skin was aflame. If it felt pain, it didn't notice. Both creatures were in the house and out of sight.

The police didn't ask questions. They all just watched the mansion burn down. Kerry and Holly were also at the funeral. Kerry took his hand and held it while stinging tears rolled down his face. The smoke and the blaring heat forced everyone back another fifty feet.

By the time dawn made its way along the horizon, the mansion was a steaming pile of white-hot coals. The house collapsed in on itself like dominos. The outer wings of the building fell inward until the heart of the mansion gave way. It was still burning in heaps and probably would for another day or so.

"At least we know that man won't be a problem anymore," the detective said.

Eton shook his head, too angry to respond. Kerry gave him a dirty look, and he realized his error. "Sorry about your friend. She seemed like a lovely lady."

Holly held on to Kerry, who just cried. He felt so bad for bringing his little sister to this place. She had never known anyone who had died before. Neither did he. The realization that Destiny was dead just felt like a punch to the gut each time he thought about it.

"Nothing left to be done here," someone shouted. "Let's get this lot to the hospital."

He didn't want to leave, and he didn't need to go to the hospital. He struggled in protest, and the medic injected a sedative into his IV. The mansion groaned in response. Everyone turned to see the whole center of the building fall to the ground.

He couldn't understand what was happening because the sedative was taking hold, but before he passed out, he thought he saw a young woman with long black hair standing in the forest.

***

People asked him millions of questions in the hospital. First it was the Coast Guard, then it was Iceland's PD, followed by Scotland Yard and a couple of private detectives from Norway looking into the fisherman for something totally unrelated. The island was closed off to all visitors. Poor Bart rolled up to the dock and found the place crawling with police and they wouldn't tell him anything. Fortunately, the old man had Eton's and Kerry's phone numbers.

They offered to show Eton the reports made by the three different investigations, but he didn't care. There were no survivors from the fire. Not even a pile of charred bones—so much for Jeremy's theory they were imposters running a scam.

Jeremy's team published his findings. They didn't need Eton's permission, they just edited him out of every frame. He learned the attorney was the one that called Jeremy and that he could probably sue him, but he hardly had enough energy to get out of his hospital bed these days, let alone start a lawsuit.

"Hey," Kerry said. He forgot she was sitting in the red upholstered seat beside him.

"They said you are okay, but they think you should go to the psych ward."

"I'm not suicidal," he said. "I'm just depressed. My friend died."

"That's what I told them," she said. "They said we could go back to the island if we wanted."

He shook his head. He didn't want to go back. He didn't want people coming to ask him questions about anything that had happened, and he didn't want to be on the island knowing she wasn't there anymore.

"Yeah, I feel the same way, but I'm going back to pack up our stuff. Bart and Holly are going to help."

He doubted she felt the same way. He was numb. It was like his brain couldn't switch on. He closed his eyes and pretended to fall asleep so his sister would leave him alone.

***

After several more days and all his lack of effort, they discharged Eton from the hospital and gave him anti-depressants. Soon, he found himself in Bart's tiny blue car.

"I'm sorry about Destiny," the older man said while they were driving through the Icelandic countryside. "She was a wonderful woman."

It felt good to be around other people who knew her. It didn't hurt to be on Bart's boat even though she was once there. It didn't hurt to be in the cottage, packing up all his shit. Even when his memories of her were all over the place. It didn't feel great, but it wasn't as painful as he'd imagined it would be.

"The UN declared the island as Icelandic territory," Bart told him. "You can't keep shop without the proper permits and whatnot."

Eton shook his head. "I just want to leave."

It was going to suck going back to his parents. He thought about extending his visa and staying in Iceland. He could get a job doing farm work or something. He was pretty good at chopping wood these days. Kerry had already been there. She had most of the stuff hauled away. He just wanted to make sure he left nothing behind.

The animal pens were empty, and all her stuff was gone. There was nothing left but some of his sacks of stuff she couldn't carry because they were so heavy. He shoved the heaviest sack in his suitcase and rolled it out to Bart before going back in with some plastic bags he took off the store shelf.

"What the fuck you pack in here?" Bart yelled as he dragged the suitcase out the door.

"It has wheels," Eton called back. "That's why it has wheels."

He stuffed the rest of his things into bags and loaded them onto the boat with one hand. The other hand held a bottle of vodka.

"Is that it?" Bart asked.

Eton unscrewed a bottle of his most expensive vodka and the top of a liter-sized bottle of sparkling water and alternated sips. Bart only shook his head and went into his cabin. The motor roared to life, and the fisherman steered him away from that god-forsaken island forever.

CHAPTER TWENTY-NINE

EPILOGUE

Eton opened his laptop and checked through his social media. He liked the pictures of friends getting married and the funny cat videos before a video call disrupted him. He accepted the call without waiting for the caller ID to show the name. He already knew who it was.

"Hey," he said to a potato-quality image of his sister. Her hair was cut to her shoulders, and she was wearing a giant puffy coat. "How's it going? Looking cold."

"I'm good. I wanted to call you as soon as I got the news," she said.

"You've got news, let's hear it."

"I signed the lease!" she squealed.

"Congrats!" he said. Eton got so excited he stood for a moment before sitting back on his cushion. "Your own store. I'm so happy for you."

"How's the west coast treating you?"

"It's good," he said. "Winters here are so mellow. Business doesn't slow down at all."

"I saw some CEO talking about your retreat. Pretty awesome."

"Yeah, well, I ruffled a lot of feathers with my instant start-up. It's not every day that a twenty-four-year-old nobody throws two million dollars into a business and becomes an overnight success."

He had brooded about Destiny for a few weeks while living with Bart and his family. When Bart's poor wife tried to move his suitcase, it finally occurred to him that one of those sacks belonged to Destiny. Two point seven million dollars' worth of rare gems and gold. It was enough to get his retreat started, buy a home, and provide his sister with some funding for her own business.

"You still think about her, don't you?" Kerry asked.

He didn't answer; he didn't need to. It was written all over his face, even through the horrid quality of the video image. He would think about the woman who died saving his life every day for as long as he lived.

"You know I dedicated this place to her," he said. "It's the least I can do. I bought this place with her money."

"Holly has a surprise for you," Kerry said. "It's why I called."

He smiled and glanced at what waited in the corner of his room. "Does it have to do with a box that says, 'Do Not Open?'"

"You can open it now."

He tore into the box. It was a large picture. Along with being a brilliant mathematician, Holly was also an excellent painter. So, he knew what it was. At least, he hoped it was what he thought it was. He gently slid the canvas out of the box to reveal a portrait the size of a fifty-five-inch TV. It was a portrait of Destiny. She had her eyes scrunched closed and was smiling like a child before blowing out the candles on her birthday cake.

He choked back the tears. She deserved to be remembered this way, not how sad she was the night she died. He gave in and watched the Jeremy Sands videos just to see her face and hear her voice even when he hated it. Nobody ever really figured out just what had happened on the island. Nobody really tried. The news stations all ignored it, and most stopped any coverage of the island. The only people who wanted to talk about it were conspiracy theory forums. The island was just a part of Iceland that emerged because of climate change. That was it.

Jeremy's team released all the information he had collected. It was a bunch of conversations recorded via Electronic Voice Phenomena and, of course, the video of when he went back. It was Destiny's and Daniel's voices on the recording, but Eton refused to confirm it to anyone who asked. The hope was that Jeremy would become a legend and prove something, but it amounted to nothing in the end. The guy Ryan killed himself not long after they released the footage. Eton never learned what became of the girlfriend.

"Thank you," he said. "Holly really outdid herself."

"She's thinking about switching majors."

"What about MIT?" he asked.

Kerry gave a coy smile, "She's rethinking it. Ever since the island, art has been her focus. That, and since I opened my store, she knows I can't just leave. Holly is opening an exhibit inspired by the island. Come and see it."

"I will," he said. "Definitely."

"Promise?"

He smiled. "I'll be there opening day."

***

She nudged the ash with a bare foot. So many years of her life were spent here, trapped in a prophecy of her own making. Here she was again, sifting through the ashes of her dead family.

The basement had fully collapsed in on itself along. She had to go to the cave in the forest to find the underground tunnels. In the dark, damp earth, bored away by the Worm, she found that there was no way to reach the Hellmouth.

"Oh, Destiny," she said out loud. "You know how to throw a party."

It wasn't just the Hellmouth that concerned her. There were several spots on the island where sinkholes had developed. It took a great deal of wandering in the dark until she confirmed her suspicions.

Her cat-like eyes reflected against something blocking the tunnel. Placing her clawed hand on the smooth, scaly heap, she confirmed it was the Worm, and her body was cold. The body so massive—even she did not know its true size—was decaying and was no longer providing the surface with the support it needed.

"You burrowed too long and too deep, my old adversary," she said with a gentle pat.

The island would crumble into the ocean as the body decomposed. There was nothing left for her in this world. Yet...

Stepping across the remnants of the mansion, she found two similar piles of ash. She kicked them, and the ruby ring surfaced. Smiling widely, Helicant Sallows picked up the ring and slipped it over her clawed ring finger. Her daughter had made her proud, but she was hungry, and there were sailors waiting at the docks.